Nobody Cares

A Driven Man

By

Claude Eldridge

ISBN: 1-4033-7490-2 (e-book)
ISBN: 1-4033-7491-0 (Paperback)

This book is printed on acid free paper.

.

1stBooks - rev. 02/10/03

Chapter 1

Young Sam Warden stood staring through the drug store window at the gallows being erected by the jailhouse wall. He counted the thirteen steps and the pain in his belly became more intense.

There were two people in the world who knew the condemned man was innocent: the young man inside the jail awaiting his fate and Sam Warden. Tomorrow, Sam promised himself, he would go to his father, Judge Henry Warden, and make a clean breast of his knowledge. He had made that promise for the past three months. Months while the trial had dragged to its inevitable conclusion.

The convicted killer was Woodrow "Woody" Baker, a grade school dropout, an overall clad redneck from the red clay, back wood hills of Warden County Mississippi. The

1

Mississippi court had convicted him of murdering his sixteen-year-old pregnant girl friend.

According to Sam's mother, Angela, all the people associated with Woodrow Baker were "White trash". And Sam had been drilled by his mother not to associate with the likes of "Those hillbilly rednecks."

Sam had disobeyed his snobbish mother's admonitions, but he dreaded her ire and that was the primary cause for his reluctance. That and his natural fear of the consequences of his acts, had sealed his lips.

As he stared sightless across the street, his bosom buddy, Thomas Jefferson"Tump" Johnson came into the store. "Sammy, whatcha doin' boy?" he called in his gravelly loud voice.

Sam turned to face Tump, "Nothing, just loafing." he replied.

"Hey, they 'bout got that sucker finished," Tump said, motioning at the gallows.

"Yeah," Sam replied. Tump's exuberance had become Increasingly annoying as the time had slipped by.

"Ya' know Sammy they tell me that big rope has got thirteen wraps in the knot they slip under a man's ear. But 'ah hell it don't break his neck, he just chokes to death."

Tump kept up an endless dialog about the up coming hanging and the more he talked the more intense Sam's pain became. Finally, without a word he turned and walked from the store.

Tomorrow, he promised himself he would go to his father and make a clean breast of the whole affair. This time he would not fail. Just believing that he would gave him a great sense of relief. The pain in his gut

3

eased a little and that night he slept through the night, the first time since he had become involved in the incident.

He was awakened by his father's loud angry voice. He caught snatches of conversation, "—hanged,—in his cell."

Angela: "Suicide?" Judge Warden: "Made to look that I—he was lynched." Sam slipped out of bed and went to the door of the living room. His father was standing with his hands on his hips facing Angela, who was sipping coffee, very calmly, the newspaper spread out before her.

"Why are you so upset?" she queried. "He's a condemned killer, what difference does it make if he decided he couldn't face the music? And what makes you think it was otherwise? He's just a dumb nobody."

Sam's head was spinning. He groped for the doorjamb to steady his swaying body. Angela saw him and jumped to her feet.

"Honey, what's the matter? You're as white as a sheet. You probably heard your father ranting and raving. There's no reason for you to be upset."

"I'm, I'm O.K." Sam mumbled.

"What happened?" he looked to his father for an answer.

Angela jumped in with, "He's too young to be burdened with this sordid mess."

Judge Warden said, "He's not too young. There's a war in Europe and the military is full of young men not much older than he. We're sure to get into that mess and he'll be affected by it sooner or later."

Angela was always upset when anything she didn't control affected her son and only child. "He's just seventeen," she snapped, "and enrolled in college. He's going to graduate, war or no war."

In a faint voice Sam asked again, "Please tell me what happened."

Judge Warden gave him the details.

"Early this morning the jailer found Woody Baker dead in his cell. His belt was buckled around his neck and the other end was tied to the top of the cell door."

"What was this business about a lynching?"

"I've seen a few hangings and there were marks on his neck that I know were not made by a belt."

Sam had great respect for his father. "Who would do such a thing?" he asked.

"There was a lot of bad feelings when Woody was first arrested for killing Camille Dotson. It would have to be some of her kinfolks and neighbors, with the help of someone in the jail. It's that simple."

"What're you going to do?" Sam almost whispered

"I'm going to see if I can get to the bottom of this scandalous situation."

Angela, with her usual cool logic, asked, "What will you do if the coroner rules it a suicide?"

Henry Warden stared at his wife. She was the daughter of a Boston attorney. They had met when he was attending law school at Yale. He always felt a certain awe of her ability to cut straight to the point. "I don't know, I can only try."

"If that bunch of courthouse bums have decided to get away with something, you can bet they will." Angela snorted.

Angela was correct. The coroner ruled it a suicide. At first Sam felt a great sense of relief. It was over. He would never be implicated. He thought. That night in his dreams he relived the entire nightmare. He was with Camille off old sawmill road, on the bluffs overlooking Squaw Creek. They were standing in front of Sam's car. He felt again his stunned emotions. Camille was crying, and in a quavering little voice she said, "But you said you loved me." She stumbled backward and fell. Her head struck the bumper guard on the car.

He lay there in the cool darkness, shaking and remembering the rest. His anxiety had given way to panic when she tumbled into the turbulent waters of the rain-swollen creek. She had just told Sam she was pregnant.

Three people. Three deaths; Camille, the baby and Woody, all his fault. He lay and cursed himself for a spineless coward. He remembered how he had gotten to this point in his young life.

Sam had grown up a privileged person. In depression ridden Warden County Mississippi, where half the population was poor black people and most of the rest were equally poor whites. The Wardens were never poor. The county was named for Henry's great grandfather who had been a pioneer settler. There was a statue on the Warden county court house lawn in honor of Henry's grandfather, Daniel Jefferson Warden, a civil war hero who "Had killed more Yankees than you could count". Angela had a trust fund left by her grandfather. Henry was a successful attorney, and later a judge. They lived at Lone Pine, a country estate, near the small town of Parkersville, where Henry had carefully planned for the sole purpose of raising his family.

Angela had black servants. They lived on the estate and were proud of their white family. Jose and Ava Williams were in their fifties and they called young Sam mister.

The house was large and roomy, with inside plumbing and running water, a rarity for a country home during that period. The grounds sloped gently to a spring fed stream where Henry had constructed a dam and made a swimming pool, with a white sandy bottom and white sand on the beach.

The water was always fresh and clean from the spring that ran through the pool. As Sam grew, Lone Pine was often filled with young people Sam's age, carefully selected by Angela. Fate had limited her to one child and she protected him with the fierceness of a lioness. Even more, she instilled in the growing youth an almost overpowering sense of duty to his mother. He must never do anything to displease her.

Sam was a happy go lucky boy. All things seemed easy for him. School was a breeze. His grades were outstanding without much effort on his part. He grew like a young colt, fast and carefree. He grew much too rapidly for Angela. At fourteen he began to shave his black whiskers, which contrasted oddly with his copper colored hair. Sam was an advanced adolescent while his parents;

especially Angela treated him as a child. He was an ideal boy. Angela told all her friends how good he was. His quick temper flashed like fire on gasoline, but it cooled just as quickly and without rancor toward the object that caused the flare up.

Sam grew up in a sheltered, protected world of plenty in a sea of poverty; when he was fifteen his life was changed forever. That was the year Ramona; his first cousin from Boston came to spend the summer with the Wardens.

Ramona was seventeen and her mother wanted her away from home because of an involvement with a married man. She was a tom boyish, leggy girl, who could outrun, swim faster and do all those boy things better than Sam or any of his friends. And she laughed about it. She also smoked, on the q.t., and she swiped booze and drank it. Sam was fascinated. He had never seen anyone who could appear so docile around the grownups and then be completely different with the young people.

Sam was a typical boy where girls were concerned. He was just becoming interested, but was still antagonistic to them in general. He was alternately intrigued, fascinated and annoyed with Ramona. And he expressed his feelings in the only way he knew; he did all he could to make life unpleasant for her. He was constantly teasing. His favorite trick was splashing cold water on her bathing suited slender form as she sun bathed by the pool.

Ramona was wise beyond her years about boys and about men. She was good-natured about Sam's boyish pranks and retaliation was not severe, but it was always instantaneous.

The water splashing would bring quick response. She would spring to her feet and give chase to the fleeing boy. When she caught him she would wrestle him to the ground and push his face into the sand.

Sam's violent temper would come boiling to the surface, but he always restrained it because he was a Southerner and shared the time-honored belief that striking a woman or girl was absolutely forbidden. He continually smarted under the realization that he was bested in each encounter with Ramona.

It should have been just another idyllic summer for Sam, interrupted by occasional bouts with Ramona, but all things changed with a single incident.

It was a sweltering July evening. Thunder rumbled in the distance. The two young people decided to take a refreshing dip in the pool before dinner. Dusk was gathering as they walked, clad in their swimsuits, down the hill to the pool.

13

Ramona said, "I dare you to go skinny dipping."

Sam looked at her incredulously, "You mean naked?"

"No, stupid, with your clothes on," she laughed. "Don't you know what skinny dipping is?"

Sam smarted under her goading. "Sure I know what it means and I ain't gonna do it."

Ramona laughed again and fell silent. At the pool, each spread a large beach towel on the sand. Sam turned and ran into the water. He turned and saw Ramona step out of her one-piece bathing suit and stand naked in the half-light of early evening.

Sam had never seen a naked female before. He watched fascinated as she walked into the water. She swam past him and rolled over on her back. Her small breasts and the dark pubic hair were clearly visible. His heart began to race for a reason he could not fathom. In confusion he swam back to shore and sat on the beach towel.

Ramona swam with the easy grace of a wet seal. She slipped through the water almost effortlessly. She glided into the shallow water and walked upright across the sand to where Sam was sitting. She dropped down beside him and laughed as she tossed her head and sprayed him with the mist from her hair.

She was so near Sam could feel the warmth radiating from her body. Without a word she reached for him, putting her arms around his neck she pulled him against her wet body. For a moment Sam started to jerk away. He said, "What do you think you're doing?"

"Don't be like that Sammy," she said. "Let me show you something. Are you a virgin?"

Sam didn't know much about girls. And what he knew had been learned from Tump, who in turn had learned from an older brother and a few older cousins. Together they had learned much from a girlie magazine, which belonged to Tump's brother. He knew that a virgin was a person who had never, "Got any."

"Naw, I'm not." he lied.

"Then that makes it easy."

"But you're my cousin."

"Haven't you heard, with kinfolks it don't count? There's a saying, the closer kin the deeper in."

Sam's racing heart was choking off his breath. He wanted to jump up and run yet he was more excited than he had ever been. Ramona pressed her firm small breasts against his chest as she pushed him flat of his back on the towel. She kissed his lips gently and slipped one of her hands inside his swimming trunks and grasped his erect penis. "My goodness, you're all grown up," she whispered. "This summer might not be a complete waste after all." She quickly pulled his wet swimming trunks off without any resistance from Sam. With one motion she swung her lithe body up and over, straddling Sam. With experienced hands she placed his penis and shoved down, hard.

For Sam it was quick and wrenching and over too quickly. It was also devastating. Ramona continued to sit on him and move roughly as she sought satisfaction. Her short wet hair hung down over her deadly serious face. All at once she moaned softly and dropped over kissing him passionately. Then she laughed and said, "My I needed that."

She rolled over on the towel and said, "Sammy, we can have a lot of fun this summer, if you'll remember a few things. Never let anyone know what we're doing is number one. Especially say nothing to that dummy friend, Tump. And if your mother ever got wind of this there would be hell to pay"

Sam had nothing to say. He had been thinking of telling Tump that he had gotten some "poontang," but Ramona had said it didn't count if it was with relatives. He was uncertain of how he felt at this moment.

At dinner that night Sam was not his usual talkative self.

Angela, always sensitive to his every mood wondered if he was feeling well.

"I'm O.K.", he insisted.

Angela placed her hand on his forehead and exclaimed, "Why, I believe you are running a temperature. You've been out in the sun too much, always running all over the place and never stopping for a minute. You ought to rest some once in a while."

"Mama, I'm O.K." Sam insisted.

Angela was about to pursue the subject when Henry quietly said, "Angie, leave the boy alone. Anyone who eats as much as he does can't be ill."

Angela had to agree with that logic. Still she worried about any and all changes in her fast growing son.

Sam stole a glance at Ramona who was quietly eating with her eyes focused on her plate. He couldn't believe this demure young lady was the same person he had encountered at the swimming pool.

Sam slept naked in his upstairs bedroom, remote from the bedrooms where his parents and Ramona slept. In the early morning hours he awoke from a deep sleep with a sudden start. Someone was in the room.

"Sssh, its me," Ramona whispered, as she slipped onto the bed.

Once again Sam seemed to have difficulty breathing as his heart raced with excitement. Even the air seemed to be charged with electricity.

"Let me teach you how to do this right".
Ramona said, as she started kissing him on the lips and moved down his body to his penis. She put it in her mouth and sucked softly. Sam's erection needed no further encouragement. She rolled over on her back and told Sam to get on top of her. She guided him in and her body undulated wildly.

When she was finished she held Sam close and whispered words of endearment and caressed his hard muscled young body for more than an hour. She held his penis in her hand all that time and massaged it until it was firmly erect again. Then she straddled his body and fucked him until he came and was limp again. She was still thoroughly aroused and Sam had to insist she leave because dawn was breaking.

Sam grew up overnight. Ramona with her insatiable sexual appetite unleashed the same characteristics in the young boy. And his personality changed. Angela, with her built in sixth sense, was worrying anew. She talked to Henry about her fears.

Henry said, "Ah, you worry too much. He's just growing up and you can't accept that fact."

"Not so," Angela retorted. "You don't see him as much as I do."

"Most of the things you worry about never happen. Why not just enjoy his youth?"

"I'm trying to do just that." she muttered.

Angela had reason to worry. Ramona continued to slip into Sam's room every night. It was a trying time for the youth. He had fallen in love with her, the heartbreaking first love of a very young person. His happy go lucky nature had undergone a profound change. Angela would often find him asleep during the day in any place where he might sit for a few minutes.

When she would try to talk to him he would stare sullenly at the floor and only answer direct questions.

"Sammy, aren't you feeling well?" she would ask.

"I'm alright," he would reply, not looking at her.

If she persisted with this line of questioning, he would snap at her and walk away.

It was an unhappy situation and one that Angela brought to an equally unhappy conclusion. One night there was a thunderstorm and she awoke and routinely checked to see that windows were closed— starting with Sam's room. She was horrified to find the two young people naked in Sam's bed.

She had quietly stepped into the dark room, and hearing an unusual sound had snapped on the light. For a moment she was speechless. It was difficult for her to think of her son as anything except a child. Then a great rage started to build; directed at Ramona.

"What are you doing in this room?" she gasped.

Ramona jumped from the bed, and quickly wrapping her robe around her slim body, fled past the furious Angela.

Sam was experiencing the worst moment in his life. He had always tried to please his mother and for her to see him in these circumstances caused him to burn with shame.

"Tell me what this is all about," she demanded of her young son.

Confused and miserable Sam looked at her and said, "I love her."

A chill swept over Angela when she thought of such an impossibility

"That girl is your cousin, your first cousin. That's almost the same as your sister."

"A lot of people marry their first cousins."

"Marry, what do you know about marriage? You're just a child."

The sullen boy, staring defiantly at his mother caused her to take a second look. He was indeed not a child and not a man, but somewhere in between and confused about his emotions.

"I'm getting your father." Angela stated.

She hurried to where Henry was sleeping soundly. Shaking him awake she quickly explained the situation. Her husband was not excitable. In fact his calmness exasperated Angela.

"Angela," he said, "It's two o'clock in the morning. What do you want me to do?"

"For heavens sake, Henry Warden, he's your son. Don't you think you ought to do something?"

"Like what? Is he hurt? Is he in danger? Is he sick?"

"Sam's entire future might depend on how we handle this," Angela replied.

"Oh, for God's sake, it's just a couple of kids playing at being grownup."

Angela knew better. "You didn't see them like I did. Sam was talking about love and marriage."

"He's just a kid. Kids fall in love every other weekend."

"Henry, what're we going to do?" Angela had calmed down some and Henry put his arms around her and held her close. He loved her dearly and the one thing that could upset him was her unhappiness.

"What we can do," he replied, "is pretty simple. First, we send little Ramona home to

25

her parents. You call your sister first thing in the morning and tell her why. We'll take her to Louisville and put her on the train. Next I'll talk to Sam. It might be a problem but we'll handle it. O.K.?"

"Talk to him tonight, Henry, he's terribly upset. I've never seen him like this." Angela insisted.

"O.K., then can I get some sleep?" he growled.

Henry went to Sam's room and found it empty.

As soon as Angela had departed Sam's room, the boy had dressed and rushed to Ramona's room. It was his first visit there since she had moved in. He was highly agitated and speaking rapidly he said, "I know they'll send you away and I'm going with you."

Ramona looked at him with surprise showing in her arched eyebrows. "You're

26

right about one thing, I'm sure I'll be taking a trip tomorrow. But you're wrong about the other. You're not going with me."

"But I love you, I want to be with you," the youth cried.

"Sammy, don't be stupid, you're just a kid. What would I do with you, put you in school? Besides, I'm in love with a guy back home and we're going to be married. I'm your cousin, remember?"

Sam could feel the hot blood of his temper spreading over him like a blanket. "How about all the things you said to me about love?"

Impatiently, the girl said, "Oh, hell kid, that didn't mean a thing. It was done as they say 'in the heat of the moment', you take things too seriously."

Sam was shaking with anger and his voice had started to rise when he saw his father standing in the doorway. He turned and rushed into the hall, ran down the stairs and dashed into the dark rainy night.

Henry had been so startled at the sight of his son's white face and wild-eyed look that he had hesitated to say anything at first. Now he called, "Sam, Sam" at the boy's retreating back.

Angela heard the commotion and came running. She found Henry still standing in the open door of Ramona's bedroom.

Before she could ask what was happening Henry explained about finding Sam's room empty and then locating him in Ramona's room.

"Where is he now?' Angela wanted to know.

"He ran out into the night." Henry answered.

"Why didn't you go after him? Why are you standing here?" her voice cracking with rage.

She turned and walked to a closet, got some rainwear and a light and went into the wet darkness to find her son. Henry followed close behind, soaking wet and thoroughly miserable.

As she walked along the driveway she called as loudly as she could. "Sam, Sam." There was no answer, only the rumble of distant thunder. She began to cry. This added to the misery of her husband, who was always unnerved by her tears. He put his arms around her and she clung to him sobbing in helpless rage. "I can't understand what is happening to us," she gasped as she pounded on Henry's soggy shoulder.

"It can't be that bad," he said, although not feeling overly confident.

"What do you mean, not bad? Our son is running around in a thunderstorm, in the middle of the night and we don't know what's happening to him."

When Sam ran out of the house, he ran blindly into the wet darkness. The familiar landmarks were illuminated by the flashes of lightening. He ran across the open pasture, his rage cooling with each step. He slowed to a walk and fell face down on the wet grass. Sobs tore through his body as he dug his fingers into the wet soil. That was the changing point in his life. The sobs subsided. He never cried again—ever.

The rage was gone, the rain beat down and Sam began to shiver. He crept to Jose Williams' house and up on the porch where he was shielded from the rain. He was still a very wet and cold boy. Jose's dog, who knew Sam, didn't bark but came up to him and with tail wagging greeted him with whining pleasure.

Jose had awakened from a deep sleep. He heard the dog whining on the porch and peeked out his bedroom window. He could see the dim outline of a figure in the light provided by the flashes of lightening. He turned to his sleeping wife and shook her awake.

"What's the matter?" Ava asked.

"There's somebody on the po'ch," Jose whispered.

They both lay quietly for a few moments, remembering strangers in the dark from many years ago when they had faced many dangers. Ava peeked through the window and saw the shadowy figure stroking the dog when the lightening flashed.

"Why, that's Mistah Sam." she declared.

"Are you sho'?"

"Co'se I am, I've knowed that boy since he was born. I'd know his ashes in a whirlwind," she said as she climbed out of bed. Lighting a kerosene lamp she hurried to the door, jerked it opened and stepped out onto the porch.

31

"Mistah Sam, what—lawsy, you is soaking wet. Come in this house this minute befo' you ketch yo death of cold." She caught him firmly by the arm and led him, unresisting into the house. "Jose, light a fire, this chile's freezing to death."

Although it was summer, Jose complied with Ava's order. And began to lay a fire while Ava got some of Jose's clothes to replace the wet things Sam was wearing. She was ready to strip him bare but Sam took the clothing and said, "No, no I can do it." Ava would not hear of him dressing himself. "Chile, I've seed you since the day you came into the world, what's one more time?" She unbuttoned his shirt and started peeling it from his wet skin.

Jose had the fire crackling in the fireplace. He said, "Wait a minute, Ava, Mistah Sam is all growed up since you dressed him. You go into the bedroom and he

32

can undress by the fire. I'll see that he gets dry." He caught his wife by the arm and led her to the bedroom. He whispered to her, "Slip out and go up to the big house and see what's happened. I see lights up there. They might not know where Mistah Sam is."

Ava stared at her husband a few moments. "Tha's right, I bet they don' know. Let's get him dry and warm and then you go see Mistah Henry. Miss Angela will be fit to be tied if she don' know where her boy is. You can handle that better'n me."

When they returned to the living room, Sam was dry and dressed in Jose's clothes, which were several sizes too large. "Lawdy, chile, you look like a scarey crow." She began fussing over him, rolling up the shirtsleeves that hung down over his hands, and turning up the pants legs

It wasn't that Sam was small, but Jose was a big man, over six feet tall and well over two hundred pounds. "Let's go to the kitchen and I'll fix you some hot choc'late."

As they left the living room, Jose slipped out the door and walked rapidly to the "big house" and knocked on the door. Henry opened it. Jose was a wise man and he never wasted words. "Mistah Henry, Mistah Sam's at our house. He alright, he in good shape."

The questioning look on Henry's face gave way to one of relief. After he and Angela had searched the grounds they had returned to the house and were preparing to call the sheriff to organize a search party.

Angela walked up just in time to hear Jose say, "Ava got him dry and warm, he probably in bed asleep by now. Why not let him stay for a while? Ava would 'preciate a chance to baby him some." The parents looked at each other for a few moments. "That

34

probably makes sense," Angela said. The unspoken message passing between husband and wife that it would be better for Sam if he didn't have to say goodbye to Ramona, who was destined to depart Lone Pine as quickly as arrangements could be made.

And so it was decided that Sam would miss seeing Ramona's departure.

Angela telephoned her sister and told her she was sending her daughter home, and why. They never spoke to each other again. Henry hired a car, which took Ramona to the railroad station in Louisville. Daybreak was turning the wet darkness in to a soggy gray dawn. It had been a trying few hours for the Warden family.

Sam had been tucked into a bed and fussed over as only Ava could do. She still treated him like the child she had known all his life. She didn't know what was troubling him and didn't try to find out. First things

35

first was her motto. Her young ward needed some sleep and she intended to see that he had the opportunity.

The warm drink and warmth of the bed lulled Sam to sleep and when he awoke it was almost noon. The storm had passed, the sun was shinning and his clothing had been washed, pressed and were folded neatly on the foot of the bed.

At first he wasn't aware of where he was. And then memory came flooding back. He lay thoughtful for a moment, then slipped out of bed, dressed, and walked the short distance to his home.

Ava was bustling around in the kitchen and when she saw Sam she began fussing over him in her usual manner.

"Lawsy Mistah Sam I bet you is starved stiff a grinning. Come sit here and let me get you some breakfast."

"I'm not hungry."

"Growing boys is always hungry." Ava caught him by the arm and led him to the table and pushed him into a chair.

Long experience had taught Sam that arguing with Ava was useless if it involved what she thought was his well being. In a few minutes bacon was sizzling on the stove and eggs were sputtering in hot grease. The aroma of cooking food was filling the air and to Sam's surprise he found he was, in the words of Tump, "Hungry as a bitch wolf."

He was devouring his second helping when Angela came into the room. She acted as though nothing had happened during the night. She and Henry had decided to "just play it by ear" until they could get a feel for how their son was going to react. "Hi, Sammy," she greeted him.

"Hi," he mumbled without looking up from his plate.

Angela walked through the kitchen and out the back door and stood on the back porch gazing across the peaceful, rain washed pasture. Sam could see her ramrod straight back and he wondered what she might be thinking.

. After breakfast he wandered around the house and out on the grounds. There was not a sign of Ramona. It was as if the past weeks had not existed. In the afternoon Tump stopped by and they went for a swim. Even he, the gabby one, didn't say a word about "The pest" as he had called her. In the evening Henry came home and acted in his normal quiet manner without any mention of what had happened. Sam began to think he had been dreaming.

The next day was the same. No mention of the girl that had changed Sam's life. But she still haunted his dreams. He would fall into a deep sleep at night and Ramona would

be making love to him. It was vivid and
disturbing. he would wake up and be
breathing hard.

Chapter 2

Henry had an easy and comfortable relationship with his son. One morning he saw Sam walking aimlessly across the yard. An idea came out of nowhere. He rushed outside and called, "Hey, Sam, come go with me."

"Where to?"

"You'll see soon enough."

They got into the family car and sped away. As they rolled along Sam's curiosity got the better of him.

"What's this all about?"

"You'll see." Henry was enjoying the interest his son was showing.

About twenty miles from Lone Pine there was an airfield, owned by Lee Brown, a man who had been a World War 1 fighter pilot. He had a crop dusting business, was a flight instructor and provided charter service for those who might be so inclined. He also had a two-pump gasoline service station and an automobile repair shop. "In the air or on the ground see Lee Brown" a big sign proclaimed at the intersection of two county roads where the business was located. He lived in a small house nearby. Sometimes he was busy and sometimes very busy. "Its a living," he would say if asked how he was doing.

Henry parked the automobile by the repair shop and turned to Sam. "How would you like to learn to fly?" He was rewarded with a wide-eyed stare.

"You mean it?"

"Would I kid about a thing like that?"

"That would be great. What would Mom say?" He knew how protective Angela could be.

Claude Eldridge

"We'll just have to work that little problem," Henry replied. He was pleased by the immediate interest shown by his son.

They went into the shop where they found Lee's legs sticking out from beneath an automobile he was working on. When he heard them walk in, he slid the creeper out and stood up. "Howdy Judge," he said, as he wiped grease from his hands.

"Hi Lee, this is my son Sam. He's interested in learning to fly."

"I'm glad to know you Sam. Any son of Judge Warden just got to be a good man." He shook hands with the boy who instantly liked the smiling gray haired man.

"Well Sam, have you ever flown before?" Lee asked.

Sam shook his head no.

"Then the first thing for us to do is check out your stomach to see if it stays in place when you get off the ground. Let's go

42

for a ride. I need to get away from this place for a while anyway. Judge, you can take care of things while we're gone. Might be somebody stop by for some gas."

Sam trailed along behind Lee as they walked to the hanger where the airplanes were housed. One of which was Lee's pride and joy, one he had built himself. The name across the engine cowling was "My Baby." Years of a labor of love had gone into the construction of the trim blue and white aircraft. Lee used it in air shows as a stunt plane. In his words it was "A hot number." Lee kept up a continuous line of chatter about flying and airplanes. It was meant to put the boy at ease as well as teach him about how to handle and care for airplanes on the ground. They pushed My Baby through the hanger doors to the ramp outside. Lee went through the preflight check, telling Sam of the importance of

43

making sure everything was shipshape before starting the engine. "Flying is unforgiving, one mistake can be your last one," he emphasized.

Sam was making a mental note of everything that was happening. He was silent all during the preparation, which was in his favor with Lee. "Climb in and fasten your safety belt," he was told. Lee pulled the prop through a couple of turns and the engine came to life, he slipped into the pilot's seat and slowly taxied to the end of the runway. He turned the craft into the wind and held the brakes as the engine roared its song of power. Sam had never experienced such noise as the plane shook and rattled. Lee was a careful man where flying was concerned, and even more so when he had a student on board. He checked every detail before the plane started to roll. He pulled the throttle back and as the engine slowed it became quiet enough to hear. He looked at Sam and grinned. "Ready?"

"Ready," it was the first word Sam had spoken.

Lee pushed the throttle forward and the plane roared down the runway, it climbed into the sky at a steep angle. They leveled out over the city and made some slow turns and gentle rolls. Lee wanted to see how his prospective student would handle the motion. "Whadda ya think?" he shouted.

"It's great," his eyes shinning.

Lee put the plane through stalls and loops. He flew upside down, watching Sam out of the corner of his eye, he dived and roared over the airfield at low level, he pulled back on the stick and My Baby went almost straight up and barrel rolled across the sky, he turned and came in for a landing without a bump when the wheels touched. They taxied back to the starting point.

45

Claude Eldridge

"How's your belly?"

"I don't have one. I left it back yonder somewhere," he said in a shaky voice.

"I think you did just fine. Did you enjoy it?"

"Its the most exciting thing I ever did. I loved it."

Henry was duly impressed with his son's enthusiasm when they arrived back in the shop. Lee's report to him was very favorable. "We can get started with the lessons right away if that's what you want. I believe he'll do fine."

Sam was ready to start at that moment. "Can we start this afternoon, Dad?"

"Don't you think we should check with your mother first?"

"I know Mom won't like it."

"We'll work that problem and get back with Lee."

46

Lee had stood quietly while father and son discussed the problem of Angela's approval. He was pleased that he wouldn't have to mention the other parent's likely displeasure. Like everyone in that part of the county, he knew how fiercely protective she could be. As Henry and Sam were leaving Lee told them when they were ready, to let him know and a flight instruction plan would be worked out.

As expected Angela was aghast. "Never, never in a million years is he going to fly. He's just a child. Henry Warden I'm shocked that you would even think of such a thing."

Henry had decided to privately explain his plan to his wife. They were strolling down the lane that led from the house to the mailbox on the county road. It was lined with trees the two of them had planted. A fence ran along one side, which was covered with honeysuckle vines, and they filled the

47

air with their fragrance. He thought this was the best place he could find to reason with Angela.

"There's danger in everything, Honey. Lee Brown is the best instructor in the State."

"I won't hear of it."

"He wants a car. Are you going to be against that also?"

"That's different."

"Angela, an automobile is more dangerous than flying."

"I don't believe it." She had a stubborn, set look that Henry knew very well. "Why do you want him to fly anyway?"

"It's not that I want him to. It's for his own good. You should have seen him. He was more like himself than he's been for days. You know how he's been moping around since the Ramona deal. I must talk to him about that episode when the time is right. He'll be busy all summer, and being so young, by the time school begins I hope he will have forgotten about her."

Angela could see the logic of Henry's argument, but she was not convinced. "One of Brown's crop dusters was killed just last summer."

"He's not going to be a crop duster. He'll just be flying one of those slow cubs or whatever they are."

Henry was becoming exasperated but he tried not to let it show. By the time the walk was finished he got a reluctant go ahead from Angela.

Sam was a happy boy when his parents informed him he could begin his flight training. He assured his mother that he would be very careful. "Mr Brown is the best pilot in the country and he won't let anything happen," he assured his mother. Lee was called and on the following Monday the instruction was scheduled to begin.

49

That night Sam dreamed he was with Ramona. It was so vivid he had an orgasm in his sleep. He awoke with wet sticky underwear. His unhappiness began all over again.

On Sunday he saw his friend Tump and asked him if he had ever had a "wet dream".

"Sure have," Tump answered, "And if I hadn't fallen asleep, I woulda had another one. Har, Har," he guffawed at his joke.

"O.K. smart ass." Sam was a little annoyed.

"Ah, it happens to everybody, I reckon. That's what my brother Joe says and he knows all about things like that."

Sam told his friend he was starting flying lessons on Monday. That got an instant reaction from Tump.

"Not me boy. If God had wanted man to fly he would have sprouted wings on his shoulders. You can have the birdman bit. I get a nose bleed from climbing a ladder."

"Ah, you're just a 'fraidy cat."

"And with damn good reason. My brother Joe helped dig that crop-duster out of the ground last year. You ought to talk to him before you start flying with crazy Brown."

"Why, he's the best pilot around these parts," Sam said, getting a little hot under the collar.

"Yeah, you can bet your ass he is. That's because he's the only one dumb enough to fly that homemade contraption he calls a plane. Why do you wanta fly, you gonna be a crop duster?"

"I just want to learn."

The two had been friends since third grade. Tump was one year older than Sam. They were in the same grade because Tump had flunked second grade due to a severe illness that kept him out of school for most of the year. He was the son of a rural route mail carrier and just barely met Angela's social standards for her son's friends. They had the easy bantering relationship that is common for teenage boys. Often they were harsh in criticizing each other but quick to defend if attacked by another person.

Tump's school grades were not good. He struggled with every subject. However, he had an ability that was outstanding. He could draw anything with amazing accuracy. People's faces, a dog or a tree. Unfortunately his school could not accommodate that talent. Tump used it for his own amusement and for the admiration he received from his peers; especially when he drew naked women.

Once he had a fifth grade teacher named Miss Houston. She was a beautiful young woman. He made sketches of her in different poses, without any clothes, all from his active imagination. He was the hero when he passed the sketches around to the other boys in his class. All was going well until one day Miss Houston walked quietly behind his desk when he was deeply engrossed in yet another drawing of the young teacher. He was jerked from his seat and led to the principal's office. He was whipped severely and almost expelled from school.

"I don't see any reason for you to learn to fly," Tump said. "What good is it? A pilot's license and a nickel will buy you a coca cola."

"You wouldn't understand, dummy," Sam retorted. The boys began to push and shove and broke into giggles as they usually did.

Sam's flying lessons began on Monday. He was an excellent student with a remarkable memory for the slightest detail. Lee would say that he, himself, had to be most careful about making mistakes, because Sam would repeat them in the exact same manner. After six hours of instruction Sam made his solo flight. In less time than Henry had intended he passed all tests and obtained his pilot's license. That was before he had a license to drive a car.

During the flight instruction a close friendship began between Lee Brown the man, and Sam Warden the boy. About the time it was over Lee's business was entering the busy season of crop dusting. He offered Sam a job as a general helper in the repair shop and service station. "You like to fly, you can take your pay in flight time," he kidded.

"Man the way you pay, I wouldn't get to fly much." The pay was twenty-five cents an hour, the going rate for that time.

Sam was a very good worker, especially for one so young and one who had been pampered all of his life. Lee would say of him that he learned faster than anyone he had ever met. "Just show him one time, or better still let him read it from a book and it's his forever. His power of retention is unbelievable," Lee told his wife.

Henry was pleased that his son was keeping busy doing something that he apparently enjoyed. Angela thought otherwise. "I think it's disgraceful, working as a grease monkey in that garage. His hands are never clean. Did you ever notice his finger nails?" she asked her husband.

"Don't worry about dirty finger nails. It could be much worse," Henry cautioned, remembering the Ramona problem of a few weeks before. He had meant to discuss that subject with Sam but kept putting it off for no good reason.

The summer slipped by with Sam becoming an accomplished pilot and an all around good helper in Lee's business. He pumped gasoline for the frequent customers, kept the place clean and the shop spotless. Lee boasted that the boy could tear an automobile engine down and put it back together as quickly as the best mechanic in the county.

When school started Sam thought that would be the end of his employment, but Lee had other plans. He had expanded his business to include stocking, selling and delivery of propane gas. "I need someone to mind the store while I make deliveries," he told Sam. "You could work anytime you are free, some evenings and on the weekend. Wouldn't want to hurt your schoolwork. Or your social life," he said with a grin.

"I'd have to talk to my folks."

"Sure thing. Probably be alright with Henry, Miss Angela won't like it."

"Well, I'll try Dad first, if I can convince him, we'll let him do the heavy stuff."

Lee patted Sam's shoulder. "A wise decision."

And that's the way it was. Angela kicked up a fuss when Henry talked to her, but she consented when it was promised that if there was the slightest decline in Sam's school grades the job was over.

Henry told Sam, "You know what you have to do. If that job is important, keep the grades up."

When Lee was informed of the decision, he agreed with Sam's parents. He squinted his eyes as he looked at the boy. "Just how good are your grades, young fellow?"

"They're o.k."

"Tell you what, let's make them better. If you start having trouble, bring your books and study here unless there's a customer waiting."

As it turned out Sam's school schedule would only permit two evenings per week. He worked a full day on Saturday. His grades were actually better than the previous year because he was concentrating as never before. Lee was pleased with his bright young employee and Sam's dreams of Ramona were beginning to diminish.

Sam's sixteenth birthday was November 11. His parents gave him an automobile for a present. It was a four door Ford V8.

Tump said, "Boy, are you lucky. That's a pussy wagone if I ever saw one."

Sam's world changed a lot after he took possession of the car. There were many girls. Tump said, "Let's try 'em all, and the easy ones twice."

They worked at doing just that. The Burton twins were frequent companions for the two boys. Tump was quick to pass judgment on the young ladies. "Boy, you can't tell 'em apart, not even on the back seat." Sam maintained a close-lipped silence. He had learned to let Tump do the talking, which he did without any encouragement.

"My brother, Joe, says make sure you use a rubber. It'll not only keep you from catching the clap, but probably save you from a shotgun wedding."

"Your brother seems to know everything."

"You can bet your ass he's been around the track a few times. Did I ever tell you about the time he got caught in old lady Jackson's bedroom when her husband came home?"

"Not over a dozen times."

Old lady Jackson was about thirty years old with a traveling man for a husband. It was rumored about town that she got lonesome

59

and some of the more adventuresome males tried to fill the void left by the absent husband.

"Yeah, old Joe just slipped under the bed. Old man Jackson got to banging the old lady and the dust made Joe nearly sneeze. Jackson heard the noise and asked his wife what that was. She said it was the puppy. Old man Jackson held his hand over the edge of the bed and snapped his fingers. Joe said he had to lick the man's fingers or risk getting shot"

Tump would nearly collapse with laughter.

"Johnson, you lying bastard. You know Joe didn't tell you that bunch of crap."

Tump would laugh all the harder. "I swear it s the truth. Joe stayed under the bed until he could hear the old man snore, then he sneaked out."

"Oh bull, you'd believe any damn thing Joe said."

Tump became defensive. "Well, buddy boy, did he ever tell you a lie, or anything wrong?"

Sam had to admit Joe was a straight shooter. And most of what he knew about girls and the raw side of life had come from Joe. His parents had avoided talking to him about the "Birds and the bees".

The two boys began building a reputation for being more than a little fond of the ladies. Their friendship, which began when they were small children, continued to grow as they approached adulthood. Tump was the more outgoing. Loud and boisterous, he had difficulty in maintaining passable grades in school. Sam was the quiet one. His schoolwork was outstanding. He often gave Tump a helping hand with tough assignments.

Sam learned to avoid the truth when his mother would question his activities. "What are you doing this evening?" was a standard query.

"Tump and I are just fooling around," was his standard reply.

"Girls involved?" she would continue.

"Nah, we just drive around, maybe shoot a little pool." he would lie, with a straight face.

Angela would have had a fit if she had known of his activities. And Sam knew that his mother had made up her mind about the girls he should date. She always invited some girls from "The best families" to the parties at Lone Pine.

One example was Alicia Steinberg. Tump referred to her as "A dog". She had braces on her teeth, wore horn-rimmed glasses and had a habit of hiding her smile with her hand. Sam agreed with his friend. Her father was the richest man in the county. And she was an only child, which made her all the more attractive to Sam's mother.

Angela did what she could, without being too obvious, to throw the two young people together. She arranged a party and invited Alicia, promising the girl's parents she would see that she got home afterwards. Sam was elected to provide the transportation.

As they drove through the dark streets there was very little conversation. If Sam asked a direct question she would answer. And that was about all.

"Would you like to drive by the lake?" he asked.

"O.K", She replied.

Sam drove to the tree lined shore of the lake and parked under the spreading branches of a large oak. The girl sat calmly and undisturbed by his side. He put his arms around her and drew her unresisting body close. He could feel the warmth radiating from her and his heart began to race. He kissed her unresponsive lips and slipped his hand between her legs. She did not resist, neither did she respond. She whispered in his ear. "I'll tell Daddy".

"What'll you tell him?"

"That you raped me."

A chill slipped down Sam's spine and in his mind's eye he could see his mother's face when Alicia's father confronted her. His ardor cooled promptly. He drew back and Alicia laughed a soft husky laugh he had not heard before. They drove in silence to her home. She got out of the car and turned to Sam. "You're the first boy that ever kissed me," and without another word she walked into the house.

For some reason Sam felt he had mistreated Alicia and he was sorry for his actions as he drove back to Lone Pine. That feeling passed quickly when he was accosted by his friend Tump the next day.

"Hey," he said, "Did you go by the lake with old gorgeous last night?"

"What's it to you, smart ass?"

"Damn. I believe you did. I can tell by the look on your face. How was it? Did you get tangled up in her braces? Har, har, har", he brayed. "Did you have to put a sack over her head? If you give her a passing grade, I'll give her a try."

"O.K., I give her a passing grade. Now its your turn." Sam grinned as he faced his friend.

"UH oh, I don't like that look. What happened?"

"Nothing," Sam replied, "Absolutely nothing."

"Well, I'll be damned, mighty Casey struck out."

"Forget it," Sam growled.

"I guess you can't win 'em all." Tump punched his friend on the shoulder as they walked across the school ground.

One Saturday Sam was alone in the shop. Lee was out making deliveries. Business was slow and the chores that were a part of Sam's duties were finished. He picked up a manual on engine repair and started reading. There was a truck in the shop for repair that Lee hadn't found time to start. After reading the manual for a while Sam cranked the engine of the truck and after some effort it coughed to life and ran roughly and sputtered when he pressed the accelerator. He quickly removed the carburetor and in a short while added new parts, for a complete overhaul, reinstalled it on the truck and cranked the engine. It ran smoothly and accelerated to full power when he pressed the foot pedal. He was making some final adjustments when Lee came in. The old truck engine was purring quietly.

"Well, what did you do to that old heap?" Lee wanted to know.

Sam told him about reading the manual and determining from that what the trouble was and described in some detail just what he had done to make the repairs. His description of the repair manual was so complete it sounded to Lee as if he were reading the manual. Lee took the manual and riffled through the pages. "Tell me what page 36 is about."

Sam started at the top of the page and quoted it, word for word, in its entirety.

"Well, I'll be damned." Lee said, softly, almost under his breath. "How long have you been able to do this?"

"Oh," Sam replied, "That's the first truck I ever worked on."

"I don't mean the truck. I mean how long have you been able to memorize a whole book in a short time?"

"I don't memorize."

"Then what do you do?"

"I just look at the page and when I want to see something on that page I just look at it in my mind."

"Does your parents know about this?" Lee wanted to know.

"I don't know. We never talked about it. I think Mom can do the same."

"How about teachers, what do they think?"

"Teachers are easily fooled. Sometimes I would give wrong answers just to keep my grades down. Tump and the others always kid the pants off the so-called brains."

Lee dropped the subject when it seemed to be getting on sensitive ground. But he was a friend of the high school principal, John Fleming, and over cocktails that evening they had a serious conversation about Lee's young employee.

"John, Sam Warden works part time for me."

"Yeah, I heard that, I believe from the Judge. Young rascal has his private pilot's license. I'm surprised his mother let him do that. She's like a hen with one chick."

"Well, for some reason she agreed for him to fly. He had a good sponsor. His father. Maybe that's the reason she didn't kick up a cloud of dust. I knew he was extremely bright when he was taking his flight instruction. But I didn't realize just how bright until a few days ago. Do you know he can read a book, a whole book of instruction, like a repair manual, and then read the entire book back to you from memory?"

"No Lee, I've never heard even a hint of Sam being capable of that. I can't remember

69

his being in the top of his class in grades. Are you sure?"

Lee looked thoughtful as he swirled the ice around in his glass. "I'm sure. He demonstrated a couple of times, not showing off, just showing he could take a manual and follow it in his head. I've heard of such things, but this is the first time I've actually seen it happen."

"As an educator I've seen it happen a couple of times. Both times they were girls. Highly motivated people who were striving to excel."

"What happened to them?"

"Both graduated from high school at a very early age, entered college, fell in love, got married and became the smartest mamas in town."

"Just like that?"

"Just like that!"

"John, a kid as brilliant as Sam could pass a college entrance exam now if he wanted to."

"Ah my friend, you've said the magic words, if he wanted to. Most people only use a small bit of their capabilities simply because its too much trouble, takes a lot of effort and people just won't do it."

"John, what is it that motivates people? Anyone, you, me, or Sam?"

"Look at it this way Lee, it could be anything, ego, wanting to excel. With the two of us its probably just making a living for the family. For Sam, who knows? I wouldn't even guess. He has it pretty soft. In this land of poor and often poverty stricken people, he lives as a young prince. Has his own car, a private pilot's license. His family has his life planned for him. Hell, there are people in this county, his age that have probably never even seen the

71

inside of an automobile. There are many who can't read and write and I don't just mean the black people. The majority of them have never seen the inside of a school. And I think that's a disgrace."

Lee knew his friend's feelings about the illiterate people in this part of Mississippi. They had had many long and often heated discussions about the social ills of the South. Lee, bred and born in this same county, blamed the conditions on the civil war and the Republican Government. John was from Kansas and he believed the complacency about education was the fault of the uncaring citizenry of the local area.

Before John really got going Lee said goodnight and took his leave.

In January of 1941, on a Saturday, Sam was working on an aircraft instrument. Lee watched as the boy moved swiftly, reassembling the complicated part. "Sam," he said, "What do you think about college?

Without looking up Sam replied, "Nothing."

"Is that right? What would you like to do?"

"Fly, be a crop duster for you."

"Now that's what I call real ambition." The sarcasm in Lee's voice wasn't lost on Sam.

"Well a guy could do a lot worse. I don't have to worry. My folks got it all planned out. I'm supposed to go back East to some high priced school."

"Well, young man, if the world situation continues on its present course you'll probably get a chance to fly a lot. I guess it would be a type of pest control. Kraut extermination."

"I'd love to fly for the army. But that's a long way off. Got a lot of school to get out of the way."

"You could speed up the school work."

"How? It takes just so many years. Gotta finish high school, then four years of college."

"You could double up on your studies. Next fall take a college entrance exam. Skip your last year of high school."

"Hah, why would I want to do that?"

"A college graduate would make a mighty attractive army air corp candidate. But you probably couldn't handle the requirements of high school acceleration."

Both men were silent for a while, and then Sam asked, "How would you go about doing a thing like that?"

Lee knew he had touched a responsive chord when he hinted Sam couldn't handle the high school work. In his most innocent manner he asked, "Do what?"

"You know, going to college early."

"Talk to your parents first. Then have your dad talk to John Fleming"

"Mama would croak if she even dreamed of me being in the service."

"I'm afraid I can't help you there, that's something you have to work out on your own."

Sam thought about their conversation a few days and then he talked to his parents about taking some extra studies just to earn additional credits. Henry was pleased, but Angela was delighted. She was sure her son was starting to live up to his potential.

For the first time in his life Sam tried doing his best. Everyone was surprised. His grades were straight A s. Through a series of tests it was discovered he had a total photographic memory. He could read entire books and recite, verbatim, page by page, the complete text. Mathematical formulas and problem solutions worked out in advance were remembered, making ordinary testing procedures, for him, obsolete.

Sam's friends, and especially Tump Johnson, were completely in shock. Tump said, "Damn, what did you do, eat some smartening pills?" Sam just shook his head and smiled a tight-lipped smile.

His parents talked to him about stopping his work at Lee Brown's place, but Sam argued that they had agreed he could work there if he kept his grades up. "That should still be a good rule." Henry and Angela were pleased with his maturity and logic.

School was out at the end of May. Sam had passed the entrance exams at Ole Miss. He would begin his college career there in the fall. He had convinced his mother that it would be like his senior year in high school and he would be prepared for Yale the following year. She was easy to persuade. It was difficult for her to believe he was grown up enough to leave home. At least Ole Miss would be nearby.

Sam was working at Lee's place when he first saw Camille Dotson. She was with a group of people riding in an old model A Ford car that had been stripped down and made into a sort of flat bed truck. It was driven by Woody Baker, filled to almost over capacity with people, one of which was Camille's father, Charlie, a large grim, overall clad, man who needed a shave.

Camille was a small boned girl, wearing cut off jean shorts and a T-shirt, which showed her almost perfect figure She walked, barefoot, across the driveway to the coca-cola machine. Sam thought she was the most beautiful girl he had ever seen. He hurried from the shop to the soft drink machine and asked, "May I help you?"

She looked at him quickly and shyly dropped her gaze. "No, I'm just getting a bottle of pop." Then she turned and walked back to the truck.

After buying two gallons of gasoline, Woody drove the vehicle, rattling, out of the driveway. Camille looked back at Sam as they pulled away.

Sam said to Lee, "Boy that was one pretty girl."

"Yeah," Lee replied. "She's a beauty—now. Not much future. That's a strange breed of people. Don't believe in schools. Marry their kinfolks. She's probably already spoken for. They kill you about their women. Don't you even think about her again."

That evening at dinner Sam said, "I saw the prettiest girl I've ever seen today." He went on to describe the events at the garage.

Angela felt a chill, remembering last year's experience with Ramona. She said, "Those people are nothing but trash. They are uneducated, intermarry, break the law by not sending their kids to school and half of them, at least, make moonshine."

Defensively Sam replied, "I didn't intend to invite them to dinner. I was just sharing an experience."

Henry spoke up, "They're probably not as bad as your mother thinks. They are very poor. Some of them are very nice people. They'll treat you good if you go to their homes. Some things are taboo for outsiders. And their women is the first no no. Anybody outside of their settlement, known as Bakertown, is an outsider. You, my boy, are an outsider. Stay that way. They have shotgun weddings when kids like you just as much as touch one of their girls. And by touch I mean just holding hands."

Before Sam could speak, Angela said, "I want you to promise me you'll never have anything to do with any of that bunch of low life trash. No, more than that, I forbid you to as much as ever speak to one of them."

Sam felt his temper starting to rise. Quietly and slowly he placed his napkin on the table and arose. "I'm sorry I even mentioned the subject. Excuse me." With that he walked into the kitchen. Ava was bustling around doing her usual evening chores. She patted Sam's shoulder and said softly. "Yo' mama is sho right about that white trash Mista Sam. Don't have nothin' to do with 'em. They's night riders and hides behind white sheets. They shoots niggers for no reason. And they shoots white people jest as quick."

"Jeez, Ava, I was just talking about how pretty she is," Sam said, defensively.

"Yassuh, I knows." with that she said no more.

The next evening Sam and Tump were cruising around the streets looking for girls to pick up and Sam was grouching about his parent's attitude when he was discussing the Dotson girl. "You'd think I was planning to bring her home with me."

"Boy wouldn't you like to do that; just imagine her in your bed at home." Tump was more than enthusiastic. "She's got the prettiest little ass I've ever seen. Her little tits stick straight out."

"What do you know about her?"

"Nothing, but I've seen her, oh hell, three or four times.

My brother, Joe, went coon hunting with some of the Bakers last winter. I went with him a few times. They got the best coon dogs in the county."

"Are they as bad as my folks say, the people, I mean?"

"My brother Joe says they are poor people who take care of their own and take no shit off anybody. And if one of them says I'm gonna shoot you tomorrow at eight in the morning; you got two choices. Leave the country or get your will made out."

Sam thought that over a little bit and said, "You can't date their women, right?"

"Oh, yeah you can. My brother Joe did. He sure didn't get any nooky. Only time he ever struck out. They chaperone the hell out of you. Have some little kid sit right in the room. And if you go for a ride the kid goes along. Joe got real friendly with this little number. Said she melted his underwear just looking at him. He knew she was ready, but nothing doing. One time he tried to bribe the kid. Gave the little beggar fifty cents. The kid left and an old, snuff dipping, hag took his place. That Joe, never quit bitching about his fifty cents. Said he coulda' got a blow job at Lulu's place for that much money."

"If you want to know anything, just ask Joe, huh, Johnson?" Sam asked his friend.

"That's about right. Joe says get all you can, if you miss some you might get some more, but you'll never get what you missed. Hold it. Pull up to the curb. Here're a couple of gals from out of town. We wouldn't want them to have a dull evening."

Tump liked to drink beer, which was the powerful home brew, made by the local residents. For more festive occasions, like out of town girls, he usually had a bottle of moonshine whiskey. "That moonshine made in Bakertown lowers the female resistance to absolute zero. Girls love it," he said to Sam.

Sam had to agree that it did seem that way. Although he did not like anything with alcohol in it, he would pretend to drink from the moonshine bottle and that gesture satisfied his companions of the day. However, Tump knew that Sam was almost a teetotaler.

Tump had learned to smoke cigarettes at an early age. It was the in thing to do. The young females they dated also smoked, but not Sam. When Tump kidded him about being so straight laced he simply said, "Not so. I don't like to smoke because a cigarette tastes like a spittoon smells."

It was a few days later when Sam saw his friend. Tump was unusually quiet. "What's the matter with you, oh silent one?"

"My brother Joe—," Tump began.

"Oh no, not again," Sam protested, in mock horror.

"He joined the marines. He left this morning." Tump said softly, almost in tears.

Sam had never seen his friend so subdued. "Hey, he'll be OK. just think how he'll make out with the girls, wearing that fancy marine uniform."

Tump brightened a bit. "Boy, he will won't he? Old Joe'll knock 'em dead." Then he bowed his head and the tears started to run down his cheeks. "He gave me his little black book—like, like he'll never need it again." His voice broke slightly as he said the unthinkable. "Joe was always there when anybody needed him, and I needed him more than anybody."

"Hell, Tump, we're not in a war, lots of guys going into the service. I see a bunch of 'em every weekend strutting their ass down the streets. Joe'll be joining that parade before you know it."

Tump looked relieved. "Yeah, you're right." He was thoughtful a moment. "I got a job. I'm gonna work nights at the soda fountain in the drug store."

"Why, you lazy bastard. That's what's the matter. You've gotta go to work," Sam growled, thankful for a change of subject.

"Yeah, I've gotta go to work and you, you smart ass prick, are going away to school this fall." Tump's voice was tinged with sadness.

Sam reached over and punched Tump lightly on the shoulder. And Tump did the same to Sam. It was the only act of affection they could muster.

Sam was driving the Lee Brown fuel delivery truck over a little used county road when he saw Camille Dotson standing by a rural mailbox. He stopped the truck without even thinking.

Never at a loss for words he said, "Miss could you tell me how to get to Baker's corner?" Even though he had been there a few times.

"Yes," she answered, "Go down about a mile to a fork in the road and turn right, about two miles on the left. There's no way to miss it." She was smiling, showing perfectly even white teeth.

"Why don't you go along and show me the way?"

"I couldn't do that. I've never met you."

"I'm Sam Warden."

"I know your name, but I don't know you."

"That makes us even. I know your name, and I don't know you either, but I'd sure like to." Sam declared in his most persuasive manner.

Claude Eldridge

Camille had been standing by the mailbox, with one hand resting lightly on its top. She started to move away from the road. Sam was completely taken by her beauty. But now she was starting to walk away and he had no idea how he would manage to see her again. Hurriedly he said, "If you'll wait I'll bring you a bottle of pop from Baker's corner." She didn't answer, but looked over her shoulder and smiled.

Sam drove to the store, made his delivery, bought two bottles of cold coca-cola and returned to the mailbox. Camille was sitting under the shade of a small pine tree. Parking the truck, he climbed out and walked over to her and looked down. She had the deepest blue eyes and as she looked up at him he became completely lost. "You're the prettiest girl I've ever seen," he blurted, and promptly felt like a fool.

"Please don't talk like that," she said softly. As she reached for the cold drink their fingertips touched and they both jumped like they had touched a live wire.

"Why not talk like that? Its true."

She took a sip of her drink, still looking up at Sam. "You don't know a thing about me," she replied. She stood and shyly looking away from his gaze she started to move toward the trail that led to her home, which was about a half mile away.

"Wait, don't go. How can I get to know you if I can't talk to you?"

"I have to go. I've been away too long. Someone will come looking for me," Camille said, as she started walking faster.

"Can I see you again?" Sam called after her retreating figure. She turned and looked back, but she continued to walk. Sam was struck by the sadness on her face.

Sam drove back to the shop and all he could think of was the beautiful blue-eyed girl. He remembered the way she walked and the incredibly tiny waist.

It was a busy time for Lee's business and a week passed before there was an opportunity for Sam to go by the mailbox at the same time of day. The Baker's corner fuel delivery was scheduled for the same day each week, and although it wasn't a part of his regular duties he was, by chance, selected for the next delivery.

As he drove the truck over the county road he wondered if he would see Camille again. As he drew near the mailbox he felt excitement building in his chest. The road wound around a bend and dropped over a small hill and the girl was standing by the mailbox just like before.

Stopping the truck, Sam leaned over and opened the right hand door. Without a word she climbed into the seat beside him. When he started to drive away she stopped him.

"No, I can't go with you. Someone might see me."

"So what? It's not against the law for you to ride with me. Is it?

"You don't understand. My father promised me to someone and he would hurt you—and me if he caught us together." She looked all around, with frightened eyes as she talked.

Sam felt his heart sink. "I wouldn't want anything bad to happen to you, but I haven't been able to think of anything but you for the past week."

Camille smiled shyly and said, "Me too, I've thought of you all the time."

Boldly, forgetting the words of caution by his friends and family, Sam said, "I'll come to your house and meet your folks, then it'll be OK."

"It won't work. My Pappy wouldn't let me be in the same room with you. I have to go." She reached for the door handle.

Sam caught her by the arm. "Don't go." She turned and then she was in his arms. She kissed him hard on the mouth, then twisted away and sprang from the truck. Standing by the side of the road she turned and said, "I'll leave you a note in that old hollow tree," pointing to an ancient oak. Then she turned and ran away.

Returning after the delivery, Sam stopped by the mailbox and found the note where she said it would be. It read:

"There is a way. I can sneak out of the house late at night and meet you here, any time after ten."

On the back of the same note Sam penciled; "Tonight, after ten."

For the rest of the day and into the evening Sam thought, what a damn fool I am.

But just thinking of being alone in the dark with the beautiful girl made his heart beat faster.

At ten that night he drove his car to the mailbox and waited. The time dragged. After about thirty minutes he was preparing to leave when the girl suddenly appeared. She slipped into the car and said breathlessly. "My Pappy was sick and it took awhile for him to get to sleep."

Sam drove quickly down the country road. Houses were far and few between. Traffic was always sparse and at this time of night it was nonexistent. The girl sat against the right hand door. He drove to a heavy grove of lofty pines and pulled off the road.

Camille said, "This is crazy. Nothing good can come of it."

Sam was surprised at her speech as he had been at the written note. He had been led to believe that the Bakertown area residents were all illiterate. "Where did you go to school?"

"I go to school at Blue Ridge I just finished tenth grade. I'll graduate in two years." She said proudly, then "I'm the only one in our family that can read and write. My mother pretends she can read. She reads the paper to my father, after I've read some of it to her."

"What will you do after you graduate?"

"I would like to leave these hills forever, but my Pappy says I must get married and have lots of grandbabies." She spoke sadly.

Sam remembered hearing somewhere that a little education was a dangerous thing. He reached over and touched the girl. For a moment she hesitated then she slipped into his arms.

They lay on the blanket of pine needles that covered the ground. The wind sighed through the pines, whispering an ageless song.

That night began a passionate relationship that would have tragic consequences for both the young people.

They met once, twice, sometimes three times each week, through that summer of 1941. Their lovemaking was almost frantic at times as if they could not get enough of each other. Camille was hopelessly in love with Sam. And Sam? Although, completely infatuated, he was more calculating. Ramona had done her work well and the girls since had added to his callousness. He would not again risk the heartbreak he had experienced the year before.

The end came abruptly. It was late August and almost time for Sam to go away to school. They had discovered a more isolated spot than the grove of trees. It was a high bluff, overlooking Squaw Creek. It had been raining upstream and the usually calm creek was a roaring torrent. Sam parked the car parallel to the rushing stream, the moon was shinning through broken clouds and heavy thunder boomed in a distant storm. Sam told Camille that next week he would be leaving for school. "I expect your school will be starting soon, won't it?"

Camille got out of the car and walked around to the front. Sam got out and walked to the front also. They were standing a few feet apart. She walked up to Sam and stood looking up for a few minutes before she spoke. "I don't know if I'll go to school. I'm pregnant." The last part was almost whispered.

"What did you say?" Sam said, the shock he felt expressed in his voice.

"I'm pregnant," she repeated, never taking her eyes from his face.

Sam stood in stunned silence. He thought he had been so careful. The consequences began to crowd through his mind.

"We will have to get married. Even then my father will want to kill us both." Camille hugged her body and shuddered as if a chill had come over her.

"Married? I can't get married. I've got to go to school. What in the world would I tell my folks?"

"What about me? You said you loved me," the girl said, piteously. She was shaking so violently Sam got her jacket from the car, an oversized Civilian Conservation Corp field jacket. She slipped it on, buttoned it up to her chin, and shoved her hands deep into the pockets.

Sam wished he could talk to Joe Johnson, who had a solution for everything. He had heard of getting rid of unwanted pregnancies. "Maybe we could take you somewhere, where they get rid of babies."

The girl reacted as if Sam had struck her. She lifted her head even higher and gasped, "I can't believe you said that. I could never kill anyone, much less an innocent baby. God would never forgive me."

Sam held out his hands and stepped toward her. Camille took a quick step back. Her heel caught on a dead branch on the uneven ground. She stumbled backwards, and with hands caught in the jacket pockets and unable to regain her balance or break her fall, she toppled over, and the back of her head struck the protruding bumper guard with a sickening crunch. She rolled to the right and the momentum took her over the edge of the bluff and she fell limply into the raging stream.

It all happened so quickly Sam was stunned momentarily. He jumped toward the stricken girl as she rolled over the edge. He saw her go under the water and he immediately jumped into the swollen creek. He was a powerful swimmer, but the current was so strong he was swept swiftly downstream. He managed to keep his head above water but he never caught another glimpse of Camille. He was carried around a bend and into the brush of a fallen tree where he grabbed a branch and hung on as his eyes searched for the girl. She had simply vanished.

He called out to her. CAM, CAM, over and over. It would be reported later by some downstream fishermen that they had heard strange screams from somewhere upstream.

Sam pulled himself hand over hand through the branches to the trunk of the fallen tree. As he moved along toward the bank, the current became less violent. He finally managed to drag his nearly exhausted body onto the partially submerged tree where he lay panting for breath. He began to shake and it became so overwhelming he almost slipped back into the water. The night was hot as only a Mississippi August night can be, but the plunge into the water and the emotion of the events had shocked him deeply. He had become disoriented and could not tell quickly which direction to travel after he moved from the tree to the stream bank. After awhile he reasoned his car was upstream and after stumbling through brush and heavy grass he found it.

He started the engine and was still shaking so badly he found it difficult to drive. He turned the heater on full blast and while the interior was warming up he thought about what to do. He would go home and tell his father. With that thought in mind he began to drive away. Then he realized he was leaving Camille somewhere in

that awful stream. He began to shiver
violently again. He realized it was warm
inside the car, as well as outside, but the
shaking continued.

Sam drove to Lone Pine, took a shower and
went to bed. He would tell his father of the
horrible experience when morning came. He
fell into a fitful sleep.

Henry had an early appointment, which
caused Sam to miss his father when he got
out of bed that morning. He dressed and went
to work without seeing his mother. Now in
the light of day, the night's events began
to seem like a very bad dream. And he began
to reason about what he should do. He could
imagine all kinds of wild consequences. He
dreaded most of all what his mother would
think and say. Old man Dotson would probably
shoot him on sight. Or worse maybe the
nightriders would lynch him. After all who
could connect him to the missing girl? By

the time he arrived at Lee Brown's he had decided to say nothing.

Lee took one look at Sam at said, "Boy, you must be burning the candle at both ends. You look like you've been ridden hard and put away wet. Are you OK?"

"Yeah, Yeah, I'm OK." For one fleeting moment Sam thought of telling Lee what had happened the night before. But then he thought of what Lee would have to do. He kept silent.

It was fuel delivery day to Baker's corner. Lee asked Sam to make the run. He did so with dread in his heart. He passed the mailbox where he and Camille had begun their love affair. He half expected to see her standing there.

At Baker's corner there was a group of grim faced men milling around outside the store. One of them was Camille's father, Charlie Dotson. A feeling of calmness came over Sam. He connected hoses with quick, sure hands and made the delivery promptly. "What's going on?", he asked the lady in charge when he presented the invoice for signature.

"Charlie Dotson's girl is missing," she said, tight lipped. "He's about ready to blow up."

Sam hurried to the truck and quickly drove away, more resolved than ever to bury his secret as deeply in his heart as he could.

That night at supper Henry mentioned that the sheriff was investigating a missing person report in the Bakertown area.

"Maybe somebody wised up and decided to get away from that sorry environment." Angela stated in a strong voiced opinion.

"You could be right. It was a really bright girl from what I understand. Good student. Good grades, never any trouble to anyone. Shame," Henry shook his head, "She was the only child of Charlie Dotson and his wife. I understand the father is about to go crazy and the mother has collapsed."

"Well," Angela said, "I can sympathize with them. But for the life of me I cannot understand why people live like they do. Was Charlie and his wife cousins or were they brother and sister?"

"Angela, Angela, brother and sister? Come now. They may be cousins, although I don't think so, but no one marries brother and sister."

"How can they tell?' Angela wanted to know.

Henry just shook his head and didn't bother to answer. He knew too well how his wife felt about some of the residents of the county.

"Sammy, isn't that the girl you were raving about some time ago?" Angela asked.

Coolly Sam looked his mother in the eyes and replied. "I think it probably is".

Two days later Camille's body was found by a fisherman, on a sandbar about a mile downstream from the bluff where it had entered the water. The corner's verdict was: Death from a blow to the back of the head. There was no water in the lungs. A closed casket funeral was held the next day. The time of death and the hot weather made it necessary. It was August 27, 1941.

The next day Woodrow Baker was arrested and charged with Camille's murder.

He protested his innocence in a loud and grief stricken voice. (After all she had been his intended)

The evidence was all circumstantial. No one had seen him the night of Camille's disappearance. He claimed he was on a fishing trip alone. It was well known he never went fishing alone. He said he was

105

alone because Camille had not been treating
him "right" and he wanted some time to
think. Tire tracks in the mud near where the
body was discovered were a perfect match for
the tires on Woody's old stripped down Ford.
He said the tracks were made when he went
fishing in Squaw Creek the week before
Camille's death. Once again he said he had
been alone. The old field jacket she had
been wearing was one of Woody's left over
from the year he spent in the Civilian
Conservation Corp. And most damning of all
was a note in the jacket pocket from Camille
to Woody, written the day she disappeared,
which said:

Aug. 25, 1941

Woody.

I can't ever marry you. I'm going
away. I'm sorry if I hurt you. You are a
good man and you've always been a good

friend. Don't be mad and don't try to find me. It won't do any good. I'm not going to live in these hills anymore.

Your friend

Cam

Woody was locked in jail without bail. At the preliminary hearing the sheriff requested bail be denied for Woody's own protection. The residents of Bakertown were almost unanimous that Woody should be taken from the jail and strung up and "Left for the buzzards to pick his eyes out. That wouldn't be half as bad as what had happened to poor Camille as she lay on that Squaw Creek sandbar in the sultry Mississippi August sun." Woody, of course, insisted he was innocent. "What else would you expect from somebody who was as guilty as sin?" One old lady asked.

Chapter 3

August was the end of summer for Sam and the end of his boyhood. In September he began his studies at Ole Miss. He was younger than the rest of the students but he didn't look it. The boyish smile was gone. Grimness had begun to show lines around his mouth. He became a loner. First of all because the other students didn't take to a young genius and second, he made no effort to make any friends.

From the first his grades began to suffer, although he spent all his time with his nose stuck in a book. He seemed to have lost the touch that had been his gift so far in life. Most of his fellow students were delighted when the posted grades showed he was barely passing.

The Woodrow Baker trial was held in October and the result was a speedy conviction. The jury was out a scant two hours. The sentence was: "You shall hang by the neck until you are dead, dead, dead."

Sam was home for his birthday when Woody hanged himself. There was a note, scrawled on a scrap of paper, "I am innosent but there aint no body cares." He was buried the next day. And the words, "Nobody cares" were inscribed on a small headstone placed there by his brother, Jacob, who had loudly protested the guilty verdict.

Sam returned to school where his situation continued to worsen. The dream of Camille's death haunted his sleep. One night he dreamed he was pulling himself up onto the tree trunk out of the water. He could hear the gurgling of the stream around the fallen tree. He awoke and found to his horror he had wet the bed. He managed to hide this embarrassing condition from his room mate by lying awake, in the wet the rest of the night, then quickly making his bed, wet sheets and all the next morning. It was the day before the Thanksgiving holidays, so at the end of the school day he went home to Lone Pine.

Sam's parents were happy to see him, although they had expected him the next day. They were both becoming increasingly worried about their unsmiling son. Angela was not one to keep her worry bottled up. "Sammy I'm worried about you. You're working too hard."

"I'm OK, Mama."

"No you're not, you mope around, never go out, look like you've lost your dog."

"I tell you I'm alright. Lay off, will you?"

Henry spoke in his usual quiet manner. "I'm afraid it was a mistake for you to go to college so early. A year makes a lot of difference in a young person's life. If your school work doesn't improve by the end of the semester I believe you should come home and go back to high-school for another year."

Sam shrugged his shoulders. "OK," he replied, in uncharacteristic agreement.

That upset Angela more than Sam's demeanor. "I was against you going to that hillbilly school in the first place. All this business about accelerating your way through the world is completely ridiculous. What're are people going to say now that you're flunking?"

"Who said anything about flunking?" Henry asked.

"What do you call it? You should have kept him from doing this dumb thing in the first place. But, no, you thought it was a great idea." Angela was beginning to warm to the subject. Sam quietly left the room.

During the evening Tump stopped by to visit for a while. They had not seen each other often since their lives had started going in different directions; Sam away at school and Tump still in high school even though he was one year older. There was never any awkwardness between them. Tump was always curious about what was happening in Sam's life.

"What's happening with you? You look like the last rose of summer. Can't make it with them older gals at the seat of higher education?" That was almost Tump's first greeting.

"Its not that," Sam replied, "I'm thinking about leaving school and going to work."

Tump showed his surprise. "Boy, that's new. I thought you were going to become a professor, or some other stuffed shirt type.

You're too young to get a real job and besides yo' mama would have a fit."

"Yeah, well if I were a year older I'd join the army."

"I know what you mean. I'd like to go into the marines, like Joe," Tump replied wistfully. "He's somewhere in the Pacific, having the time of his life. He writes me where he is the native women run around naked. If Joe was here he would know how to get you a fake birth certificate and you would be one year older, just like that," Tump snapped his fingers to emphasize how quickly it would be.

Sam was instantly interested about the fake birth certificate. He hadn't really been serious about joining the army but now the germ of an idea began to take shape in his mind. "I could probably get by with a fake driver's license."

"That might be easy to do," Tump replied, "I'll check with one of Joe's old buddies and see what could be done."

The friends parted company because Tump had to go to work at the drug store. His parting words were, "I'm sorry about that, if I didn't have this crummy job we could pick up the twins and have a roll in the hay, just like old times, eh, Sammy?"

Angela could not believe her son could be having a learning problem at school. She had no way of knowing the emotional struggle Sam was enduring. Therefore, she continued to talk to him about how disappointed she was that he was going to drop out of college.

"What good would it do for you to go back to high school, as your father suggested? You've taken everything they have to offer. I think we should send you to a private school, or get you a private tutor."

Sam did not respond to his mother's continuous chatter. He simply walked out of the room, got in his car and drove back to Ole Miss, even though he had one more day of the Thanksgiving holiday left.

On December 7, 1941 Sam was in his dormitory room reading and the radio was playing the latest hit tunes when the announcer broke in and said the Japanese had bombed Pearl Harbor. He began to pack his belongings. He called Tump and said, "I'm joining the army." Tump's response was, "Me too."

Then he said to Sam, "You're too damn young. How you gonna get around that?"

"How about the guy who sells fake driver's license? I've an idea the army might not check age too close."

"I think it can be done. It'll cost you a hundred bucks."

"Do it," Sam replied, I'll see you tonight, we'll go together."

"OK, one other little detail, what'll your folks say?"

"They won't know."

Tump said, "I'll see you tomorrow, I'll have the driver's license ready, we'll catch a bus to Meriden and be in the Army tomorrow night."

"Right," Sam replied, a feeling of excitement caused his voice to sound more like the boy Tump had known for so many years.

The next day, without a word to anyone in the university, Sam loaded his car and left for Parkersville. He found Tump had done his work well. He had purchased two bus tickets to Meriden, Mississippi, the nearest recruiting station. He had packed a small bag with a few articles of clothing and a razor and toothbrush. "We won't need much,

Uncle Sam furnishes everything," he told Sam.

The fake driver's license cost Sam fifty dollars.

Tump became very serious. "I feel bad about leaving without saying goodbye to our parents. No telling when we'll see them again. I know if I told mine they would have a fit and my mom would call Miss Angela and then she would have you locked up for being insane." He raised his voice, trying to imitate a woman, "A chile like you got no business running off and joining the Army."

"Well thank you, grandpa Johnson. You're not so old yourself."

Tump waved his hand at Sam's packed automobile. "What're you gonna do with your stuff?"

"I'm parking it on the street over by the drug store. Somebody'll find it in a day or two." Sam was thoughtful for a few moments.

"What we need to do is get someone to drive us out of town a few miles and drop us off. Then we could flag the bus down. Everybody in this burg knows both of us and if we go to the bus station, it'll be all over town before we get seated."

"Yeah, that's good thinking. But who can we trust to be quiet for a few hours?"

"How about some of your old girl friends?"

"Nah, they'll be too sad to see me go," Tump replied with a twisted grin. "Alicia Steinberg works as a soda jerk in the evenings at the drug store. She used to have the hots for you. Maybe she would do it."

"That would be risky. Her Ma and mine are good friends. She'd probably enjoy blowing the whistle on me. We'll just take the car out and park it along the road. I'll leave a note."

"Thieves'll pick it clean, note and all."

Tump looked at his watch. "We got a couple of hours before the bus leaves. Let's drive around and maybe inspiration will strike."

Sam drove out of town to a small farmer's market, with the intention of getting something to eat. When they pulled into the parking lot, Alicia was walking toward her car with a bag of produce in her arms. She saw Sam and Tump at about the same time.

"Sam, what are you doing at home? I thought you were in school," Alicia said, stopping and setting her bag on the ground.

Sam got out of his car and walked to where she was standing. He thought she looked different and then realized her braces had been removed. "I've quit school," then he blurted," I'm joining the Army."

"Aren't you a little young for that? It'll come around soon enough without you rushing things."

Sam decided to risk it all. "I need help, your help."

"What do you want me to do?" She asked, puzzled.

"I need you to take Tump and me out of town and drop us off on the bus route, then bring my car back to town and not say anything to my parents for a few days."

Alicia smiled a twisted little smile that turned her lips down at one corner of her mouth. "You want me to help you put something over on your parents? Why? Angela is my friend. I drive your car back to town, and then what? What am I supposed to do after that?"

Sam felt anger rise in his chest. "Forget it," he turned on his heels and started walking back to his car.

"I'll do it," Alicia called after his retreating back.

Sam turned and saw she was still smiling the same little smile without showing her teeth. She had worn the braces so long she had made a habit of smiling that way.

"No, forget it. I'm sorry I didn't mean to get you crosswise with Mom. It's not fair to you."

"I'll do it," she repeated.

"Mom'll be mad at you."

"You can fix that."

"How?"

"Write her a note and tell her where she can find the car. I'll drop the key in the envelope and mail it to her after I park the car. That way she'll never know I'm involved."

Sam felt a surge of admiration for the quick thinking girl. "OK, that's a deal. And thanks."

They drove a couple of miles out of town and Sam parked the car off the main road. It was about fifteen minutes before bus time. Alicia said, "I bet you fellows are hungry." She had put her bag of groceries on the back seat with her when she got into Sam's car.

Both boys said in unison, "I'm starved." It was late afternoon and they had forgotten to have lunch.

Alicia made thick sandwiches from cold cuts and bread she had in her grocery bag. She gave each an apple and they drank milk from a quart bottle. Tump declared it was the best food he had ever tasted.

When it was time to say goodbye, Alicia shook hands with each boy and said gravely, "Take care of yourself. This isn't a Boy Scout trip, you know."

Tump said, "Yeah, we know. You be good and have fun. Or maybe just have fun." He was laughing and anxious to be on the way.

Sam said nothing. He waved his hand and Alicia pulled away and left them standing by the side of the road. Sam watched until the car was out of sight.

In a few minutes the bus came to an air brake hissing stop. The boys paid their fare to Meridian and they were on the way. It would be a long time before they saw this part of the country again.

The recruiting station was closed when they arrived. Tump was ready to get a room for the night but Sam said, "Johnson, let's go on to Jackson. It's further from home and we're not likely to bump into anyone who knows us."

"That's OK by me. That'll give us time to get some real food." Tump replied, then added, "I need something besides the horse cock sandwich Alicia gave us."

"Johnson, you've got hollow legs, Uncle Sam'll go in the hole just feeding you. It was pretty nice of Alicia to feed us and take the car back. You shouldn't be bitchin'."

"I don't have to be overcome with gratitude. I'm old enough to go into the marines without all this hidey hidey stuff. I'll admit that old Steinberg is a good scout. She's sure improved in looks since she got the braces off. She looks almost good enough to screw. I might try that when I come home on leave from the marines."

Sam smiled a tight-lipped smile. "I'm sure you'll dazzle the hell out of all the females when you show up wearing the uniform of the United States Army."

"You got that wrong, old buddy, I ain't going into the army. It's the marines for me. That army is your stuff."

Sam said, "I'm going into the Army Air Corp, why don't you go with me?"

"Why Samuel Warden, you know how I feel about flying. If God had intended for man to fly he would have sprouted wings on his shoulders."

"You don't have to fly. There are lots of things for people to do besides fly. All planes have ground crews."

"Sam, I ain't gonna be a grease monkey for a bunch of fly boys. Besides, every time the infantry needs some more cannon fodder they look right in the Air Corp. Joe wrote me just how it is."

The lifelong friends looked at each other and realized they were destined to travel different roads. Tump stuck out his hand and Sam reached out and hugged him. Tump turned away with tears in his eyes. And the next morning in Jackson Tump became a Marine and Sam joined the Army with the hope he would be accepted into the Air Corp after basic training. The recruiting Sergeant declared, "They are getting younger looking every day" when Sam filled out his application.

Sam wrote a letter to his parents and mailed it to Alicia with a note to her saying he had forgot to leave the letter with her when they parted company on the bus route.

Sam's parents had received notification from the university that their son had been absent from classes for three days. They had immediately driven to the university. They examined the dormitory and found all of Sam's belongings missing. They questioned his roommate who could shed no light on his disappearance.

Angela was absolutely frantic. "What in the world could have happened to him? You can't just disappear from school like that, leaving no trace. Let's call the law and have them search for him."

"Wait, there's got to be a logical explanation," Henry said, "Sam had his reasons for doing this. Let's go home and see if his friend Tump can shed any light on what's going on"

"What do you think happened?" Angela asked, suspiciously.

"Many young people are rushing to join the military service," he replied as calmly as he could.

"No," Angela gasped, "I won't hear of it. He's too young. Henry Warden what do you know about this that you're not telling me?"

"You know everything I know," he replied.

They drove back to Parkersville in almost complete silence. At Lone Pine, the first thing Angela did was call Tump's mother who told her she had received a letter from Tump that day telling her of his joining the marines. Her heart sank. She turned to Henry who was sorting the mail. He had the letter from Sam. Silently he handed it to her.

It was short and simple. It said:

Dear Mom and Dad.

I've joined the army. I did it this way because I knew you would never agree for me to join. My car is parked behind the drug store. Please don't try to stop me.

Love

Sam

Angela read the letter and burst into tears. 'What are you going to do about this?" She demanded between sobs.

"I don't have the slightest idea what you're talking about," the miserable Henry replied.

Angela was almost hysterical, gasping she shouted. "Our only son has run off and joined the army and he'll probably be killed and you don't know what I'm talking about. I can't believe you Henry Warden."

"There are a lot of other only sons in this mess. Don't you understand we are in a war?"

"The others are not seventeen year old children," the distraught Angela fairly screamed at her husband.

"The military is accepting eighteen year old volunteers and Sam will be eighteen next year."

"That's next year. I want him out of that place now. I'm calling our congressman and demanding that he get Sam discharged, or whatever it is they do. I can't depend on you to do anything, so I'll just take care of it myself."

Angela was thoroughly angry and that had help dry her tears. She began trying to locate the congressman of that district. He was on a fact-finding trip to Europe and it was several days before she could contact him. When she finally reached him he was not enthusiastic about getting a volunteer discharged from the army during the time of war. But he promised to try.

There were long lines of young men everywhere Sam looked as the youth of America responded to the Japanese attack. They were rowdy and full of fun and adventure. Sam was more somber and quiet. His was a spirit of escape. He was struggling with the bad dreams and each time he dreamed he was in the water clinging to the fallen tree trunk he would start to wet the bed and would awaken just in time to prevent a major accident. At other times he would dream of Camille, of making love to her, complete through orgasm, then he would see her tumble down the bank into the swollen creek. He would awaken drenched with perspiration and shaking as if he had a chill.

Sam began to realize he would never be able to fly for the Army unless he was able to control his feelings of guilt. He tried to bury all feelings in extremely hard work. Where goofing off was army tradition, he never shirked any detail. A dread of sleep caused him to stay up late at night. After bed check he would slip out of the barracks and shoot pool in the recreation area. He discovered he could do well on three or four hours of sleep and in an exhausted state the dreams began to diminish.

Sam's serious attitude and close attention to duty was sure to attract the attention of the officers, and it did, but it was the aptitude tests that made his a special case. One officer said, "That kid made the highest overall score I've ever seen." As a result several different officers interviewed him, each trying to place him in a different part of the Army.

Each time Sam said, "Sir, I volunteered for the Army for one purpose; to fly." On his application he had stated he had taken flying lessons and had soloed, but didn't have a private license. After basic training he was assigned to the Air Corp and stationed in Arizona.

Sam's flight instructor was a salty old army pilot whose first instructions were, "Forget what them civilian instructors told you. You're harder to train than a green horn who has never seen a damn airplane. We've gotta unlearn you all that shit before we can ever get started. You understand?"

"Yes sir," Sam agreed

Some trainees in Sam's group had no prior knowledge of aircraft at all. And so Sam acted the same. He followed instructions carefully and completely. Bookwork was completed on time with accuracy. It was the same with in flight instruction. He quickly adapted to the instructor's methods and even his whims. He got words of praise, not to his face, but to other officers in the training group. "That Warden kid flies like he was a part of the plane," his instructor, Lieutenant Jack Wilson, told the other instructors over cocktails one evening. "And on the written work he scores one hundred percent. He took the night flying test and damned if he can't see in the dark."

"Maybe you've got a candidate for the Night Hawks," one of the other officers said.

"Yeah, I've heard of that group. Some brass hat got the idea of a group of night fighters, not just the ordinary run of the mill type, but people who have the ability to see in the dark and function like it was daylight," Jack shook his head, "Sounds a little far fetched to me. Most flyers do ok flying in the dark on a set course and on instruments, but more than that sounds a little spooky. I don't know much about it, probably just a rumor anyway." Jack stretched and yawned. "It's time to put these old bones to bed." He got up and walked away.

Nearby, within earshot, Captain Ted Davis heard the comments about the ability to see in the dark. On a note pad he wrote the names, Jack Wilson, recruit Waldon. Or Warden.

The next day Captain Davis pulled Sam Warden's file and after examining it he called his Superior in Washington, D.C.

"General, it looks like we might have found one," he reported.

"How good does it look?" the General asked.

"As good as I've ever heard of and maybe better."

"Give me his name and serial number."

Captain Davis passed that information to the General.

It was two days later; Sam had just completed his Army solo flight when he was called to report to the day room.

The next morning he was on a military flight to England.

He was just a few hours ahead of his parents. It had taken the congressman a while to find where Sam was stationed because the fake driver's license, his only identification, had an Alabama address. He had filled out the next of kin properly on his application and that's how he was located. Proceedings to have him discharged for being under age were in process. When they were told his whereabouts was a military secret, Angela was livid with rage. Her ranting to her husband and to the congressman had no effect. The door had closed behind the young man. The weeping

Claude Eldridge

Angela said, "I'll never see him again, the army will just use him for cannon fodder."

Chapter 4

Sam was mystified about his status. Nothing was explained for the first few days. He was hustled off to Keswick, England where a special training cadre had been established. He was the only private soldier in the group. All the others were officers; their ranks were lieutenant to major. He didn't ask questions, but listening to the other men talk he found they were also uninformed about what was happening.

They were billeted in a hotel, two men to the room. Sam's roommate was Captain Karl Mimba, a black South African native. He was twenty-one years old and had been serving in the English Royal Air Force. He had flown spitfires and had been credited with shooting down two German aircraft.

"Soldier," Captain Mimba said to Sam, "You look a little young to be in this group."

"Yes sir, I mean I'm older than I look sir." Only the way Sam said sir made it sound like the Southern "Suh"

Captain Mimba grinned and said, "And a bloody Yank at that, a Deep South Yank, eh Yank?"

"Yes sir," Sam replied nervously.

Captain Mimba stuck out his hand and said, "Well, we're in this together, whatever it is. I guess we'll find out together. Right? Until we find out what the bloody hell is going on we can skip the formalities. Call me Karl."

Sam shook hands and was grateful for someone to talk to. The sudden departure from the States and the hotel with rooms filled with military personnel from different countries had thoroughly confused him. Sam told the Captain about his short time in the military service and how, without explanation he had been whisked away before his training was complete.

Captain Mimba frowned, "It makes no sense, it was the same with me, except I was told to report here. I rode the train down from London. I've talked to some of the other men, even the Major knows nothing, or at least he's not talking."

The hotel dinning room had been converted into a mess hall. There were fifty men at the evening chow. The hall was buzzing with speculation. Just before dinner was served a United States Army Brigadier General strode in. Someone called "Attention" and the entire group started to rise. The General held up his hand and said, "At ease men." He waited until a hush fell over the room and then he began to speak.

"I'm General Joe Lockwood, United States Army Air Corp. I know you men have all been wondering just what the hell is going on. And I don't blame you. But for security reasons, we felt it best to do it this way." He paused for a few moments and you could have heard a pin hit the floor. The General continued, "You have been selected for a very special and most important role in the war. Each of you possesses some special qualifications. You are pilots, you have more than average intelligence, but most importantly you have the unique ability to see in the dark." He paused again. "I'm not talking about just seeing in the dark as all normal people do, but the ability to see and to function as though it were broad open daylight." The last few words were spoken forcibly and emphatically.

The General continued to speak." Now you know what this clambake is all about and why you are here. All of you, from that young private to the oldest officer were given tests that show you have extraordinary night vision. Of all the hundreds of thousands we have tested in the allied armies only you fifty have the vision we think is necessary for the mission. The mission is to form a unique night fighter squadron, one that will act as the eyes that see what the enemy is doing under cover of darkness. Troop movements, supply trains, night bombing raids, the possibilities are endless. But first we have to see if you have what it takes. Some of you have had combat experience, but this is going to be the most stressful duty a person can be put into. And we know some of you won't make it. We hope we can salvage twenty-five out of fifty. You will be known as the Night Hawk Squadron. We will select your commanding officer from your ranks. I will be in charge of your training. Reveille is at five AM tomorrow morning. Chow at six. Enjoy your dinner."

Noisy chatter broke out immediately. Some of the men laughed nervously. Karl Mimba looked at Sam and said, "Well, I'll be damned."

The next morning at chow time The General outlined the training plans. "I want this group to be as informal as possible. We will dispense with the usual military protocol. Everyone should be on a first name basis. We will break into groups of five, with a ranking officer in charge. Training will be geared to correcting any perceived weakness. Here are the groups and the group leaders. Where there is not a ranking officer, we have appointed a leader. After chow all groups get together and stay together. Eat, sleep and work together."

Sam was assigned to Captain Karl Mamba's group.

After breakfast men shuffled around, moving to their respective groups. Sam was dinning with Karl and he waited with interest as the other three men found their way to the Captain's table. There was one other American, James Andrew Holland from Wichita, Kansas. Of the other two, one, Bryan Eugene Cochran, was from Australia and the other one was Simon Pulaski, from Poland.

Sam felt like the odd man out. The other four were all officers. Holland, Cochran and Pulaski were Lieutenants. All, except Holland, had served in some branch of the Royal Air Force. Pulaski had escaped from Poland when it fell to the Germans.

Captain Mimba made the introductions. Then with a slight smile and in his best-clipped British accent said. "What a group; the fearless five from four different countries. Let's start by talking about ourselves." In a few terse sentences he told where he was from, what his flying experience had been and his combat duty to date.

Cochran had seen some combat, Holland was fresh from the states and Pulaski was a veteran flyer with fifteen combat missions. He was reluctant to say how many enemy planes he had shot down, but after some encouragement from Karl he admitted to five kills and three assists. In talking about Germans he became red faced with anger. Karl was making mental notes as each man talked. Then it was Sam's turn.

Captain Mimba had noticed that Sam never smiled. While other men laughed and joked, smoked, and drank anything available, Sam wore a poker face. He didn't smoke and he didn't drink alcoholic beverages, not even beer; that drink soldiers considered their own. He said, "I haven't done anything, I— (Holland guffawed and a hard look from Captain Mimba silenced him)—had a private pilot's license, was going to college, joined the Army Air Corp, soloed, one flight, and here I am."

Captain Mimba said, "We are different in a lot of ways and Sam is the young one in the group. I'll work on the assignments for you old timers and have them shortly, but Sam and me are going to go flying together."

The experienced flyers were given immediate flying assignments. They were expected to fly, in the dark, without lights, a fixed triangular course and identify established markers at given points along the route; return to base and land without the assistance of runway markers or landing lights. The U.S built P38 Lightening was the airplane assigned to The Night Hawks.

Sam was given the P38 manual to study while Captain Mimba was trying to decide what should be done about his young charge.

He told the General, "I think this is a good fellow, but he's not had the experience. I wouldn't want him killed just because he can't fly one of these hot planes."

The General pulled Sam's file and studied it for a few minutes. "This young'un has the highest I.Q. of any man in the group. His night vision is phenomenal. He's exactly what we're looking for. All he has to do is fly a P38. Can you take care of that little chore, Captain?" The General's voice had grown dry and crisp when he asked the question.

"Yes sir. I believe I can." Karl said quickly.

"Karl," the General said," you can have anything you need."

"Yes sir," Karl answered as he turned and walked away. "We'll just see if I can have anything I want," he thought as he hurried to flight operations.

"I need a P38 trainer," he told the Sergeant in charge of supplies.

"You got it Cap'n. You wanna have it delivered or wanna pick it up?"

Karl started to say have it here tomorrow, but then changed his mind as an idea began to form. "I'll pick it up, you fix up the paper work. What kind of transportation do you have from here to wherever this trainer is located?"

"Not much, 'cept the General's got a C47 for his own private use."

"Get it ready, he said I could use it." Captain Mimba had decided to test the General's words.

The Sergeant raised his eyebrows, but said, "OK. Cap'n, it's your funeral."

Karl hurried to the room where Sam was reading the manual a page a minute, or more. "I didn't mean for you to just thumb through that manual. You're supposed to be studying it." Karl was becoming a little irritated.

"I am studying it," Sam quietly replied.

"Bring it with you, we're going to take a ride."

As they walked briskly back to flight operations, Karl explained what they were going to do. "I can get a trainer, but instead of having it flown in, we're going to pick it up and you are going to fly it back."

The General's C47 was always in a state of readiness, and when they arrived it was waiting with the engines running and ready to go. A one-hour flight across the beautiful green English countryside brought them to a remote air base where the trainer was waiting and ready for flight.

Karl soon found why everything had been so easy. None of the flyers had been checked out in the P38 and a number of trainers had been prepared and were waiting for use by the Night Hawks. Before they could leave with the trainer Karl had to have a check ride with a qualified pilot before they would assign the plane to him.

"You fly it to home base," Karl told Sam when they were ready to depart.

By the book, Sam did the ground check, the walk around complete, he climbed into the front seat and ran through the instrument check. He started the engines and began to move to the end of the runway, he turned into the wind and did the engine run up, released the brakes and began to roll.

He advanced the throttles, by the book, and the big Allison engines roared with power; he climbed out sharply, banked left, leveled out and headed for home. As they barreled along, Sam eased the throttles forward until they were at full power. In thirty minutes they were back at the base.

He circled the field and came in for a smooth landing.

Not a word had been spoken during the flight.

An attendant directed him to a parking place, he shut down the engines, turned off switches, climbed out of the cockpit and made sure the plane was secure.

Captain Karl Mimba looked at him closely, rubbed his chin and said, "I almost feel like I've been, how you say it, had?"

"Captain, I read the book," Sam replied as he started to walk away.

"Wait," Karl said, "Let's take it up again." He had decided to see just how well Sam could fly.

Sam went back to the plane and went through the entire preparation procedure again, even though the plane had just been parked. They climbed in and Sam started the engines and taxied out onto the runway. As he turned into the wind and started his takeoff roll Karl said, "I want you to take it up and wring it out. Give it the works." Sam shoved the throttles to the firewall and the big engines roared to life. When the plane gained takeoff speed, Sam pulled back on the stick and headed almost straight up. The altimeter spun as he gained altitude. At twenty five thousand feet he pushed the nose down and the plane hurtled toward the ground. He held it there until the instrument neared the red line, then he pulled out and rolled to the right in a tight turn. He did everything he had learned from Lee Brown while flying the little biplane "My Baby." His final move was flying low over the field at full throttle, then pulling out and climbing at a steep angle. The engine noise rattled all windows in the complex.

General Lockwood heard the noise and told his aid, "Find out who that pilot is and write a directive for my signature forbidding buzzing the field."

The aide came back in a few minutes and said, "The pilot is private Warden with his instructor Captain Mimba."

"As soon as they land have Mimba come see me,"

When Sam taxied to the parking slot and cut the engines Karl said, "A private pilot's license, eh?"

"I had a good instructor," Sam replied.

When they climbed out of the plane General Lockwood's aide was waiting. "General Lockwood wants to see you," he told Karl.

"I'm not surprised," Karl said, in his dry South African manner. As he walked with the aid he thought of the numerous grievances the General might have: The C47, the trainer plane, buzzing the field with a green young pilot at the controls.

The General met him at the door to his office. "How'd it go with young Warden?" were his first words.

Karl shook his head. "That fellow is unbelievable. This morning I left him with the '38 manual, when I went to pick him up, I found him turning the pages a few seconds apart. Apparently he has a photographic memory. When we got to the plane, you would think he had flown it for years, just from the book, he checked it out and flew here without me saying a word. When we landed I decided to take him up again and just let him to whatever he wanted. It's been awhile since I've had a ride like that."

"Well now, seems like your man is the first to get checked out on the P38. I like your initiative. I'm appointing you commander of this group. The appropriate promotion will go with appointment. As of today Private Warden is Lieutenant Warden. You might like to pin his bars on." The General slid a pair of 2nd lieutenant bars across his desk and continued.

"It's our intention to promote people as rapidly as they qualify. I want you to get this group functioning as quickly as possible. If there is any thing you need let me know, and let me know if you need my C47 again." He grinned slightly when he said the last words. He picked up a paper and started reading. "That's all Colonel." And that's the way the new commander knew what his rank would be.

That evening at chow Sam had his new officer insignia attached to his uniform. The other members of the group of five were impressed at how rapidly events were moving. Yesterday Holland had laughed when Sam had related his lack of experience, now he was qualified in the late model P38 trainer before any other member of the group.

The General made another brief speech and introduced them to their new commanding officer. A part of what he said was; "We don't have the luxury of time. We must move rapidly. Decisions must be made, sometimes, on gut feel alone. We believe what we're doing is vital to the war effort. After dinner I want to meet with Colonel Mimba and the other group leaders. We will plan each group's activities for tomorrow."

The night flying began the next night for the experienced pilots. For one week Sam flew mock combat missions with experienced pilots as the "enemy." On the last day of the week Colonel Mimba played that role. The planes were equipped with gun cameras that would record the "kills".

Before they took off the Colonel said, "You have to make a flight with me without getting "shot" down. If you pass that you are on your own."

Sam said, "What if I shoot you down?"

"The same thing. But you've got to be first. We won't know who did what to whom until we see the film. Then we can tell by the sequence. OK?"

"Right," Sam agreed.

"You take off first, I'll give you a two minute start then I'm coming to get you," the Colonel said with a big grin creasing his face.

Sam took off and climbed at maximum speed as steeply as the plane would climb. It was a bright sunny day and he remembered all the tales Lee Brown had told him about hiding in the sun and waiting for the enemy. Maybe, just maybe it would work, just this once.

From his vantage point he could see the Colonel's plane climbing into the clear blue sky. As it passed under him and was going away Sam pushed the nose down and dived at full throttle. He caught the Colonel completely by surprise and had him firmly in his gun sights before he could react. He roared over his opponent's plane and peeled off steeply to the left. "You're dead Colonel," he called over the radio.

"Why you so and so," Karl growled back. "At least we could have had a little fun before you pulled that stunt."

"We can anyway. See if you can do me in," Sam replied.

"OK, smart boy, give me your best evasive action, I'm coming after you."

Sam pushed the plane into a steep dive and leveled out just above the ground and for about fifteen minutes he flew that way. It was a reckless and foolhardy way to fly and one the Colonel would not duplicate. The Colonel called Sam on the radio to tell him he was in violation of flight rules. There was no answer. Sam had conveniently turned off his radio.

The two planes careened through the sky; Sam just above the ground and the Colonel several feet above the fleeing plane. At one point Sam flew under a bridge. The Colonel continued to try to contact him on the radio, while maintaining a safe distance above the reckless young flyer.

Sam roared over the farming countryside, sending startled sheep scurrying in every direction.

Colonel Mimba decided enough was enough when Sam flew over a farmyard, so low that chickens ran squawking, blindly into fences and the side of the barn. A farm lady was in the barnyard and she shook both fists at the airplanes. The Colonel peeled off and headed for the base.

Sam spotted the departing Colonel, and climbed to a higher altitude and cruised to a gentle landing at the base. A grim faced Colonel Mimba met him. "You're grounded, and I'll tell you for how long when I'm not so angry."

Sam was the picture of innocence. "What's the matter? What did I do?"

"Don't give me that baby faced innocent act. You know damn well what you did. Let me name just a few of the things you did. First you either turned off your radio or you would not respond to my call. You flew too low; you flew under a bridge, thereby endangering government property and your life. You probably caused a bunch of sheep to kill themselves. You plucked the feathers off that farmer's chickens and that woman was mad as hell. Every phone at the base is probably ringing right this minute."

As if right on cue, an orderly walked up and said to the Colonel, "The General wants to see you."

Colonel Mimba glared at Sam and said, "What do you think this is about?"

Some of the line mechanics had heard the grounding order and the ass chewing Sam had received. When the gun camera film was developed, showing Sam's "kill" of the Colonel and the voice recording saying, "Give me your best evasive action." Sam became the celebrity of the day. On the achievement board his name climbed to the top of the "day" flyer's list.

In General Lockwood's office, the still fuming Colonel Mimba Said, "I know what you want and let me assure you it won't happen again."

"What happened?" General Lockwood asked.

Colonel Mimba gave him the story— straight, from beginning to end.

"How long you gonna keep him down?" the General asked.

"I haven't decided."

"Well, make it as short as you can. Give him the benefit of the doubt, maybe he really didn't know he was violating all the rules." General Lockwood grinned, "I can't believe he got to you with that old hiding in the sun trick. Wonder where he heard of that?"

"Probably some comic book," Colonel Mimba growled. He was starting to cool and his sense of humor was beginning to be restored. "I think he'll make a hell of a good pilot." He pondered a moment then, "That is if he don't kill himself first."

Sam was grounded for two days. Mimba had moved to different quarters and Sam's roommate was the Kansan, Jim Holland from Wichita. They became close friends. Jim had begun the night flying. His comments, or some of them were; "That's a hell of a way to fight a war. What the hell good is it anyway? And besides that it scares the piss out of me. I don't mind sitting in wet pants but when I fly upside down it runs down the back of my neck and I don't like it a bit."

Sam listened to Jim's gripes with somber interest and continued to study the P38 manual. He spent a lot of his two-day suspension at the hangers watching the mechanics keep the planes in tiptop shape. The mechanics were impressed by the young lieutenant, his interest in their work and his willingness to help and get his hands dirty. It was there he met Sergeant Fred Wilson, who would become a part of Sam's life while he was in the service.

When the two days were over Sam was assigned to night flying. His first night out it was pitch black dark. It was during the dark of the moon and the sky was heavily overcast. He flew the course in record time, identified the markers correctly, landed without a ray of light showing on the runway and made his report to the operations officer.

It was the night when three pilots could not locate the markers and five pilots radioed for lights on the field to assist them in landing. The ranks were beginning to thin.

In two weeks Sam was among the top five in the group. Where most of the others had had some actual combat flying, he had never seen an enemy plane. That was the next phase of making him what destiny had decided for him.

It was a bright English morning when Colonel Mimba called Sam to report to flight operations. "This is the day we've been waiting for," he told Sam. "Now we're going hunting. I understand the Boche have a lot of birds flying. Let's see if we can find a couple."

They flew to the English Channel where they joined a daylight-bombing group on the way to Germany. In a short time the sky was filled with German fighter planes. Colonel Mimba had given Sam instructions to stick close to his wing until he gave the signal to scramble and then it was to be every man for himself.

The German fighter planes made a savage attack on the bombers and their escort planes. In Sam's field of vision he could see two bombers going down in flames. Colonel Mimba gave the scramble signal and Sam elected to dive at the same moment a German plane passed under a bomber and headed right in front of Sam's plane. He pressed the twin triggers and the fifty calibers stitched rows of holes in the enemy fuselage as the plane passed in front of him. He turned in pursuit and the German fighter exploded just as he pressed the triggers again. There was no time to think as he jerked the P38's nose up to avoid the debris of the stricken German plane. Steel jacketed slugs tore through the aft fuselage of Sam's plane as he rolled sharply to the right. He went into a shallow dive with the enemy in close pursuit, sending short bursts of bullets into the American P38. Sam cut the power to the engines and employed the speed brakes; then jerked them off and reapplied the engine power, almost in one motion. The German plane passed over the top of him and then Sam was close behind the enemy.

The German plane swung wildly from side to side as Sam bore in for the kill. Short bursts from the fifty caliber machine guns tore holes in the fleeing plane; smoke began to pour from the engine cowling. The German pilot rolled his plane on its back and spilled from the cockpit. Sam followed the cripple toward the ground; still giving it short bursts from his guns. About two thousand feet from the earth the plane burst into flames and exploded.

As Sam peeled off and headed back upstairs he saw a parachute floating down with the enemy pilot alive and well. He flew by and waved. The pilot saluted.

In a few moments Sam caught up with the bombers. The fighter escort had successfully driven the enemy fighter planes away and all was calm as the B17s droned through the sky. He flew over and under, above and by the side of the big planes. He could see the crewmembers; each one giving him a smart salute and a cut throat sign. They had seen the action of Sam's plane.

Colonel Mamba's voice crackled over the radio. "Time to go home. Fuel." Sam looked at his gauges and turned sharply toward home base.

Colonel Mimba landed ahead of Sam. He was in good shape, no damage to his plane and no kills to his credit. When Sam landed and came to a stop at his designated parking place, Sergeant Wilson was waiting. As he looked over the bullet shredded metal he said, "Damn, Lieutenant, you were getting close to the pearly gates. I thought this was supposed to be a training mission."

"I guess it was," Sam replied, as he headed for the debriefing room.

Colonel Mimba made his report about the more than expected concentration of enemy planes. He had engaged the enemy, sustained no damage, and made no kills.

Sam reported he had engaged the enemy, had sustained damages, he did not mention kills.

When the gun camera film was developed it plainly showed two German planes shot down by Lieutenant Warden. The information ran through the establishment with the speed of a rumor.

When Colonel Mimba got the gun camera report, he walked over to Sam's quarters and said, "Lieutenant, the debriefing is for the purpose of telling what happened. Don't you understand that?"

"How could I know that? You never told me. This was my first time. I thought you were supposed to wait for confirmation. I'd look stupid if I reported a kill without verification. Wouldn't I?"

The next day it was reported in the papers: ROOKIE PILOT MAKES TWO KILLS, FIRST TIME IN COMBAT. Then it gave the details, pilot's name and hometown, the usual stuff.

In Parkersville, Mississippi, the story was carried in the Parkersville Journal. It showed a picture of Sam, bare headed, standing by a P38, wearing his flight suit and parachute. Judge Henry Warden was eating

168

breakfast when Ava brought him the paper. From the front page his son stared back at him.

"My God, Angela, come here," he cried, with tears running down his face. "Look at this."

Angela looked over his shoulder and together they read of their son's achievements. Angela said, "I can't believe it. Look at his eyes. He looks so sad. He's just a child."

Henry wiped his eyes and said, "He'll never be a child again."

Alicia read the article to her father at the breakfast table. "That's the man I'm going to marry," she announced.

"Does he know?" Her father asked.

"No, but he will," the girl replied.

A few days later the real mission of the Night Hawks became abundantly clear. Twenty men had qualified. Sam included. It was top secret and each one was cautioned to never even mention what they were doing to anyone. There would be no glamour and no publicity. Each pilot would be in grave danger if there should be a leak.

General Lockwood gave the briefing; "Men I've heard the bitching and griping about flying in the dark. And I know you are all wondering what we're up to. It's a simple plan.

Many key people are behind enemy lines. Downed pilots, informants, spies, and maybe most importantly, defectors from the German high command. We want to get them out. That's where you come in. It is most dangerous. We don't always know how reliable our source of information might be. The French underground is doing a fine job of smuggling our people out. But as you might guess it takes a while to get one person out. We want to speed that up. The communication apparatus is in place. Obviously we can go to a landing site just once in a given period, because it will be guarded for a while after that.

We have modified some P38 planes to carry the pilot and one passenger. We'll see how it works. Any questions?"

There were none. But there was plenty of conversation after the briefing.

"That's the craziest damn thing I ever heard of," Jim Holland said flatly "After a week of that shit there won't be a Night Hawk left."

Colonel Mimba shook his head, "I didn't' expect everyone to be in love with the plan. But we'll see just how crazy it is, tonight. Five of us are going to the same landing site. There are five people there. We will go in at two-minute intervals. I will lead then Warden, Cochran, Holland and last Pulaski. Questions?"

"Two minute intervals? How you gonna pick up somebody, taxi back and take off before the next guy runs into you?" Holland wanted to know.

"Good question," Colonel Mimba replied. "You go straight ahead. The underground people have prepared a runway of steel mesh. It's narrow and short. Use it sparingly. You must be correct when you land, pick up your passenger and come home. And, oh yes, fly low, both ways."

The Colonel gave them the coordinates, the ground markers and the location where each passenger would be standing.

Sam took off two minutes behind Colonel Mimba. He flew at tree top level and came into the landing site just as the Colonel's plane was picking up speed for take off. He slipped to the makeshift runway, popped open the canopy and a figure clambered in. He was moving before the passenger could fasten his safety belt. The canopy snapped shut and he roared away. From wheels down to wheels up thirty seconds had elapsed.

When Sam landed and taxied to the parking area, the military police were waiting. The passenger climbed out and was whisked away before Sam got a good look. All the other pilots experienced the same thing.

At the debriefing all agreed it had gone very smoothly.

"Fair dinkum," Cochran muttered.

"Hell, that was a piece of cake,' Holland declared.

"I saw a long column of German soldiers marching down a road," Pulaski stated. "It was so tempting to turn and mow them down."

True to form Sam had been quiet.

"Warden, what do you think?" Colonel Mimba asked.

"It went ok. I was a little disappointed at not seeing who any of the passengers were."

"Well, maybe it won't always be that way. I don't know. Somebody is making the decisions. You fellows did a good job," the Colonel stated "We have time to do that one more time, same place, same method. If you see soldiers nearby, come home quickly."

The next trip was a carbon copy of the first. The five Night Hawks had removed ten people from behind the German lines in one night.

Back in their room Sam was so keyed up, sleep was out of the question. Holland pulled a bottle of cognac from his duffel bag and poured a big slug in a water glass. "I've been saving this for a special occasion. The special occasion is that I'm still alive. Here 'Sippy have a drink," he offered Sam the bottle.

Sam shook his head, "I'm going out to the flight line. I want to talk to Sergeant Wilson."

"Warden, you're a fugging weirdo," Holland said as he took a big swig of cognac.

Sam didn't bother to answer. Dawn was breaking as he walked into the hanger where Sergeant Wilson was working on the plane Sam had flown. "Hi, Lieutenant, I hear this was a real milk run. How does it feel to go to hell and back twice in one night?"

"I'm pretty sure it won't always be that simple. What if one of the pickups decided he wanted to fly the other way and had a gun to enforce his wishes?"

"I'm afraid the pilot would have damn few choices. He could crash and probably not survive. He could follow the passenger's instructions and then I wouldn't even guess what would happen if the Krauts got their

175

hands on him." The Sergeant was looking at Sam with grave concern in his eyes and in his voice.

"Let's think of a way to give the pilot a way out if it should happen a bandit tried to take over," Sam requested.

"Let me give it some thought," Sergeant Wilson requested.

Sam went out onto the runway where he started to run at a pace that was called a dogtrot in Mississippi. He had found that exercise was a great tension reliever. It had started to rain. And as he splashed through the puddles that were beginning to form, he gained some degree of peace in his mind. He began to run at a ground-covering clip. He ran around and around the buildings and after about thirty minutes Colonel Mimba noticed the slogging figure.

The Colonel prided himself on being able to figure anyone out in a short time. But

Sam had him baffled. All the other pilots were either sleeping or were in the recreation area drinking beer. He knew that all soldiers avoided exercise whenever possible. But here was Lieutenant Warden, on his free time, and in the rain, doing the unthinkable. As Sam came slogging along he called out to him. "Hey, Warden, why aren't you resting?"

Sam slowed to a walk and replied, "Don't need much rest, Colonel. Just knocking off the sharp edges so I can sleep."

Colonel Mimba fell into step with Sam and they walked along in silence for a few minutes. Sam spoke first, "I've been talking to Sergeant Wilson about a concern I have." He went on to explain his opinion about the Night Hawk pilots being vulnerable to hostile passengers. The Colonel listened intently.

"That's something we've failed to consider," he said. "We even have the passenger seat behind the pilot which makes it worse. Have you any ideas?"

"Bullet proof glass between the pilot and passenger," Sam replied dryly.

From that conversation there were two innovations added to the planes; bulletproof glass behind the pilot's head and nerve gas, controlled by the pilot, routed into the passenger compartment. The gas not only was vented into the compartment but also into the passenger's oxygen mask, which was on a separate system from the pilot's.

The other pilots thought it was being overly cautious. Most agreed with the outspoken Holland when he said, "Hell, the jokers we pick up have only one thing on their minds; that's to get out of that mess as fast as they can. That's just another Warden bad dream."

The operation became highly successful. They changed pickup places constantly. General Lockwood made a hard and fast rule: only one pickup at any location. Using paved roads solved the problem of landing strips. Most were at a crossroads in the flat countryside, where there were no obstructions to interfere with the airplane wings.

The Allied Air High Command was very pleased at the success. Over one hundred people had been rescued right from under the German occupation force's nose in the first month and not one Night Hawk casualty.

On the other hand it was driving the Germans crazy. They could hear the planes pass overhead, see no lights, hear them land and take off again. They could find tire marks where the planes had landed. They suspected some sophisticated secret weapon and made plans to find what it was.

179

It first happened to a British pilot named Martin. It was a routine pickup, in a remote countryside at an open intersection. Martin landed and turned his plane to take off on the left hand roadway in the still air. The passenger clambered aboard and as he strapped on his harness the plane was moving rapidly on its takeoff run.

Martin climbed out sharply and headed for the English Channel when he heard the chilling words, in perfect English, "I've got a gun pointed right at your head. Turn around. We're going to Germany."

Martin was so startled he momentarily forgot the procedure and started to make the turn. He quickly flipped the switch to turn on the gas and almost instantly the passenger's head flopped against the canopy.

As Martin approached the field he radioed. "It's sweet dreams for me tonight." The military police were waiting when the plane landed. The passenger was still unconscious when he was dragged from the plane, but a little while in the fresh air and he began to regain his senses.

By the time the passenger was fully conscious General Lockwood and Colonel Mimba were present in the hanger where the military police were holding him.

General Lockwood stood staring at the young dark haired man. "Would you like to tell me why you pulled a gun on our pilot?" he asked softly.

"Would you like to take a step to hell?" the young man asked defiantly.

General Lockwood smiled a thin-lipped smile. The young man was sitting in a chair and a burly military policeman was standing on either side. He suddenly popped something into his mouth and jumped to his feet. Through clenched teeth he said, "Heil Hitler," as he gave the Nazi salute and immediately fell dead at the General's feet, even as the military policemen reached for him.

The General skewered his military police with a long stare. "I'm sure no one thought to strip search him," he gritted.

"No sir. We took his gun. Our briefing said if this should ever happen we should disarm the prisoner. He only had the one gun," the military police Sergeant said, miserably.

"By the book, nobody ever thinks," the General growled as he walked away.

The prisoner had popped a cyanide capsule into his mouth while standing within reach of the Military Police.

General Lockwood promptly called a meeting of all the Night Hawk personnel. His message was short and to the point. "The enemy is now aware we are doing something extraordinary. They will spare no effort to discover what that is. We must, and I emphasize must, prevent the Night Hawk secret from falling into their hands. They probably think it is some new aircraft technology. Let them think that. It is obvious they are after an airplane. And one day they will succeed in disabling one. You are charged with the responsibility of destroying your aircraft if capture is imminent."

Before another Night Hawk flight all aircraft were equipped with destructive charges that could be triggered by a simple hand held electronic device.

A few days later as Sam approached his designated landing area on a remote country road, he spotted a squad of German soldiers crouched in the road ditches near the pickup spot. He gave the plane full throttle and roared away. He turned and came back over the area, thinking of strafing the soldiers.

He could see they were holding civilian hostages. He pulled up sharply as the soldiers began small arms fire.

He made his report at the debriefing and other pilots reported the same thing.

Colonel Mimba said, "I'm afraid our source of information has been contaminated by the enemy. From now on it will become more and more hazardous to pick up anyone."

The French underground was informed of the turn of events and they requested Night Hawk flights be suspended until further notice.

Colonel Mimba assembled his pilots and gave them the information. "Don't fuss about it," he said, "The French underground people have a way of taking care of traitors in their ranks. We'll have a chance to get some rest. We'll start with some two-day passes. About half of you at a time."

Jim Holland was ecstatic. He said to Sam, "Damn, Warden, let's go to town. Do some serious drinking. And if we're lucky get some of this English pussy that's running around without any men to take care of it. Oh, I remember, you don't drink. Do you like girls?"

"I like girls," Sam replied.

Chapter 5

Sam Warden and Jim Holland were in the second group to get a two-day pass. When the first group returned to camp they were full of stories about the friendly people and the beautiful willing young girls.

"Lying bastards," Holland growled. "Guys that talk about getting a lot of pussy, ain't getting none. I'm going to get me some if I have to go to a whorehouse. What about you Warden?"

"Well I don't know. I've paid a high price, at times, but I've never been to a whorehouse," Sam replied.

Sam had never ceased to have dreams about having sex with beautiful girls. Just the two days of inactivity had made it worse.

When they arrived in the city, Holland wanted to go to the nearest pub. Sam said,

"Nah, you don't want to go to a pub. Everybody goes to pubs, they'll be full of G.I.s, we won't stand a chance."

"Whatta ya mean won't stand a chance? They'll serve me drinks, I'm damn sure of that."

"I thought you wanted to get a little nooky," Sam answered.

"Well listen to the expert. Pardon me. What do you suggest, oh wise one?" Holland was at his sarcastic best.

"First, let's go to the park." Sam had noticed one as they came into the city. It was nearby and what had attracted his attention was a group of girls, some playing tennis and others just lolling around.

"You're kidding, aren't you? You gotta be kidding." Holland was just about ready to strike out alone.

"Trust me. What've you got to lose? You've got two days to fill up on beer, or whatever you want to drink." Sam was convincing.

They walked the few blocks to the park and as Sam had observed, there were many pretty girls. All young and as Holland said, "Not an ugly one in the bunch."

They were friendly. They smiled and nodded as the two young American officers strolled by. Under his breath Holland said, "What now brains? Just grab one and run off?"

"Don't be so impatient," Sam cautioned. "Just look around. The girls are more interested in us than we are in them. If that's possible."

And it was true. The two young men were creating quite a stir among the girls as they strolled along. Sam spotted a beautiful brunette, seated on a bench reading a book. She wore glasses and as she bent over the book her dark hair fell around her face. Sam walked over to where she was sitting and said, "Pardon me ma'am."

The girl quickly looked up. Her eyes were deep blue. Sam continued, "We're strangers in town. Could you direct us to the library?"

She smiled and replied, "I sure can, better than that I'll show you where it is." She stood and she was almost as tall as Sam. Introductions were made. Her name was Helen Nelsen.

They started walking across the park grounds toward the street. A pretty red haired girl came trotting toward them.

"No fair Helen, you can't have two," she called to her friend.

"Come join us Maryann, I'm showing the fellows the library."

"I'll join you, but what I want to know is why these yanks want to go to the library?"

"Maybe it's just an ice breaker," Helen laughed when she answered.

Maryann fell in beside Jim Holland just as Sam was explaining to Helen; it was their first liberty and they were strangers, didn't know anyone and really didn't know a thing to do in this strange country.

Helen took Sam's hand and said, "Let us show you this part of our country. You've probably seen it from the air, but we'll show it to you at ground level."

It was the beginning of a great two-day pass. The girls showed them the city and took them to Helen's home in the nearby countryside. Maryann was a houseguest there. They had dinner with the family. Helen's two brothers were serving with the British army in North Africa, so there were only six for dinner, Mr and Mrs Nelsen and the four young people. The British people were completely intrigued by the young Americans. Holland spoke in the crisp hard Kansas sound and Sam in the soft slurring Mississippi accent.

There was wine after dinner and much talk of the war. Mr Nelsen noticed the Night Hawk insignia and asked, "Do you chaps fly the ghost ships?"

The two pilots looked at each other and Sam said, "Ghost ships?"

"That's what the kids call them. They have no lights, fly in the darkest of nights, no one knows anything about them."

"We vote with the rest of the population, we don't know anything about ghost ships either," Jim Holland replied.

Mr Nelsen smiled slightly and dropped the subject. "Will you gentlemen be our guests for the night, or for the duration of your leave, if you like? We've plenty of space and would be ever so pleased to have you. We've never had American guests before and we so enjoy the different accents."

Sam was watching Helen as her father spoke. She smiled and nodded her head ever so slightly. He spoke quickly before Jim could reply. "If you're sure we wouldn't be imposing. We had planned to get a hotel room or go back to the base, but it is getting late."

"No bother at all," Mr Nelsen replied, "We have a guest house with lots of room. It's away from any noise; you can catch up on your sleep. Helen, why don't you show Sam and Jim the guest house and make sure they have whatever they need."

"All right father, "she replied, "This way gentlemen."

The two men said goodnight to Mr and Mrs Nelsen and followed Helen across a small courtyard to a cottage behind the main house. Helen gave them a tour of the fully equipped house. There was a well stocked bar for the likes of Jim Holland. Each man had a separate bedroom and bath. When she was sure they would be comfortable, Helen said goodnight. Sam walked to the door with her, she turned and kissed him and whispered in his ear, "We'll be back in a little while."

Jim went to the refrigerator and began making a cocktail. As he poured scotch whiskey over ice he looked at Sam and said, "Well, this ain't exactly what I had in mind. Nice, very nice, all we need now is go to church tomorrow and this leave will be complete. At least the booze is good and it's hard to beat the price."

Sam was all innocence as he asked, "Don't you like Maryann?"

"Yeah, I adore her, I also adore the movie stars in Hollywood, but they are out of reach. I'm leaving here bright and early in the morning, I'm going where there's some action, girl type action, without a chaperone." The scotch was beginning to do its work and Jim was showing his disappointment.

Sam said, "I thought things were going so well, nice girls, nice family, good food, low cost. What else can you possible want?"

Jim was thoughtfully forming a scathing retort when there was a soft knock on the door. Sam opened it and the two girls walked in. Jim stood with his mouth half open, his drink in his hand, Maryann took it and after a sip said, "Where's mine?"

Jim came quickly came to life and said, "Ma'am, its coming right up." While he was preparing a drink for Maryann he said, "Helen, can I get you something? I'm a good bartender"

"I'll have a glass of wine later," she answered.

The house had a recreation area, with a pool table and a tile floor. There was plenty of room for dancing. Helen put music on the phonograph and as the strains of Moonlight Serenade filled the room the two couples danced easily and very close.

One time the girls were selecting the music and the two men were out of hearing distance from them. Sam asked, "Well, what do you think, Holland?"

"I think I've died and gone to heaven. I take back every bad thing I ever thought of you. If you ever want someone bumped off just let me know."

Sam smiled a tight-lipped smile. Jim said, "That's the nearest thing to a smile I've ever seen on your ugly mug. Tell me Warden, why are you so damn grim."

Before Sam could reply, the girls were back and the dancing began again. They changed partners and Maryann pressed her body so close to Sam he could feel her legs and her breasts pushing against his chest. When he danced with Helen, she was more

195

distant. When he would hold her close she did not resist, but she still did not melt against him either.

Jim and Maryann drifted out of the room and Sam and Helen continued to dance. He kissed her ear, then her neck, ran his hand down her slim back and caressed her round bottom.

Excitement ran through him, his heart began to race; it had been such a long time since he had been with a beautiful woman, any woman. They were near the pool table and Sam pushed her against it and started raising her dress. His hand found her scanty underpants and felt the wet pubic hair.

"Wait," she whispered, "Let's not spoil it. Let's find a more comfortable place." Then she gasped as Sam entered her, around the loose leg of her underpants. And for a few moments they were completely lost in each other.

"I'm sorry," Sam whispered as they clung to each other, "I just couldn't wait."

"Don't be sorry, it was wonderful. Maybe we can try that again sometime. But for now let's find a more comfortable place."

In Sam's bedroom, Helen began to undress. She slipped her dress over her head and unsnapped her brassiere and let it fall to the floor. She stepped out of her shoes and dropped her panties and stepped out of them. Her beautifully proportioned body was milk white with dark nipples on her uplifted breasts and her pubic hair was black as coal.

Sam had been watching Helen, fumbling with buttons as he undressed. Excitement began to race through him and by the time he was undressed his erection was complete.

Helen stood close to him and took his penis in her hand. Squeezing it, she said,

Claude Eldridge

"I do believe it's true what they say about Americans."

Kissing her passionately, Sam asked, "What do they say about Americans?"

Helen mumbled between kisses, "Over paid, over sexed and over here."

Sam laid her slim body across the bed. Slowly and carefully he caressed her, kissing her eyes, her throat, her mouth and moving down her throat he kissed her breasts, each one, then each one once again. He kissed her navel and bit her, hard on her flat belly.

Helen gasped, and moaned, "Oh please, please take me."

Sam placed her beautiful long legs over his shoulders and bending her back he gently entered her and pushed and pushed. Helen stifled a scream of ecstasy.

They made love until the early hours of the morning. Helen said, "I never thought it

198

could be like this, and I've had a little experience."

Sam rolled her over on her belly and began to kiss the nape of her neck. He moved down the small of her back, across her buttocks, on down her legs and then he began to gently bite the soft skin on the back of her knees. Helen began to make little moaning sounds and beat her feet against the bed. Sam stood on his knees between her legs and raised her body. He entered her from the back and slowly but firmly stroked back and forth. With one of his hands between her legs his fingers massaged her clitoris. The girl had one orgasm after the other.

Finally they lay side by side. Their sweaty bodies pressed close to each other. They began to drift to sleep.

Helen sat up in bed. "I must not go to sleep. I have to go to the house." She jumped out of bed and took a quick shower.

Got dressed and leaned over Sam and pressed her lips hard against his. Then she was gone.

After a hot shower, Sam dropped into bed and his sleep was dreamless. When he awoke, sunlight was streaming through the windows and someone was knocking on his bedroom door. He slipped his pants on and opened the door. Helen was standing there, beautiful, fresh and cool. She said, "Good morning sleepy head." He reached for her and she pushed him back. "No, no, no time for that. Father and mother are leaving and they would like to say farewell."

"It'll be a few minutes, I have to shave."

"Don't rush, I'll wait for you at the house." With that information Helen turned and walked away.

In record time, Sam showered and shaved. He knotted his necktie while remembering the night before. Helen seemed so cool this morning. When he arrived at the main dwelling house, the Nelsons greeted him warmly.

Mr Nelsen said, "I trust you slept well."

"Best night's sleep I've had in ages," Sam acknowledged.

"Good, good," Mr Nelsen was all smiles. "The wife and I have to run out into the country to see her mother who is doing poorly and we wanted see you before we left. We would like to invite you back any time you can get some time away from your duties."

Sam's manners had been drilled into him by his mother from an early age. He thanked the Nelsons graciously for their hospitality and finished by saying, "I'm so sorry circumstances prevent me from reciprocating, but if you are ever in America, stop by Lone Pine near Parkersville, Mississippi, and even if I'm not there my parents will see that the county is yours."

Mrs Nelsen was so touched by his statements, especially "if I'm not there" and its implication, she began to weep. She embraced Sam and said, "We are so grateful for what you are doing for us and the world and we will pray every day for your safety and implore almighty God to return you to your family."

Sam glanced at Helen and she was dabbing at her eyes. Mr Nelsen said gruffly, "We'd best be going, it's getting late." He grasped Sam's hand in both his and said, "Do come again, we won't take no for an answer."

Sam nodded in agreement. Mrs Nelsen presented him with a bag of goodies the cook had put together, kissed him on the cheek and said goodbye.

"They have adopted you, at least in their hearts," Helen told Sam after her parents had departed.

"How about you? You seem pretty cool this morning. I thought last night was special."

"It was special, but I didn't intend for it to happen. That bit up against the pool table caught me off guard. And after that I thought why not." Helen was looking out the window. She said, "I bet you're starved. I'll tell cook to prepare you some breakfast."

"I'd rather go back to the guest house with you," Sam replied.

"After we eat," Helen replied.

While they were eating Sam asked what had happened to Jim and Maryann.

"They were up early this morning and went into the country to see Maryann's parents," Helen answered with a smile. "Looks like love to me. Maryann was simply glowing."

"Never fall in love with a soldier," Sam admonished.

"I believe that, you're wise for one so young," the girl said with a touch of sadness in her voice.

"Did one break your heart?" Sam wanted to know.

"Not yet, I'm married to one."

There was a long silence. Finally Sam said, "Well, I guess that explains some things."

"I expect so. He's in North Africa. I haven't seen him in eighteen months. I just lost control last night. You seemed like such a young boy I thought we would show you fellows a good time. I can't be having men friends around my parents."

The words came in a rush.

"I'll go, I'll get my things." Sam arose from the table and started for the guesthouse.

Helen walked with him and stood watching as he packed his toilet articles. "I don't blame you for wanting to leave. You must have a terrible opinion of me," she said sadly.

Sam stopped his packing and turned to face her. "I have a great opinion of you. That's the reason I'm leaving. I thought you wanted me to go. I don't live for tomorrow. Right now is all I have. I'd like to try the pool table again."

Helen started unbuttoning her blouse. "The bed is much better," she said.

Sam was back on base in the evening after his two-day pass had expired. He had an understanding with Helen that they would meet whenever he could get away. But not at her parents home.

Jim Holland came in later. With great exuberance he talked of his outstanding liberty from duty. "Boy, I never dreamed of anything like that. I think I'm in love. Warden, you son of a gun, I've never seen such an operator. Ma'am can ya'll tell me how to find the liahberry?" He was having great fun imitating Sam's Mississippi drawl. "How'd you make out with that cool tall Helen?" he wanted to know.

"She's married to a British soldier."

"Well I'll be jiggered," Holland said with surprise.

After the two-day leaves had expired the Night Hawks spent their time honing their skills. Once again they were flying the observation course and being scored as though they were in training. A new element was added. They flew mock combat missions against each other. An infrared gun camera recorded the "kills". This exercise was discontinued when there were four midair collisions in one week. All four pilots were killed.

When the records were checked, it was discovered, at least one of the pilots in each collision had marginally passed the night flying training. And all of them were at the bottom of the scale of proficiency rating.

Two weeks passed before the French underground reported it was safe to resume the rescue missions. Once again the Night Hawks were in action. And once again it became almost routine. They moved in quickly, picked up their passengers and were airborne in short order. The French underground reported the Nazis were offering a two million dollar reward for a Night Hawk plane. Caution became the watchword. General Lockwood sent a directive to all operations personnel: "Be extremely cautious. If you see anything suspicious, abort the mission. Take no extra chances and above all make sure the plane is destroyed if its capture is imminent."

Sam had developed a sixth sense about the unusual. On one pickup he was coming in for a landing when he noticed heavy grass concentrations on either side of the road where he was designated to land. He pulled away and flew back to base and made his report. There were cryptic messages from the underground about leaving that passenger stranded.

It was two weeks later when a message was received to pick up a very important person at the same location. Colonel Mimba asked Sam what he thought about making that run.

"I think it's a trap of some sort and a mistake to go there."

"I'll ask for a volunteer," Colonel Mimba said a little bit caustically.

Bryan Cochran stood. "I'll go," he said.

Sam stood and said, "Let me fly cover for him, if something goes wrong we'll know it."

Colonel Mimba said, "We can't afford to let both of you go on this one mission. We need you to fly into a different sector, Warden."

Cochran flew out and did not return. Each flight had a time schedule. A few minutes were allowed for unknowns, such as wind changes that would affect times, but the flights always returned within ten minutes of the schedule. After thirty minutes Cochran was presumed lost.

Colonel Mimba called Sam to flight operations and said, "Looks like you were right. He's not coming back. What do you think happened?"

"I believe those clumps of grass were camouflaged soldiers lying in wait. When he landed they shot out his tires, or disabled the plane in some other way and probably captured Cochran."

Once again the Night Hawk operation was suspended because in some way the underground had been compromised.

Concerned messages were sent to the highest rank in the French movement. What had happened to Cochran was of major importance. A few days later a message was received. Enemy ground fire had shot Cochran's tires full of holes. He had been killed when the plane was destroyed.

Once again General Lockwood assembled his Night Hawk personnel. As usual he was brief and to the point. "Men," he said, "Your accomplishments have exceeded out expectations. We knew the enemy would retaliate. For the time being, that is until our contacts can assure us the Nazis are not controlling them, we are going to suspend our rescue mission. Until further notice you will use your skills in destroying the enemy's capability to sustain his war effort. Good hunting."

Colonel Mimba asked the pilots to remain after the General had finished his talk.

"I'm not happy about what's happening to us. We had twenty of the best and brightest. We have lost nine. We have eleven left. I hope that's a lucky number. We will fly search and destroy missions. As before we will fly individual missions. We will sector the target area to avoid duplication. Are there any questions?"

Jim Holland stood and asked, "Sir, could I have a week's leave?"

The Colonel smiled and said, "We'll work out something for some time off."

Back in their quarters Holland said to Sam, "I need to go see my girl. Why didn't you say something? The Colonel gives you a lot of attention."

"Yeah," Sam replied, "Like the attention he gave me when Cochran went for his last ride."

The Night Hawks entered into the search and destroy phase with the same enthusiasm they displayed for the rescue missions. Generally they selected targets away from the heavily protected enemy installations. Their flights for the most part were unchallenged as was expected because of their ability to operate in the blackest of nights. Their actions had a demoralizing effect on the Germans. A long column of soldiers, marching under the protective cover of darkness, would suddenly and without warning be raked with machine gun fire from a Night Hawk plane.

Sam earned high praise, commendations and a promotion to captain for his outstanding contribution to the search and destroy effort. The many missions he flew and the supplies he destroyed became legend. He had the ability to find the most cleverly camouflaged train.

On one occasion a one hundred car train pulled by four locomotives, loaded with fuel and ammunition, was moving rapidly across the French countryside. It was running without lights and had spotters with radios in two different engines at half-mile intervals in front to warn of any danger. The train rounded a bend in the railroad and began its journey over a long curving trestle across a swiftly flowing river. Sam had spotted the fast moving train some minutes before it arrived at the trestle. He lurked overhead until about half of the train was over the river. Then he hurtled his P38 straight at the lead locomotive with all guns blazing. The steam boiler ruptured and blew the locomotive off the track and it fell two hundred feet into the river below, dragging the other locomotives with it as it fell. The wrenching action of the locomotives took a section of the railroad track with them and as each following boxcar hit the broken track it fell into the river. Tank car after tank car piled into the river on top of each other. Many ruptured and the volatile fuel caught fire. Loads of ammunition piled into the conflagration and began exploding. The railroad trestle crumbled under the heat of the flames and the heavy explosions of the ammunition. And still more and more falling cars added fuel to the raging inferno. The towering flames consumed the few railroad cars that remained on the track after the crew managed to apply the brakes and get part of the train stopped. The river became a stream of swiftly moving destruction as it ignited, first the woods, and then buildings along its shore. At one point a fuel storage area was set ablaze. The exploding tanks added their light to the already brilliantly lighted sky.

Sam made his report at the debriefing. As usual it was unassuming. "A train had been damaged. There was a fire."

The airplane's cameras showed most of the details in all their fiery brilliance.

The French underground reported a tremendous loss to the enemy and had words of the highest praise for the Night Hawks. The Germans down played the debacle, calling it a train accident.

Colonel Mimba called Sam into his office and said, "Tell me about the train at the river trestle."

"What can I tell you that you don't already know?"

"In your own words, tell me the way it happened."

215

"Well," Sam said, "There was a long train, it was going over a railroad trestle. I attacked the first engine. It fell into the river. Other things fell on top of it. There was a fire; the flowing water carried burning fuel downstream. Other things caught on fire. That was all there was to it."

Colonel Mimba smiled, "That must be the understatement of the year. The French underground thinks it was a blow to the Germans of the first magnitude."

"Yes sir, that's the same underground that said it was safe for Cochran to land. Isn't it?"

"At least the same organization. You blame me for Cochran's death, don't you?"

"I don't blame anybody for anything. I just say the French underground people exaggerate," Sam replied.

"The French want to make sure the Night Hawk responsible for the train destruction is amply rewarded," Colonel Mimba said.

"OK, I've been rewarded. Can I go now?"

The Colonel smiled again. "Dismissed," he said, then added, "Happy birthday." It was Sam's eighteenth birthday, even though the record showed it as being number nineteen.

Sam's train destruction caused a stir among the pilots and the ground crews. Sergeant Wilson said, "That Lieutenant Warden is like a frigging bat. He misses nothing." That remark gave birth to a nickname that was to become a part of Sam's military career. More and more people started calling him Bat. Writings would refer to him as Lieutenant Samuel "Bat" Warden.

When Sam had free time he spent it with Helen, there were no more visits to the guesthouse. They would get a hotel room and make passionate love throughout the time they had together.

Time passed swiftly for the Night Hawk squadron, as it did for all men engaged in destroying the enemy. The great industrial might of the United States was beginning to make a difference and by mid 1943 it was obvious it was just a matter of time until the Nazi regime would be smashed. It was in mid July of that year when the love affair with Helen came to an end. They had spent the night together and were having breakfast in a restaurant when Helen said, "My husband is coming home next week."

"Then I guess this is goodbye," Sam said, without a trace of emotion.

"I think it must be," Helen replied.

Sam got up and walked away. He saw Helen one time after that. Jim Holland married Maryann and Helen and her husband were at the wedding. She was as cool looking and as beautiful as ever. She introduced Sam to her husband as gracious as a person could be. Later there was dancing and Sam danced with her. There was no indication on her part that Sam was anything but a casual acquaintance.

There was no shortage of girls and the handsome young Lieutenant had his pick from many. And he played the field. But there was never another Helen.

New recruits had swelled the ranks of the Night Hawks. They numbered thirty by the end of 1943. The rescue missions were scheduled to resume. The underground forces reported they had discovered the German agent in their ranks and had purged him in a decisive manner.

Three new members were added to the Warden, Holland and Pulaski group. One was a Frenchman, Jean Claude Petrie, one was a Palestinian Jew, Sharon Rosen, and the other was an Arab, a Saudi Arabian citizen named Mohammed Acumed.

Each new member was assigned to an older member to expedite his training. Jean Claude Petrie was assigned to, now Captain, Sam Warden. And Petrie was a natural. If Sam was like a Bat in the dark, Petrie was a jungle cat. His hatred of the Germans burned white hot. His assignments were performed with flawless perfection. He was a great asset to the Night Hawks. He knew France as only a native could.

Petrie also knew England. He had spent many years of his youth there, on vacation with his parents, and going to college. He knew all the right places to visit and took a lot of pride in showing Sam where to find the most beautiful girls.

The Night Hawks resumed their rescue missions whenever it was decided by the commander it was safe for the flyers. Sam had become the scout for the group. He would fly over the landing site and decide whether or not the rescue pilot should go in. Unfortunately he could not see everything.

The underground contact requested a pickup of a very important spy. The time and location was specified. Sam checked it out the night before the pickup was scheduled. It was a wide-open intersection of two level roads. On one side a half-mile away there was a heavily wooded area. He reported to Colonel Mimba that he was uneasy about the heavy woods. "Soldiers could hide there and not be detected from the air."

"Did you see anything suspicious?" he asked.

"Just the heavy woods."

Colonel Mimba sat in silent thought for a good two minutes. "It's most important we get this person out of France,"

"Give me the assignment. I've seen the terrain, it should be easy."

"No, we'll send the new man, Petrie."

Sam stood and started to walk away. He paused and turned to face the Colonel. "What is it Sam?" the Colonel asked.

"Let me follow Petrie. If something should go wrong we would know what happened. If nothing is amiss, well, I just took an extra plane ride."

"You know that's not the way we operate."

"I know, I know. But I'll give up a day of my next leave. You can't lose like that."

"Man, I never thought I'd hear you give up a day of leave for anything." The Colonel was thoughtful for a few moments. "That's what we'll do. I don't know what you expect, but it can't hurt. Go ahead and follow Petrie."

"Thanks," Sam said as he walked away.

Before they departed he talked to Petrie about a plan of action. "If something goes wrong, if your plane is disabled on the ground, get out fast. Set the demolition charge timer and run north as fast as you can. There's a hill about a quarter mile away, then the road flattens out for a way. I'll pick you up as soon as I'm sure you are not being pursued."

"Mon Dieu, what do you expect to happen?" The Frenchman was a little excited.

"Nothing, I'm just saying what if? We gotta have a plan just in case. If the Germans are wise to this operation they'll come out of the woods to the South of the pickup site. I'll slow 'em down and give you a chance to go over the hill. If I can't get to you, shuck your flight suit and join the peasants. You should fit right in."

"I remind you of a peasant, eh?"

"I meant the language, French you know."

223

Petrie looked at the unsmiling Captain Warden and said, "I'm glad you're going along for the ride. This is not standard operating procedure, is it?"

Sam replied, "I think I talked the Colonel into doing it this way. But he probably had it planned all along."

Sam was one minute behind Petrie as the Frenchman slipped to a landing at the pickup site. His plane touched down and began to roll when both main gear tires blew out. The roadbed had been covered with the steel devices made like a child's toy jack. No matter how they fell there was a sharp point sticking up.

The plane slewed to the right and stopped in the road ditch. Petrie set the demolition switch, jumped out and started running north, dropping his parachute as he ran.

Sam came over the site just as the German soldiers, with lights, came rapidly out of the woods on the South. He roared skyward to gain altitude, turned and bore down on the row of lights with guns blazing. The soldiers fell like grain before a scythe. He wheeled around and came back, picking up any stragglers. Some were running for the shelter of the woods, all lights were now out, but he could see three who were crawling toward the plane. He made one more pass, strafing the prone forms as he passed. In the distance he could see Petrie running at the hilltop. As he turned and passed over the pickup site, he could see two figures huddled in the road ditch.

He flew past Petrie, turned and landed and rolled to meet him. Petrie ducked under the wing of the moving plane and scrambled through the open door.

"Let's get the hell out of this place," he said over the intercom.

"Right," Sam agreed. He shoved the throttles forward and the P38 jumped into the air. He swung wide over the pickup site where he saw a lone figure climbing into the cockpit. "Oh, hell, the demolition charge didn't go off. Petrie," he shouted, "Did you set the charge?"

"Yeah, yeah I did."

"How about the hand held trigger?"

"Gad, I forgot all about that. I was too busy getting my ass out of there."

Sam turned and headed for the crippled bird. The big fifty calibers stuttered their deadly song. The first pass didn't seem to have any effect. As he turned for a second run, a wounded man was struggling to get out. As he dropped to the ground something struck a spark, perhaps his boot hit one of the steel tire traps, there was an instant flash as spilled gasoline ignited. The sky lit up with the explosion.

"Now, let's go home," Sam said.

The two pilots trudged into the debriefing room and made their report to a grim faced Colonel Mimba. He sat silent until they were complete. "Lieutenant Petrie you're excused. Captain Warden, please stay."

When they were alone, Colonel Mimba said in a deceptively soft voice. "Captain Warden, what authorized you to make an unscheduled landing and pick up a downed pilot?

"I've never heard of a rule against it. So I authorized myself."

"You know its not part of the operating procedure. That's what rules are for. So we know what to expect from everyone."

"You authorized me to go with Petrie. You are always telling everybody to use their heads. That's what I did. Rescuing one of our own should be a part of the operating procedure."

"I'll talk to the General and get back to you," Colonel Mamba's voice seemed to hold a veiled threat.

When Sam got to his quarters Jean Claude Petrie was waiting. "What did the old man have to say? He queried.

"Oh, he's pissed off because I picked you up. It's not in the rules. You can bet your sweet ass he'll be on your case about the demolition charge when he's had time to think about it."

Petrie was easily excited. "What do you think he'll do?'

Sam was growing weary; it had been a long day's work. "I don't give a big rat's ass what he does. He can send me home. I'm going to bed."

Colonel Mimba had the greatest respect for his young Captain. He was more strict with him for two reasons. He didn't understand what made Sam run and he had heard rumors that the other men thought the Colonel was partial to Sam because they were once roommates. He had these things in the back of his mind when he briefed General Lockwood.

"There are two issues from this incident. Lieutenant Petrie failed to destroy the stricken plane, and Captain Warden made an unauthorized landing to rescue Petrie. Now the question is; what should I do about these serious infractions?"

"Ground them both. Ground them for three days and sentence them to spend them in London," the General said, gruffly.

Colonel Mimba was taken aback by the General's attitude.

"Are you serious?" he asked, incredulously.

Claude Eldridge

"I'm serious," General Lockwood, replied, "Warden is probably the most outstanding man we have, he did caution us about that pick up. He did three things that deserve a commendation. He read the danger signals correctly, he took immediate action to pick up his downed comrade, and he destroyed the crippled plane. If we'd been following strict operating procedure, he wouldn't have even been at that site when Petrie's plane was crippled."

Colonel Mimba could feel himself smarting under the General's statements, especially the one about following strict procedure. He knew he was responsible for that part.

"You think I'm being too critical?"

"No, I think it's difficult to manage a group such as this and then you throw in a maverick like Warden that doesn't fit the mold and that adds to the difficulty. I admit I can't figure this guy out. He's a textbook soldier. And he works extra hard at doing everything right. If this were the major leagues in baseball, he would be playing errorless ball. Doesn't drink, doesn't smoke, the only vice I can find, if that's a vice, is a strong liking for the ladies." The General was thoughtful for a few moments. "And he never smiles and I would like to know why. Colonel, you do what you think you ought to do. You have my opinion."

Colonel Mimba rose to leave when the General stopped him.

"One other thing I think you should know. Looks like we'll be losing Warden. There's a need for leadership because of the heavy influx of new inexperienced pilots. The high brass has tapped Warden for one of those slots."

Sam and Jean Claude were given a three-day pass. They went to London where the girls were. Sam was in a USO building sitting at the bar sipping a coke when a voice from the past said, "I can't believe it's the pride of Parkersville, Mississippi." He turned and for a few moments he couldn't place the owner of the soft southern accented voice.

"Alicia, Alicia Steinberg! What in the world are you doing here?"

"I'm working for Uncle Sugar." She was trim and neat in her Wasp uniform. An overseas cap was perched over one eye and she was not wearing glasses. "Don't I rate a hug from an old friend?"

Sam held out his arms and she walked in. He held her close and his heart started to race. He held her at arm's length and said, "Look at you, I can't believe it's you. My gosh you've changed."

"It's been over two years Sam, that's a long time in a growing girl's life. And look at you. You're not the sad sack I drove out into the country back in '41, you look great, a Captain and all that stuff. Everybody at home is so proud of you"

Alicia had changed. Her teeth were beautiful she no longer wore glasses over her wide spaced gray eyes, and her body was all long slim legs, well rounded hips, narrow waist and large breasts the uniform could not hide. Her lips were full; her nose was large and slightly crooked. She still smiled a twisted smile that Sam remembered.

For a while they both talked at the same time. There was a lot of news that, to his surprise, Sam was interested in.

"I saw your parents about a month ago. They are well. Angela was terrible unhappy when you left like you did. They worry so about you. Parkersville has more than it's share of gold stars in the windows of homes. Joe Johnson was killed in Guam. The last I heard Tump was wounded. They did get to see each other before Joe was killed. Tump was just so crazy about Joe. I know he must have been devastated. You know he was like you. He never came home on leave after he joined the marines."

"Tell me about you," Sam insisted.

"I can't believe it's been over two years. I graduated from high school the year you enlisted. That summer I worked for Lee Brown. You remember him?"

Sam nodded his acknowledgement.

"Well, I learned to fly. He's a great instructor. Then I started to college in the fall, went one semester and it seemed so useless. The war was so terrible, every day another one of our boys was listed as missing in action, or worse. I just wanted to do something to help, so I enlisted and because I had a private pilot's license, they put me in the Air Transport Command and

234

after a lot of hard work and training here I am." Alicia was almost breathless as she finished her statement.

The band was playing "Harbor Lights," and Sam said, "Would you like to dance?"

"I sure would like to dance with you Captain Warden. I never danced with you when you were a civilian, so this will be a first."

Sam followed her as she walked to the dance area. It was hard for him to believe this beautiful creature was someone he had known since childhood. She turned into his arms and they danced so close Sam could feel her legs against his, her breath was warm on his neck. He kissed her cheek and she turned her face to him and kissed him on the lips, long and hard. Her mouth was slightly open and he could feel the tip of her tongue. Excitement began to build in him. "Let's get out of this place," he whispered.

"I can't Sam, I have an early flight to Goose Bay. All my people are standing over by the door looking at their watches, just waiting for me to say goodbye to a friend from home. There's just no way, some other time. O.K.?"

Sam watched her hurry across the floor to join her group and walk out the door. He had a sad letdown feeling. Jean Claude sauntered by with a pretty girl on each arm and said, "Hey, soldier, I need help." Sam shook off his feeling of sadness and volunteered to help his friend. Their three-day leave passed rapidly.

Chapter 6

When they returned to base Sam's orders were waiting. He was being transferred to a unit stationed near London. That city was being pounded nightly by German bombers and some thing new to modern warfare, buzz bombs. The jet-propelled bombs were launched at the city indiscriminately. Sam's new unit was assigned to night flying to help make the German effort as costly to them as possible.

Sam was assigned as squadron leader. The planes they flew were the new American P51 Mustangs. From the beginning Sam fell in love with the Mustang. He named his, "My Baby II". And instead of the figure of a pretty girl painted on the nose, as was the custom, he had a small biplane painted on the nose and up close you could read its name, My Baby.

Sam's squadron distinguished itself from the start. The slower German bombers provided ample opportunity. The string of "Kills" painted on his Mustang increased on a daily basis.

Sam's squadron was over France when the fabled Warden luck ran out. Sam was making a tight left turn; the P51's engine was at full throttle when he ran into a bursting shell from ground fire. The engine was disabled and a part of the canopy was torn off. A shell fragment struck Sam in the face, gashing his right cheek from hairline to the edge of his jawbone. He was momentarily knocked unconscious. When he regained consciousness he was floating down through the darkness. He never remembered exiting the plane or opening his parachute. He landed in an open field.

He lay on the ground for a few minutes trying to get his bearing. He was bleeding from the head wound and his right eye was swollen shut. Almost automatically he began following the training provided for a downed pilot. He disengaged the parachute and using his sheath knife, cut bandages and wound them around his injured head trying to staunch the bleeding. He then rolled the parachute into a tight bundle and concealed it under a nearby stone fence.

Sam began walking across the field to a country road where he had a difficult time deciding which direction he should go. He was in shock, he was bleeding and the early morning chill caused him to shiver. He was in enemy territory and fear of the unknown filled his heart with dread. His misery increased when it started raining a slow drizzle. He walked more slowly, sometimes only half conscious as the approaching dawn started chasing the shadows of the night.

A French farmer, Pierre Duloc, doing his early morning chores saw the injured flyer stumbling down the road. Rushing into his house he told his wife, Nicole "Look Mama, there's a wounded man walking down the road."

"Maybe he's German," the wife said, gazing into the dim light.

"No, no, he's American, I can see the insignia on his jacket. We must help him."

"It's very dangerous, the Boche will be looking for him and you know the penalty for aiding the enemy."

"It's a chance we have to take. We can hide him in the wine cellar. It has a secret door; they'll never find him there. I know who to contact to get him back to his home base."

The couple, which could speak English, hurried to Sam's side. Weak from loss of blood, shock and fatigue, he was barely able to walk. Without resistance he allowed himself to be led into the modest home where he collapsed upon the floor of the living room.

"First let's stop the bleeding," Pierre said, as he stripped away the crude bandages Sam had applied. "It doesn't appear to be a serious wound. His eye is swollen shut."

Nicole bathed the injury with warm water, she applied some medicated ointment and with sure fingers wrapped Sam's head in clean cloth bandages. His weakened condition and the damp clothing caused him to shiver as though he had a chill. Pierre stripped away the wet clothing and they wrapped the barely conscious man in a warmed blanket and dragged him to the kitchen and placed him near the heating stove.

Pierre held Sam's head while Nicole feed him some warm porridge and encouraged him to take a few sips of a dark red wine. Sleep overwhelmed him.

Sam drifted into wakefulness. There were farm sounds, a hen clucking, a rooster crowing and somewhere near a cow was lowing. For a moment he thought he was at Lone Pine in Mississippi, then memory came flooding back. He moved gingerly to see if all members were functioning, it was then he realized he was naked and wrapped in a blanket. He pulled it tightly around himself and sat up. A little girl who had been watching his every move, jumped from her chair and ran outside yelling, "Papa, Papa, he's awake."

Pierre hurried into the house and asked, "How are you feeling?"

"I'm O.K., where're my clothes?"

The Frenchman smiled, "Oh your clothes, they have been cleaned and are still wet, I will get you some of mine." Pierre brought some of his clean rough work clothes and handed them to Sam, who took them with one hand while holding the blanket with the other. He sat on the floor waiting, while the little girl stared at him with big curious eyes.

Pierre smiled and said, "Out, out Simone." And the child scampered away.

Sam stood and swayed for a moment until Pierre caught his arm and steadied him. He slipped into the clothing, which was tight in the shoulders and loose in the waist.

Pierre said, "Not a good fit, but your uniform will be ready soon. We have to make sure the Germans don't find you. We have a perfect hiding place."

Pierre led Sam downstairs to the cellar. He pressed on what appeared to be solid stonewall and a section swung inward revealing another room. Shelving supports hid the cracks made where the door met the rest of the wall. To anyone examining the wall the shelving and all supports would have to be moved before the door could be discovered.

Sam looked around and saw row after row of bottles of wine. There was a cot for sleeping and blankets for warmth.

"We think you will be safe here," Pierre said, "I've been in touch with some people who will see that the underground knows your whereabouts. Your people will be notified by the code we use. It is a combination of your serial number and other information scattered through the message so that it makes sense to only those who know the code. Such a simple system, but it works. I'll leave you here for now. I'll bring you some food shortly. Will you be alright?"

The question was asked anxiously.

Sam nodded his head affirmatively. He sat on the cot and assessed his situation. He was deep in enemy territory, on a farm, hidden from the German patrol, in a wine cellar. He switched off the light and was pleased to find that his night vision in his one good eye was as sharp as ever. He realized his fate was in the hands of the French citizens.

He stretched out on the cot and fell fast asleep. He dreamed he was at home in Mississippi. He was walking along the garden path at Lone Pine and his mother called him to supper. He could smell Ava's fried chicken. He awoke with a start when the light was switched on. Pierre was at the door with a farmer-sized meal. Sam realized he was ravenously hungry.

Pierre watched as Sam wolfed the meat and bread and vegetables. "Drink a little wine, it will be good for your stomach. You are not a drinking man, eh?"

"I'm not a drinking man," Sam admitted.

"This is not drinking, this is medicine."

Sam sipped the dark red wine and felt the warmth spread through his body. He suddenly felt very comfortable. He was well fed and warm—and sleepy.

The next day Sam was much improved. Nicole came to the cellar with his breakfast and his clothes. She dressed his wound and clucked over him like one of her barnyard hens with one chick. "You need a shave, but it'll have to wait awhile. Not much use shaving just one side. You're healing up nicely, but you will have a lasting scar to mar that handsome face."

Sam spent the day pacing back and forth in the narrow cellar. His strength was back to normal and he was anxious to see what lay ahead. During the night he was awakened by the light being turned on.

Pierre and two other men stepped into the room. "These men are from the French underground. It's best that you don't know their names. Go with them. They know how to get you back to England."

"I want to thank you for all you've done for me. I'll never forget it," Sam said, as he was getting dressed.

"No, we thank you. You risk your life for our cause. Maybe we will meet again under better circumstances."

Sam followed the two men into the dark night. They walked across the field and continued for about two hours. Finally one of the men spoke, "We will rest."

They sat on the ground and Sam leaned against a tree. The same man said softly, "Do you know the operation called Night Hawks?"

"Yeah, I know about Night Hawks," Sam replied.

"We have you scheduled for pickup in about thirty minutes. There's a road just over that hill where the plane will land. It's a shame only one person at a time can be picked up, there are so many who could be saved from the horror of the Nazi camps," the Frenchman said.

"You could fix it so more could be picked up," Sam answered.

"How could you do that? We are watched so closely. We are lucky to get a few downed pilots out safely."

"You could use steel landing mats. Find a field or pasture level enough, place the mats on the ground, cover them with about an inch of soil, plant grass or wheat in the soil, which would hide it from the Germans. When it was ready the Night Hawks could land a C47 and take out twenty-five or thirty people at a time. You might get in three or four flights before the landing site was discovered."

There was a long silence. Then the Frenchmen talked to each other in their own language. The one who had been acting as the spokesman to Sam said, "You might have an excellent idea. Now it's time for us to go."

They walked over the hill and Sam saw a paved road stretching across the level plain. It reminded him of the rescues he had made when he had been a Night Hawk. As he approached the road his heart raced with anticipation.

"It doesn't really matter which direction he comes from. There's no wind," the French spokesman said.

The three men walked through the tall grass and crouched in the ditch by the side of the road. Each one of the French men anxiously looked at his watch and then at the sky. Suddenly there was a swooshing sound and an airplane slipped through the darkness, landed on the road, rolled to a stop just opposite where the men were waiting.

"Go, hurry, bless you, return to the skies and rid the world of the German scourge," the English speaking Frenchman said as he shoved Sam toward the road and the airplane.

The plane was moving as Sam clambered aboard. It was roaring into full power by the time his safety belt was fastened. Over the treetops it soared, in the ink black darkness, as it headed for the English coast.

Sam turned the intercom microphone on and said, "Where the hell have you been? A person could starve waiting for one of you bastards to show up."

The French accented voice of Jean Claude Petrie came over the mike. "Your gratitude touches my heart. What the hell are you doing hiding in a road ditch in the French country side, with a couple of men yet, when there are so many gorgeous women in this great country?"

"Some people don't have such a cushy job as you. There are pilots who have to work for a living."

"Look Bat, my friend, I'm happy you made it out of that pickle you were in. The old Night Hawk outfit has not been the same without you."

The plane roared across the English Channel and slipped into a landing at its home base. It was met by the military police who hustled Sam to the base hospital before he could thank Petrie for bringing him back to friendly territory. He was found to be in good health except for the long cut across his face and a very black and swollen right eye.

The cut had started to heal and the doctor said, "You're going to have a dandy scar, but it's not going to damage your good looks. The ladies will think it makes you look wicked. What we have to be concerned about is the sight in the eye. It'll be a few days before we know for sure."

A chill ran down Sam's spine. Until now he had given little thought to the possibility of a loss of eyesight. Not flying was a real possibility. What would he do if he were shipped back to the states, or worse, given a desk job in Europe?

He was placed in a hospital ward with other injured men. During the night he got out of bed and slipped out a door into the darkness. He pushed his swollen eyelids apart and found he still had his night vision. He went back to bed and immediately fell into a deep sleep.

Sam was hospitalized for a week. All the Night Hawk personnel came to see him, the line mechanics, the clerks and even the cooks. All wished him well and urged him to transfer back to "His old home base." He began to realize he missed being a part of the unusual group called the Night Hawks.

Back at his fighter wing base he was not approved for flight status. He was given a two-week recuperation leave.

He had a letter from Alicia saying she was arriving in England the day his leave began. When her flight arrived he was waiting in the flight lounge.

She came walking from the flight line in her baggy flight suit, her hair smashed down by the helmet, her face lined from fatigue. He thought she was beautiful.

He stood directly in front of her so she would have to step around him. She looked up and froze in her tracks. Her eyes brightened like stars. "Sam," she gasped, and then she was in his arms. She pushed back and asked in a shocked voice, "What in the world happened to your face?"

It's a long story, I'll tell you about it."

Sam held her close, his heart bursting with joy.

"How much free time do you have?" he asked.

"Three days, I can get three days."

"Let's make the most of them."

"Let's do," she replied her eyes shinning.

After Alicia checked out and they were in the bus headed for London, Sam said, "I have a room in a small hotel, there is a good restaurant nearby. We can get you some food and a good night's sleep and we'll see what tomorrow brings. What do you think?"

"I'm too excited to think, or to sleep. Does your room have twin beds?"

"Yes, as a matter of fact it does."

"You think of everything, don't you?"

"Probably not, but I try."

It was a nice room, with twin beds, an oversized bathtub with a shower. Sam had bought a bottle of wine, "I thought you would like a glass of wine and a bath before dinner."

"That would be great, Sam," Alicia had become thoughtful and quite somber.

Sam poured two glasses of the red wine. He passed one to Alicia and held up his glass, "A toast, to you."

Alicia touched his glass with hers and said nothing; she took a few sips of wine and was still quiet.

"I'll go downstairs and make some dinner reservations. You get your bath." He spoke gently. "I'll be back in about an hour. Will that be enough time?"

"Don't go," she whispered," I've waited long enough for this and I don't want eating and sleeping to interfere." She spoke seriously and unsmiling. "Help me undress."

Sam's heart began to race. He unbuttoned her tunic, then her shirt, as he fumbled with the snaps on her brasserie she stepped out of her trousers and stood before him in her underwear. She turned her back for him to reach the unruly brassiere hook. And when she turned to face him she was completely naked. Sam thought she was the most beautiful woman he had ever seen. "Now I'll help you," she said.

She stood close to him and her warm breath was sweet in his face. Sam's clothes were cast aside and they stood in close embrace. He kissed her full lips, hungrily and repeatedly. Her hand found his erect penis and she held it firmly and gently. Sam lifted her and laid her on one of the beds. He kissed her throat and her full breasts and taking one of them in his mouth he gently massaged it with his tongue. He put his hand between her legs and she spread them eagerly. He found it difficult to penetrate her. Alicia arched her back and gave a mighty shove and screamed with ecstasy from the result.

Breathing hard they rested and whispered terms of love.

"I love you," Sam said, it was the first time he had meant it.

"I've always loved you, you are the only man I've ever loved. This was my first time. And it was just like I had dreamed it would be."

The three days were spent, mostly in bed, getting to know each other and trying desperately to pack months of separation into a few hours of being together.

On the last day Alicia was sitting at the mirror putting her long hair up in braids, which she wound around her head. Her naked back was turned toward Sam and he could see her face in the mirror. She had bobby pins in her mouth as she said, "Sam, marry me."

"You're leaving today. There's a waiting period here." he replied.

"Oh, I don't mean today, when you come home is what I mean. My daddy says this war will be over and there will be a lot of exciting things to do. He says there will be a great demand for everything. He thinks real estate will boom. He would love to have you go into business with him."

"Marrying you is one thing, going into business with your father is another. I'd

258

love to marry you today, or when I get home. Your father doesn't know a thing about me. All I know how to do is fly an airplane, and kill people"

"Oh, he knows a lot about you. I told him when you left for the army, you were the man I was going to marry."

"You're pretty sure of yourself, aren't you?" he teased.

"I've always known that if I didn't marry you there would be no one. And after these few days together I know I could never love anyone else."

Before Alicia's flight departed Sam purchased an engagement ring and slipped it on her finger.

"Give my parents a hug for me," he said, as he kissed her goodbye.

"Please take care of yourself," Alicia said as she touched the scar on his cheek.

Then she walked away with tears streaming down her cheeks.

Sam went back to the room where they had shared their joy in the love of each other. He had never felt so alone. He visited the usual places where he had been with friends. It was not the same. He had changed. He knew the aching longing for someone he loved. After two days he reported for duty.

He was given a task of supervising the repair of battle-damaged aircraft. He was not just a figurehead. In his usual thorough fashion, he read the repair manuals and knew what was required. He was extremely strict about doing the utmost to assure pilot safety. The mechanics learned to respect the decisions of the quiet unsmiling Major.

It was a month before Sam returned to flight status. He returned to the battle in the skies at night. He received letters from

Alicia, letters of endearment and wrote letters to her in the same vein.

It was two months to the day from the time Alicia had departed when Sam was shot down again over enemy territory. His squadron had been taking a heavy toll of German bombers when Sam flew into a shower of debris from an exploding German plane. His propeller was damaged and the plane began to vibrate violently. He cut the engine but the propeller continued to spin. He baled out and as he swung on his opened parachute he saw his plane explode in the air. He floated to earth and into the hands of a German patrol.

He was taken to a prisoner of war camp and interred with a large number of allied military personnel, many of them pilots.

The prison had an internal organization with a British colonel in charge. Colonel John Montrose had one purpose in mind. Keep everyone busy doing something to keep morale at a high level. He had been a prisoner for two years and he knew it was nearly impossible to escape, but he continually clung to the hope that a way would be found for at least one prisoner to escape.

During his time in the prison ten men had tried to escape and ten men had failed. Two had died in the attempt. Each time an escape had been tried, the German commander had made sure all the captives had paid a big price. Some of which included a severe limitation on food and a complete confinement to barracks. That confinement period got longer after each attempt. The recaptured escapees were placed in solitary confinement for an ever-increasing period, which began with thirty days. The severe penalties, levied on every man made it necessary to get agreement from the other prisoners before any attempt to escape was made. The Germans had done their work well. Initiative to escape was almost nonexistent.

Sam slipped quietly in to the prison routine. Colonel Montrose assigned him to a group whose duty was to keep the parade grounds cleaned. Everything picked up and the soil raked over and over. Then in the afternoon his group exercised for two hours. In the evenings there was a discussion session, which included reading the available books and reporting on their content. The King James Version of the Holy Bible was available as was Mein Kampf.

Sam's extraordinary reading ability and his photographic memory came to light early in the first session. The moderator gave twenty minute reading assignments and then each man was called on to report on what he had read. Most of the time, reporting took a couple of minutes. The time limit was five minutes.

Sam being the new man was assigned Genesis. His report time began: "In the beginning God created the heaven and the earth and the earth was without—." For five minutes he continued, far into the book of Genesis. He was quoting, verbatim the scripture as written.

The moderator was Lieutenant William "Tex" Malone. He cocked his head to one side and said, "Major Warden, you a preacher, or a bible student or something like that?"

"Nope," Sam replied, "I never read that before."

"Well, I'll be damned," Tex exclaimed.

After that first session there was a new form of entertainment. Sam was given a part of the bible to read, or a part of another book to read the night before the session began. Then during the session there was a period of "Stump Sam." The participants would select a page and verse, or sentence and ask Sam for an exact quote. He never failed.

The boring routine of the camp made this a major event. More and more of the prisoners began to crowd into the session until it was to the point of overflowing. In a few days it came to the attention of Colonel Montrose. He called Sam into the corner of the barracks he called his office.

"Warden, that's an unusual talent you have. I understand you've read about all the books we have in the two weeks you've been here. How do you do it?"

"I don't really know. I learned at a pretty early age I could remember about anything I saw and after some practice it just got better."

"What do you plan to do with that ability?"

"After the war I'm going to finish my education."

265

"And what is that education?"

"I thought I knew, but I've been doing so rethinking."

"Finance, the business world. That's the ticket. You would have a decided advantage. Be interesting to see. For the time being, how would you like to get out of this hotel?"

"I think it would be great. But I've heard how tough it is. The rest of the men won't agree."

"The men need for someone to be successful. In the past they get away from the camp, but they can't elude capture, primarily because they get lost. Get fouled up on the maps we give them, get hungry and try to steal food. All those things lead them right back. The two that got killed made the mistake of running from the soldiers who called for them to halt—the

Germans said. How long can you retain this memory of things you see, or read?"

"A long time, I've never tried to see how long. I can remember whole books I've read before the war."

"What I was thinking, if you could remember maps and landmarks from crude drawings we can make, you might stand a chance, you and one other man. I know for sure a very large number has no chance."

"Why not just take the maps with us?"

"German reprisals. The camp commander has decreed a map on a prisoner is a death warrant. You will be shot on the spot. Furthermore, they pull a surprise search every once in awhile. Maps found in the barracks is cause for severe penalties."

"How would you get maps for me to study?"

"We have a map that's in five pieces. Hidden by the person who has each piece. No one else knows where it is. I have one piece. The other four are in the possession of four of the most trusted men."

"Why me? There must be other men here who can remember a map."

"Probably, but I'm not sure they would be willing to try. Are you?"

A tinge of excitement began to run through Sam. He was thoughtful for a moment.

"Under the right conditions, I would be interested," he replied.

"What are those conditions?"

"Under cover of darkness, cloudy, moonless, dark."

Colonel Montrose looked at him intently.

"Don't tell me. I don't want to know. The Germans have a million pound reward for the capture of a Night Hawk pilot. But you're not one of them. You're from a fighter group."

Sam nodded his agreement. He had decided not to reveal his Night Hawk experience.

"If you try this escape attempt, do you have a choice of a man to go with you? Another American, Perhaps?"

"Yeah, I believe Lieutenant Malone. We at least speak the same language."

"Well that should work. Speak to him about it. And whatever his decision might be, make sure he keeps it quiet. The fewer who know the better off we'll be." Colonel Montrose was thoughtful for a few moments. "We know there's a mole in the camp. We even know who he is. We've decided not to take care of the bastard—yet. We find him useful, especially when we want the Boche to know something they think they're not supposed to know. For that reason this deal must be kept top secret. Only the two men who are involved and the F.O.M."

"What is the F.O.M?" Sam asked.

"That stands for the Five Old Men. I'm one of them and there are four others. All over twenty five and we make the decisions for the group. The other four will probably approve of the plan, when it's final. But if it were left to a vote of the men in general, it would not pass. The prison officials are most harsh on everyone when there is an attempt to escape. That's the reason we need a success.

The camp commandant brags that no one has ever escaped Raven prison and no one ever will as long as Von Stutz is in charge. Maybe if you're successful the Nazis will send him to the Russian front."

"How will you know if we're successful? Von Stutz is not likely to tell you."

"Oh, we'll know. If you're captured, alive, he'll parade you in front of the assembled prisoners. If you're dead, he'll parade your dead bodies before the assembled prisoners. So, the longer you stay away, the more hopeful we will be. But just to make sure we do know that you are successful, get word to the R.A.F. or to the American Air Force. Have them fly a plane over Raven and goose their engines, twice, if you both make it."

Sam asked, "When do we get started? The sooner the better, as far as I'm concerned."

"Patience, is the word, it'll be awhile, first things first. You talk to Malone. I'll work on the F.O.M. approval. My one vote needs two more. We have to think about the welfare of all the men. Let me know about Malone."

At the exercise period the next day, Sam jogged along side Malone. As soon as they were out of earshot of the other men, Sam got right to the point.

"How would you like to escape from this hole?"

Malone shot him a quick glance. "What the hell have you been eating? You're serious, I

271

do believe. I been here eight months. The fellows tell me you can get out but they bring you back, dead or alive. And its pure hell for everybody for a mighty long time."

Sam gave a brief outline of his conversation with Colonel Montrose. He said, "You were my choice, when he asked for a second man."

"Well, thanks a hell of a lot for volunteering me to get killed."

"I'm not volunteering you. It's your choice. If not you, we'll find someone else." Sam's voice had grown harsh.

"Don't get hot. O.K., count me in. It's crazy but I was never known for being long on brains. What do we do?"

"We wait for the Colonel's go ahead."

Sam passed Malone's decision to Colonel Montrose. The waiting stretched into days and then into weeks. Malone and Sam jogged together each day and only once was the plan discussed. Malone said, "I didn't think the man was talking about the war being over before we went over the fence."

The waiting ended with Sam being summoned to the Colonel's corner office. A blanket was hung to provide some privacy. A map was spread on a makeshift table. The Colonel motioned for Sam to take a look. "This is it," he said, in a low voice.

Sam stood staring at the map. Every detail was etched firmly in his memory. Realizing the importance of the occasion, he gave it more attention than he had ever given anything he wanted to store in his mind. After a few minutes he turned to Colonel Montrose and said, "OK."

"Do you need more time?" Colonel Montrose asked.

"I think not."

"Some of the F.O.M. think it's impossible for anyone to do what you are attempting.

The doubters would like to test your memory in a few days before they give the final go ahead. Is that alright with you?"

"Its OK."

"We'll be in touch in a few days."

Sam walked across the exercise yard where Malone was playing catch with a fellow prisoner. As he walked by he said, "It's working."

The waiting began all over again. Days passed and Sam was becoming more impatient. "At this rate the war will be over before anything is decided," he told Malone, one day as they jogged around the grounds.

"That might not be all bad. I've thought about this a lot. The probability of success is slim and none. At least in here we're still alive," Malone said.

"You're not backing out, are you?"

"Oh no, it's just that nothing happens. I've always heard the British are cautious. But this is ridiculous."

A week later Sam was summoned to Colonel Montrose's office. "Let's get on with the memory test," he said as a greeting. The map was spread before him. "The other members of F.O.M. have decided to accept my opinion of your ability. We believe the fewer people involved the better it will be for everyone. Are you ready?"

"Ready," Sam shrugged.

"Begin here at Raven and describe the map's details in a counter clockwise direction. Expand the circle each revolution. If you make five complete revolutions without error, or missing a detail, that will be sufficient." Montrose was crisp and spoke almost angrily.

Sam began describing the details of the map. The five revolutions were made without hesitation. As he completed the last one, he stared hard at the Colonel and said, "What's bothering you?"

"The other F.O.M. members want to scrub the attempt. They think it has no chance. They also believe I'm letting my personal feelings get in the way of my judgment. One member thinks I would do anything to beat Von Stutz. He says I'm sacrificing you two men and jeopardizing the welfare of all the prisoners just to satisfy a personal grudge. What do you think?"

"I think all prisoners are duty bound to constantly strive to escape. I don't know anything about personal hatreds or any of that junk. If we can get from behind this wire fence and get a few minutes away from here, in a dark night, we have a chance. Forget that sacrifice crap."

Colonel Montrose relaxed a little and smiled a tightlipped smile. "You're a man

after my own heart Warden. That map reading
demonstration beats anything I've ever heard
of. In about a week it will be the dark
phase of the moon. We'll plan for that time.
We need an air raid so the lights will be
out. Are you ready?"

"Yeah, I'm tired of waiting. Give me the
particulars."

"The F.O.M. has prepared an escape kit
for each of you. It has rain gear, a
blanket, a water canteen and a small amount
of food; also some first aid items, pills to
put in water to kill the bugs and stuff like
that. When the air raid warning sounds, the
Boche rush a guard to the barracks doors, so
each night until we get a raid you and
Malone wait outside in the shadow of the
building. When the raid occurs and the
lights go out rush to the southeast corner
of the yard. There'll be a man there with
the packs and a wire cutter. He'll snip the

fence, you'll pass through, he'll pull the wire back together so it won't be so obvious and you'll be on your way back to England."

"How will the wire cutter get back into his barracks? And how about bed check after the lights go back on?"

"Don't worry, the cutter has a way back in and the empty bunks will have a sleeping dummy in them."

"How much time do you think we'll have before we're missed?"

"Depends on how long the lights are out. With luck, maybe three or four hours."

Sam rose to leave. Colonel Montrose held out his hand and said, "Might not get to talk again. Good luck. Get in touch again—some day."

Sam briefed Malone on the plan and the two men began, once again, the waiting game.

The dark phase of the moon began and each night the two waited in the shadows of the building. It was four days later when the sirens wailed and the lights were snuffed out. With pounding hearts they rushed to the fence. A man was waiting. In a calm voice he asked, "Is this the night?"

Sam assured him it was and in an unhurried manner he began to clip the wires in the fence that separated them from the outside world. In mere moments, although it seemed like an eternity, there was a hole in the fence, which permitted them to slip through. The packs were passed through the hole and the fence cutter said, "Go, and Godspeed."

They ran through the darkness to a nearby road. Sam said, "Stay close and right behind me. I'll warn you of any uneven ground or holes you might fall in. We don't need any sprains or broken bones. That would be the end of the road."

Malone's teeth were chattering as if it were cold weather, "Don't fret I'm right behind you."

They were both in very good physical condition because of their attention to the exercise program they had established in the prison camp. They jogged at a mile eating pace through the dark German countryside. There was no traffic and no lights from any of the buildings they passed. An hour passed, then two hours, lights began to spring up as the all clear was sounded. "So far, so good," Malone said, as he matched Sam, stride for stride.

"Yeah," Sam replied, "But there'll be hell to pay in the camp some time soon."

It began to rain and they didn't bother to get the rain gear from the pack. The running was causing them to perspire and the cool water felt good to their warm skin. They kept going until almost dawn when Sam began to look for a place to hide during the daylight hours. He chose a deep wooded area near the road. They crouched under some low hanging branches and in a short time they were shivering from the early morning coolness and the wet clothing. They opened the packs and ate some of the dried fruit that had been prepared for them. Toward noon they became warm enough to fall into a fitful sleep.

The rain, although uncomfortable when it came time to sleep, gave them their first lucky break. Back in Raven prison, the guard missed seeing the cut in the fence when he walked around it after the air raid. The barracks inspection guard assumed someone was in their bunks when he made his walk through.

Commandant Von Stutz had a camp policy of calling the roll and accounting for all prisoners the morning after an air raid.

They were lined up single file and required to take three steps forward when their name was called. There was no way to beat the system and fake someone being present when they were not.

Von Stutz was furious. Livid with rage, he sent his guards to bring Colonel Montrose to his office.

"You can stand here at the window and watch your men stand at attention until we find Warden and Malone. It won't take long. Then we'll deal with all of you."

"This is clearly a violation of the Geneva convention. You will be held responsible for the mistreatment of prisoners of war."

"Ha, you and your people brought this on yourselves.. And this is just the beginning. How will you like going without food and water?"

Colonel Montrose turned to face the window and stood at attention as his men were doing. Silently he prayed, "Please God let Warden and Malone escape."

The commandant ranted and raved and ordered his men to bring the escapees back "Today, or else." German soldiers were scurrying in all directions.

On the parade ground the morning passed into afternoon and the afternoon into early evening before the first man fell. Then in a short time another one went down and then the frequency increased.

Colonel Montrose was suffering with his men, but he was feeling better. The escapees were still at large.

Sam and Tex awoke in the late afternoon and ran an inventory of their supplies. They arranged the rain gear where it was easily accessible and decided they had enough food for four days if they skimped on everything.

"We're about four days from the Rhine River, five at the most. We might just have enough if we swipe any fruit and vegetables from the local farmers. Otherwise, we'll go hungry," Sam said, in a matter of fact tone.

"Go hungry, hell I'm starving right now. I could eat the biggest steak in Texas. And they got some big 'uns down there."

"Don't think about it. Think about Raven Prison," Sam admonished.

"Boy, you're a hell of a lot of fun," Tex shot back.

They went back onto the road and began the jogging that moved them swiftly along their journey. They hid in road ditches when any traffic came along. They slept in secluded places during the daylight hours. Their meager supply of food was augmented with what little they could filch from the fields and fruit trees along the way. Although they had seen many German patrols

284

along the roads, and low flying aircraft in the sky, their progress had not been slowed to any appreciable amount.

They first saw the Rhine River in the early morning of the fourth day. Daylight was approaching too rapidly for them to attempt a crossing. They hid in a clump of trees and watched the river traffic go by.

"I see some row boats along the shore, just south of that dock," Tex reported.

"Maybe we can borrow one when it gets dark," Sam replied.

"Take a look at this," he added, pointing to a truck loaded with soldiers.

The truck parked and for a while the soldiers walked around, bending over and stretching and doing the things men do after being cooped up and riding for a long time.

"I guess they're not looking for us Tex. Why don't we get some rest?" We're sure a scruffy looking lot. Be nice if we could get cleaned up before we go visiting."

The soldiers got back on the truck and it growled away, leaving a lot of quiet behind. The two fugitives drifted off into an uneasy sleep, Tex to dream of Texas and his blonde girl friend and Sam to go back to Squaw Creek, off old sawmill road.

It was his first recurrence, since he had been in Europe, of the nightmare that haunted his life. He was in the water, trying desperately to find Camille. He broke out in a cold sweat. He sat up and looked around. The river traffic was moving along and nothing seemed out of the ordinary. He looked back in the direction they had come from and froze at what he saw.

Two armed civilians were walking toward them. Sam reached over and placed his hand over Tex's mouth, who was awake instantly.

Sam held his finger to his lips for silence and pointed toward the two men.

The two escapees had been furnished a knife with their pack of supplies, a long bladed, dagger-like weapon. Sam slipped his out of the scabbard and whispered close to Tex's ear, "Take the one on the right, if they discover us."

Tex nodded his agreement and crouched ready to spring, with the knife held at the ready. The two German civilians walked to the edge of the brush where the fugitives were hiding, then they turned and walked along the edge until they were out of sight over a small hill.

"Damn," Tex breathed, "That was close. They didn't seem to be looking for anything, maybe they were hunters."

"I hope we never know," Sam replied. "The thought of killing someone with a knife is a little unnerving."

"You do look a little shook up. I thought you had ice water in your veins until today. I'd been thinking that you were no nerves Warden. Hell, I've been scared to death ever since we left the prison camp."

Sam just shook his head and didn't reply. The two men had been talking in a low voice while their eyes scanned the area for any sign of other people. Sleep was out of the question now. They tried to relax and waited for darkness.

After awhile Tex broke the silence. "If we get across the River, what then? The Swiss will intern us until the end of the war. That might be a hell of a long time."

Sam was thoughtful for several minutes. "Maybe we should try some other way. Don't just waltz in and surrender to the authorities, although, that would be the easy way. We could get some food and housing immediately. But we might be able to contact some allied sympathizers; then we'd have a chance to get across the French border and into the hands of the underground forces. I've had some experience with them. They know how to get things done under the absolute worst conditions."

"I've been hungry so long, I guess another six months won't make a lot of difference," Tex sighed.

They watched a beautiful sunset and a long twilight before darkness settled in. There were rowboats along the river's edge, but the cautious owners had taken the oars and paddles with them. That problem was solved by prying the pickets from a fence. With the make shift paddles they proceeded to propel the small boat they had stolen toward the Swiss shore and freedom from the Germans.

It was fairly easy to move the boat with the make shift paddles. As they approached their goal, Sam could see a heavy patrol of Swiss soldiers any place where a dock existed. In the heavy darkness they paddled near the shore until they came to a cliff overhanging the water. Nearby the shore was strewn with small boulders and rocks. They came ashore and pushed the boat back out into the current of the river. "Damn, I think we made it," Tex breathed.

They struggled up the cliff and found a winding road; by sheer guesswork they selected a direction that would take them toward the French border. Dodging and hiding from traffic and police patrols they made their way through the darkness. Near dawn they came to a small village. Shopkeepers were beginning to open for the day's business. Their hope of avoiding the authorities was beginning to fade.

"A lot of these people speak English," Tex said, "Let's just walk up to someone and ask them to help us."

Sam was near exhaustion and he knew his companion was also. "That sounds good to me. Let's do it," he replied.

They walked into a bakery shop, where the smell of hot baked goods almost overpowered the two starving men. The proprietor, an elderly man, looked up in surprise at the bedraggled flyers. Before he could say anything Sam asked, "Do you speak English?"

The man nodded his head and said, "Yes I do. What can I do for you?"

"We are American soldiers, escaped from a German P.O.W. camp. We'd like to get back to our unit. If we surrender to your authorities we'll be out of business for the duration. Can you help us?"

"Yes I can help, come with me." He led the way into a back room, which served as living quarters for he and his wife.

"First, let me get you some food. That looks like the first order of business."

He spoke quickly to his wife, who motioned for the two Americans to sit at the small table. In a short few minutes a mug of hot coffee was steaming in front of each. Hot pastries with thick butter, then a bowl of porridge, followed that. And that was just starters. There was sausage and eggs, ham and hot breads. It was difficult for the two, ordinarily well-mannered men, not to wolf the feast set before them.

Stuffed and groggy from the food and from fatigue, they tried to thank their benefactors. The man held up his hand.

"Later, we talk. You need rest. Come." He showed them an upstairs room with a big bed. "The bath is there," pointing to the corner.

"Plenty of towels. Leave your clothes outside the door for cleaning. Use my sleeping clothes hanging in the closet."

"I think we've died and gone to heaven," Tex said as he headed for the shower. By the time Sam had his shower Tex was sound asleep.

Sam lay in bed staring at the ceiling and thinking about the escape from Raven prison. He knew how the remaining prisoners were suffering because of what they had accomplished. What would the next few days bring? With that thought he drifted off to sleep.

Even in his exhausted state, Sam required very little rest to be completely restored. After five hours of deep and dreamless sleep, he awoke. Tex was breathing deeply and had not moved since going to bed. For a moment Sam was lost. The unfamiliar sounds, a bird singing outside the window, automobiles on the street below and the murmur of voices from the shop. Then memory came flooding back. Quietly he got out of bed.

He was wearing the proprietor, Mr Morison's, pajamas. He found his freshly washed and pressed military uniform just inside the door. He shaved and dressed, feeling almost normal he descended the stairs to the dinning area where they had eaten a few hours earlier. Mrs Morrison looked up from her task of preparing dough for baking bread. "Did you have a good rest?" she asked.

"Yes I did. I can't thank you folks enough. We were pretty tired."

"You don't need to thank us. We should be thanking you. Its young men like you who are carrying the heavy load. I'll get you a cup of coffee and then I'll fetch Joseph."

"I'm surprised to find people who speak English so well, and the very first people we met."

"Oh, we lived in England a long time. Joseph is a British subject and we live here because it is my home and Joseph loves it so. But he loves England also, and would do anything to help defeat the Germans. I've never seen him as excited as he is about you boys escaping the German prison camp."

Mrs Morrison bustled around and brought a pot of black coffee and a plate of breads and cakes, she then went through the door to the shop area. In a few moments Joseph Morrison entered the room.

He cocked his head and said, "I do believe you look better."

"Yes, thanks to you and your good wife," Sam replied.

"We're happy to help the cause any way we can. We are surrounded by a merciless power.

Any time they chose, we could be overrun in one day. Our government must be extremely careful not to give cause for an attack. But what the government doesn't know won't hurt if we handle it properly. We have established an organization to help people like you, fighting men who need to be back with their unit."

"We are most anxious to be back. We are also anxious to send a message that we have escaped. Can that be done?"

"We can't help with the message. That would involve the U.S. embassy and they in turn would involve the Swiss government. The message will just have to wait."

"If it can't be done, it can't be done. We don't want to be locked up just to get a message out. How do we get back to England?"

"What we do is smuggle you across the French border. The German occupation forces have it closely guarded. But we have ways.

For you it's like jumping back into the fire, but the French underground is highly successful at eluding the German soldiers."

"I've had some experience with the French underground," Sam replied.

"It will take a few days to get everything set up. In the meantime you two will have to stay out of sight of the general population."

They were with the Morrisons for three days. Mrs Morrison almost overwhelmed them with food and attention. Tex declared he was ready to be adopted by her. At one meal she had served a thick steak, not mesquite wood grilled Texas style, but good enough to win Tex's heart, or at least his stomach.

On the fourth night, Joseph arranged transportation for them to a village near the French border. There they were turned over to a group of Swiss and French young people. Sam and Tex were dressed in their

American military uniforms that had been provided by Colonel Montrose's people in Raven. Their appearance created no curiosity because the group was used to seeing military people seeking a way back to England. The group leader was a French woman named Violet.

Living quarters for the group was a house with a large room that served all purposes. It was a dinning area during the day and at night it was the sleeping quarters. Everyone used sleeping bags. It had a common bath, showerheads around the wall. No privacy.

Violet was brief and to the point. "We are here to help you get safely into France. We've had a lot of success and some failures. You will stay here tonight. Tomorrow night we move into the mountains. We're informal here. There's no place for false modesty. We've had some experience with that too. You fellows have been away from women for a while. If you see anyone you want to sleep with, just ask. She might have a husband here, but he probably won't mind. And one of the girls, or maybe more than one, might decide they would like to sleep with you. Get a good night's sleep."

Tex looked at Sam and said, "What the hell do you make of that?"

"When in Rome," Sam replied.

After dinner the members of the group striped and took showers in plain sight of all. None of them seemed to notice. Tex said, "What the hell," peeled off his clothes and sauntered into the shower area.

When he came out Sam asked, "What're you doing? Advertising?"

"Can't hurt. When in Rome," Tex replied.

Sam undressed and wrapped a towel around his middle. One of the girls was in the shower. Seeing her naked started a shiver of excitement through his body. He averted his eyes to avoid the embarrassment of an erection. The girl smiled and rubbed a soapy washcloth over her breasts. Her eyes were inviting.

"You don't have to wait until bedtime," she said.

Without a word Sam crushed her wet body to his. His mouth found hers and days of pent up emotion poured through his body. The small sized girl wrapped both legs around his hips and from that position Sam thrust into her savagely. She moaned with pleasure. Such intense emotion could not last long. Both were trembling when it was over.

"What's your name?" Sam asked.

"Marie, can I sleep with you tonight?"

"I wouldn't miss it for anything."

Marie made it an exciting night for Sam. Tex got very little sleep. He told Sam the next day that it really does pay to advertise.

Violet briefed them on what to expect. "We will move out tonight. From here we go into the mountains. There is a series of caves near the border. One group extends under- ground and into France. It has remained a secret from the Germans. We call it Freedom Fighter Road. That's the route you will take. We'll get you safely into France. The underground forces will take it from there."

They spent one night at an underground camp in the caves. The next day they were told that the cavern was a top-secret route and only the people involved in their transfer knew its location. After traveling, on foot, through a wooded area, one full day, they arrived at a camp that had once been a hunting lodge. It was a Free French controlled establishment used for the purpose of helping fugitives fleeing from the Nazis. They said goodbye to the Swiss guides who had taken such good care of them and had advanced their cause so much.

The leader of this French underground group was a man named Paul. A rough looking, balding, bearded fellow who carried a flask of wine instead of water. That was in addition to the sub machine gun slung over his shoulder, an automatic pistol in a holster at his hip and a long knife in a scabbard on his belt.

Tex said in a low voice to Sam, "That joker is loaded for bear. And he's a mean looking sonofabitch. I'm glad he's on our side."

"At this time I'm afraid we don't have much to say about who is controlling our destiny," Sam replied.

"We will stay here tonight. And tomorrow night we will split into two groups." He motioned toward a young woman. "Luda will take the Lieutenant and I will take the

Major. We will head for roughly the same
destination."

"Why are we splitting up? Sam asked.

"If by chance the Germans catch one, the
other would still be free. There is no
safety in numbers here. What we're doing is
very dangerous. When the Germans catch one
of us, its instant death if we are lucky. In
Luda's case it would be a fate worse than
death. She would be assigned to the
soldier's barracks. She carries a cyanide
pill to help avoid that situation."

The sincerity and simplicity of Paul's
statements was touching.

"I guess it makes sense," Tex said. "I
was hoping we could make it all the way
together, but getting back to England is the
main thing."

"Yeah, I was hoping the same. Let's make
sure we get in touch as soon as we can."

Sam and Tex had been together for four months. Now that parting was near they realized how close they had become. They strolled around the lodge and talked about the war and what they each planned to do when it was over.

Tex said, "My old man was a driller in the oil fields. He led a rough life. He was a good provider, but I don't plan to follow in his footsteps. I'm going to get a degree in geology and start my own oil drilling company. Why don't you join me? You can work the night shift. You do so good in the dark anyway, it would be a natural."

"I don't know what I'm going to do. I'll finish my education, I think. The folks want me to be a lawyer like my dad. If the war is ever over, I'll give it some serious thought."

"You got a serious love back home?"

Sam told him about Alicia and how they had an understanding. "She's not really pretty." He was thoughtful for a few moments. "She's just gorgeous. From the ugly duckling as a kid to this outstanding swan now that she's grown up. I'd give years off my life span just to see her now."

"Sounds like a vine covered cottage and a house full of kids to me," Tex grinned as he spoke. "That's not for me. Texas is full of the world's most beautiful women and it would be a shame if I missed any of them as I travel through life."

They kidded around awhile as men do who are uncertain about their future.

When parting time came, they shook hands silently and Tex turned and followed Luda into the darkness.

Paul motioned for Sam to follow him and they began the journey of walking toward the English Channel. Paul used a small flashlight to guide him through the familiar trail. He said nothing as they trudged along, hour after hour.

"Are we going to walk all the way to wherever it is we're going?" Sam asked.

"You'll have transportation later," Paul curtly replied.

They walked for about five hours without stopping, except when Paul would stop to relieve himself and take a big swig from his wine jug. They had reached a road and followed it, now walking side by side without a light. They came to a small house, set back from the road.

"We stop here for the rest of the night. Transportation will come here tomorrow or the next day," Paul said.

In the vacant house there were sleeping bags and food supplies and signs of neglect. There was dust on the floor and cobwebs on the dirty glass windows.

Paul flashed the beam of his light around the area and pointing it at a sleeping bag said, "Take that one."

Sam unlaced his shoes and stretched out, fully clothed. In a few minutes he could hear the deep breathing of his companion and he drifted off to sleep. He dreamed his recurring dream. Once again he was on the bluffs by Squaw Creek, sliding down the bank to rescue Camille. He awoke with a start. He could not hear Paul. He turned and looked where the man had been sleeping. He was gone.

Quickly tying his shoes he slipped to the door and saw a truck by the roadside. It bore the markings of the German army and German soldiers were getting out. Paul was standing in the road pointing toward the house.

Paul had left his weapons lying on the floor by his sleeping bag. Sam quickly grabbed the submachine gun and the pistol and ran silently into the darkness as the German soldiers crept up the lane toward the house. He could hear the shouting in German and French when they discovered he was gone.

For the first time in his life Sam was lost. Even when he was shot down he had known the directions of the compass when he hit the ground. He could see the stars. He took a bearing and headed west. He knew the German army would be searching the entire area as soon as daylight would permit. Some way he must distance himself from this area.

Sam ran through the brush and then across a field. In the distance he could see a railroad. Maybe he could get to a village that would give him some help. He ran along the railroad, jumping from cross tie to cross tie. It would not be long until dawn and in his mind he could hear the gates at Raven clanging shut behind him.

He had read the bible when he was in prison and now some of the words came back to him. "Ask and you shall receive" came into his mind. "Please help me," he prayed, "I don't know anything else to do."

Behind him he heard a train in the distance. He slowed to a walk and then stopped. The train came laboring up the grade. It was moving at a fairly fast pace. Sam hid in the grass by the railroad tracks and as the train rumbled past, he sprang to his feet and ran as fast as he could. He grabbed the ladder of a passing car and swung his body against the steel side of the car.

Sam clung to the boxcar for dear life. His arms felt as if they had been wrenched from their shoulder sockets. He was putting some distance between himself and the certain pursuers. He knew it wouldn't take a genius to figure out how he had left the area. His only hope was population and their hatred of the Germans.

The train whistled through one small village after another. "Good," thought Sam. "The more villages we pass the more places the Krauts will have to look." He had moved in between the rail cars to avoid detection.

Dawn was approaching when Sam dropped off the train as it slowed for a small town. He ran to a nearby barn and climbed the ladder into the haymow. He lay breathing hard from the run and from climbing the ladder. The sounds of the train became more faint as it moved on. He was thirsty, tired and hungry. His bed of hay smelled of clover dried in the sun. Weariness overtook all other senses and he slept.

He awoke with a start. A young boy, about ten years old, was standing staring down at him. Sam suddenly opening his eyes startled the boy and he drew back a couple of steps.

"American, American soldier," he said in schoolboy English.

"You speak English!" Sam stated.

"Oui, yes," the boy replied.

"I need help. Could you get me some water?"

"Yes, and food." The boy turned to go and Sam stopped him.

"Wait," he said, "Don't tell anyone I'm here. The Germans are looking for me."

"Tell no one," the boy replied, as he scampered down the ladder.

In a few minutes he returned with a pitcher of water, a bottle of wine and some cheese.

Sam took a long drink of water, paused a moment and drank some more.

"You very much thirsty," the boy said.

"I was very thirsty. Thank you for everything. What's your name?"

"Charles."

Sam began eating the cheese and washing it down with the dark red wine. Charles was sitting on a pile of hay, watching with great interest.

"Charles, I know how dangerous it is for you to help me. But I need to know where I am. Maybe you have a map. I'm trying to get back to England."

"My Uncle will help you. He's a very good man. Hates Germans. I will go bring him here."

Remembering his experience with the traitor Paul, Sam was cautious.

He told Charles, "Maybe we should wait until it's dark. How did you know to look for me in the haymow?"

"I have a dog and he kept whining around the ladder. We don't need to wait until dark. Uncle Frank will know just what to do."

"I have to go into town. Uncle Frank has a shop there." Charles' eyes were dancing with excitement.

Sam thought about it for a moment and then said, "OK"

"OK, Joe," Charles said, and scampered down the ladder once again. He was gone for more than an hour. Sam was beginning to have an uneasy feeling. He moved to a window, which gave a view of the street going into the town, and the house where Charles lived. There was no sign of life anywhere. Then he saw Charles riding his bicycle toward the house. He went inside and after awhile he came out and played with his dog and kept getting closer to the barn.

Sam watched the boy toss a stick and the little dog fetch it time and again. He threw it into the barn and followed the dog inside. In a moment his head popped up into the mow.

Claude Eldridge

"Uncle Frank says he heard about an American soldier escaping from the Germans. They're looking everywhere. They think it's very important they catch this one. He say for you to stay here until dark. He don't want any activity around here He's afraid someone might be watching."

"Is your uncle a part of the underground?"

"Don't know about the underground. He's important man with Free French."

Charles reached inside his shirt and pulled out a foot long length of sausage. He handed it to Sam and said, "You hungry. Uncle Frank said for me to come back to shop and stay with him until he comes home from work."

"Is it just the two of you living together?"

"My aunt lives there. She works at the shop with Uncle Frank."

"Where are your parents?"

The boy looked away before answering. Sam knew what to expect.

"The Germans killed them both." Hatred twisted his young face and his eyes grew hard. He turned and slowly descended the ladder.

Sam watched as the boy rode away. He continued his vigil as the afternoon wore on. He saw the family come home and darkness began to obscure the landscape. He saw the boy and his uncle come to the barn, and then Charles called softly for him to come down.

Frank was a small elderly man who spoke no English. Sam shook hands with him and Frank spoke in French. Sam had learned some French in his association with Petrie, back in his Night Hawk days. Charles acted as interpreter.

Frank asked about how he came to be hiding in his barn. Sam quickly told of his escape from Raven and the route he had taken. He concluded by describing Paul's betrayal. He handed the submachine gun to Frank and told him why he had it.

Frank listened intently and his face hardened when he heard about Paul. Frank said that explained why there was so much interest in locating Sam. The Germans were afraid Paul would be exposed. The French would take care of Paul. There could be no doubt that his double crossing days were over.

Frank led the way to the house where he met Jolene, Frank's wife. Sam was given a warm meal and told he would have to move to a new location that night.

Their route to the city was through a series of dark alleys and side streets. The new location was a cellar in a house occupied by a member of the underground. He was told he would have to stay there until it was safe to move. He said goodbye to Frank and when he shook hands with Charles, he said, "I'll never forget you my young friend."

"Come back some day," Charles invited.

"You bet I will," Sam replied. He then reached out and embraced the boy who clung to him for a moment. Then they were gone.

Sam was hustled into the hiding place and began a long wait. Days passed. One week went by and the only person he saw was an elderly woman who brought his meals. When he tried to question her she said, "Germans everywhere. They search all houses. Paul is taken care of. It will quiet down in a few days."

Sam's nineteenth birthday passed while he was in hiding. He had plenty of food and water—and wine, which he drank sparingly. The boredom made the stay seem longer than it really was. There was reading material, but much of it was in French. He read everything he could find. He paced back and forth in the small cell like room. He did pushups by the hundreds.

After three weeks, he was beginning to think he would never leave. A man came into the hideout and told him it was time to go. They walked most of the night and then he was passed to the driver of an automobile, who drove through the night, without lights. He was hidden for one day and the next night it was the same. And the next, it was the same. Each day he was passed to a different person. They didn't speak. He was treated well, but with almost studied indifference.

On the fourth night, they traveled for two hours. The driver parked by the side of the road. The driver then spoke in perfect English. "This is the pickup point. The ghost flyer will be here shortly. Get out."

"Well, thanks a lot," Sam replied, as he got out of the car.

The driver started the engine and drove away, leaving Sam standing in the road, alone.

He heard the drone of an airplane engine and in a few minutes the plane slipped to the road and he clambered aboard and closed the door. The engines roared as they picked up speed and Sam's long ordeal was over.

He had been missing in action six months.

There was a reunion of Night Hawk flyers when Sam arrived back at the base. All the pilots, the mechanics and ground crews had assembled in the flight hanger. Even General Lockwood was there. The plane taxied to a stop in front of the hanger door, and Sam climbed out and dropped to the concrete runway. He walked into the hanger and was greeted by a mighty cheer; he stood, dirty and unshaven, completely stunned by the

319

attention. Everyone rushed to greet him, shaking his hand and pounding him on the back.

The French underground had reported a day-by-day account from the time he had been taken from Frank's barn until the pickup by the plane. They reported the execution, by the French, of the traitor, Paul. Tex Malone had filled in all the other details. He made Major Warden sound like a magician.

Jim Holland embraced him and said, "You are without a doubt the saddest looking specimen of an Air Force officer I've ever seen."

Sam was provided with clean clothing and a private room. After a shave and a shower and a long sleep he emerged a crisp clean-cut officer in need of a haircut. He was summoned to General Lockwood's office.

"How are you feeling Major?" He asked.

"Not bad, sir, a little groggy from too much sleep, but not bad at all."

"Good, good. Glad to see you survived the whole ordeal. Only a Night Hawk could have pulled that stunt. That Lieutenant Malone swears you can walk on water."

"Tex is from Texas, you know. A little exaggeration goes with the territory."

General Lockwood smiled and his steel blue eyes almost twinkled. "We've arranged for you to be transferred back to the Night Hawk squadron. What do you think of that?"

"I do what I'm told."

"The French built that landing strip you talked about when you were their guest the other time. They've got it ready to go and have asked that you personally lead the mission."

Sam was too surprised to say a word. He had long forgotten that conversation with the French underground men. Now it came back to him with a rush.

"We'll have your gear moved over right away. Malone told us about the signal Colonel Montrose asked be sent to Raven prison. We'll have that done. We were just waiting for your return."

After Sam left the General's office he walked slowly around the parade ground. He breathed deeply of the cool British air, the free British air. A flood of relief swept over him so intense it left him shaking. He went into the Day Room and began to write a letter to his parents. His shaking hands made the writing completely illegible. After a few minutes of rest the shaking passed and he wrote the letter to his parents and one to Alicia.

Chapter 7

In Raven prison Colonel Montrose had continually protested the treatment of the prisoners. Some became ill from malnutrition and two of them had died. Commandant Von Stutz had relented somewhat after the second death. As time passed Montrose had about decided that something had gone wrong. If the escapees had followed the plan they should have been interned by the Swiss after, at most, two weeks. The signal should have followed in about the third week.

Whatever had happened, the F.O.M. had decided the price of escape was too high. In a meeting the vote had been four to one against any further escape attempts. Colonel Montrose was the dissenting vote. "You're doing just what that bastard, Von Stutz wants you to do," he growled to his companions.

The prisoners were all on the parade ground when it happened. A lone P38 swooped low over the treetops and the pilot goosed the engines, once and then once again. He also let loose a blizzard of leaflets and newspapers. On the front page of the papers were pictures of Major Warden and Lieutenant Malone. Bold headlines proclaimed: AMERICAN OFFICERS ESCAPE RAVEN PRISON; TELL OF ATROCITIES BY CAMP COMMANDANT VON STUTZ. In smaller writing, but still bold print, "International Red Cross to protest, demands investigation." The leaflets contained excerpts from the Geneva Convention on the treatment of war prisoners.

Chaos reigned in the prison for a while. The papers were scooped up and a mighty shout went up as they read the headlines.

Guards were rushing around trying to confiscate the papers and leaflets.

Von Stutz had heard the plane and had rushed to the office window. He could read the headlines and see the pictures clearly. He rushed onto the parade grounds, screaming like a maniac. The next day his superiors removed him from the camp and Colonel Montrose never saw him again.

The plane had been specially modified for the flight, with added fuel tanks that could be jettisoned. It had been approved by the Air Force high command for propaganda purposes. It served its purpose well and improved the lot of the Raven prisoners.

Sam was promoted to Colonel and put in charge of the multi-engine rescue effort. After he was briefed on the size and location of the make shift landing strip he devised a bold plan to rescue as many people as possible before the Germans discovered the location.

In the past, single engine planes had swooped down and rescued one person at a time. They were fast, modified fighter aircraft, and they were armed. This mission would be with slow, unarmed C47 aircraft. They would be easy prey if discovered by German fighters.

General Lockwood put the entire Night Hawk squadron at Sam's disposal. He was told to come up with a plan and then clear it with the General before execution.

Sam held a meeting with all the pilots. He stood and began to speak. "Fellows, we have an opportunity to rescue a very large number of refugees from the Nazis. They are mostly helpless women and children and some elderly men. Nearly all are Jews. In the past we have rescued a lot of people, one at

a time. This time it will be about twenty-
five at a trip. We'll use C47 planes."

The pilots started shaking their heads.
"We'll be sitting ducks," one of them said.

"What do you think of this?" Sam queried.
"We take four C47 aircraft and go in thirty
minutes apart. That'll give just enough time
for the people to get on board and take off
before the next plane arrives."

"Hey, Colonel Sam, how the hell are we
going to keep the Germans off our ass?"
Petrie wanted to know.

"Our success has always depended on speed
and stealth and of course the cover of
darkness. Now this time we'll keep the
darkness and run the mission under cover of
all the airplane noise we can muster. Night
bombing missions are going on almost every
night. They travel right over that landing
strip. We'll get the R.A.F. and the U.S. Air
Force to stage a massive air raid. Using

327

hundreds of planes, one wave after another, and hundreds of fighter planes flying escort. The Germans will be too busy to notice another. We'll use our own Night Hawk fighter cover—just in case."

Sam walked over and sat down with the other men. There was complete silence for a few minutes, and then everyone started talking at once.

Colonel Mimba stood and the other men fell silent. "You know, that's just crazy enough to work," he said. "How in the name of all that's scared do you think you can get the bomber flights you are talking about?"

"I don't know that we can. What other ideas do you have? Think about it. We have to come up with a plan and sell it to the General. Maybe we tell him it can't be done. That's an option. A lot of Frenchmen took a lot of big chances to steal the material and build that strip. Maybe the Germans already know it's there and are just waiting to pounce on whoever shows up. It's the light of the moon now, so we have a little time."

They met the next night, and the next. Almost half said it couldn't be done. The rest of them said Sam's idea had the best chance of having any success at all. Sam went to the General with the plan to fly under cover of the bombing missions.

General Lockwood listened to the plan of action with studied patience. When Sam had finished there was a long silence. The General looked out his office window and rubbed the back of his head. "It's a long shot, but it might work. Let's get our people to contact the French underground and see how they react. I'll let you know what they say. In the meantime, have your guys rehearse as if it's a go."

Claude Eldridge

Three days later Sam was called to the General's office.

"The French like the plan, but they say it won't work, simply because they think it would be too dangerous to try and assemble that many people. They think it would be sure to attract attention they don't want. They suggest we make it one flight every other day. They will keep us informed if there is a problem. How does that sound to you?"

Sam shrugged, "If that's the way it is, who can argue?"

"When can you be ready?"

"Whenever there's a heavy bombing run."

"I'll work on that issue. I guess you know there's a lot of Air Force people who could give a damn less about small side issues like saving a few people. You can't blame them, when our people are being killed by the hundreds. But, we are fulfilling our mission. And it's not going to cost one bit more to help this cause."

Sam knew the General was catching a lot of flak from the Air Force. When he had been in the fighter squadron he had heard the snide remarks about General Lockwood being a do-gooder, out to save all the down trodden and helpless. He thought the strain was beginning to show.

That afternoon Sam received a telephone call from the General. He said, "There is a heavy bombing run tonight. I've notified the French. Seems there's a very important Jew who is about to be separated from his family and sent off to some camp. That carried some weight with the Air Force. I'll let you know as soon as I hear from the French."

Sam notified his pilots. The C47 would take off ahead of the bombers and plan to arrive at the target at the same time the lead bombers arrived. They would load the passengers and be airborne as the second wave arrived. They would fly home under cover of the third wave. The Night Hawk fighters would fly cover for the C47. Twelve P51 mustangs would escort the C47 to the destination and stay in the area until it took off. Twelve additional fighters would relive the first twelve and return to base to refuel. The third twelve would fly out to intercept and relieve the second squadron. The fourth would fly to meet the incoming plane and provide cover if needed.

"Who has the honor of flying that bus? Jim Holland asked.

"Petrie will pilot and I will be co-pilot," Sam replied.

Some of the men started to protest about Sam going on the flight. Even Colonel Mimba volunteered to be co-pilot.

Sam held up his hand, "I want to see if this hot shot Petrie can fly and land this so called bus." He turned serious and continued, "I want to see first hand what the situation is. I've already cleared it with the General, so it's all set. Be ready to go at ten thirty. Any questions?"

The pilots had been through the drills so many times and had asked so many questions there was little room left for any new questions.

At ten o'clock Captain Petrie and Colonel Warden were sitting at the end of the runway with the engines of the C47 ticking over like clockwork. Petrie stretched and yawned.

"I can see you're really excited about this mission, "Sam said.

"Ah, it's a piece of cake. What the hell am I doing in a deal like this? I signed up to shoot Germans out of the French sky. Here I am rescuing some little old lady."

"My heart bleeds for you."

Petrie grinned. "Yeah, I bet you bleed for me. What I can't figure is what you're doing here. You are the frigging Commander. And on top of that you've got enough points to go home. How come you're not back in that south land of yours enjoying corn pone with that cute little bird you're so crazy about?"

"It's time to go," Sam replied.

They took off and flew over the channel into French air space at a low altitude to avoid detection. Overhead the fighter planes of the Night Hawks whipped back and forth to make sure the slow C47 was not attacked by enemy fighters.

As they approached the pickup area, the first wave of bombers overtook the slower plane and the air became alive with flak from anti-aircraft guns. The night Hawk fighters stayed back out of range and the C47 slipped in to a landing without mishap.

As the plane rolled to a stop, Sam was out of his seat and had the door open. The steps dropped down and people started getting on board. There were low lights to mark the seats and Petrie was there to instruct them, in French, to fasten seat belts. The underground French members were urging haste. In less time than Sam had allotted for the operation, everyone was strapped in, the door closed and the plane was on its takeoff roll.

The landing strip was grassy with the firm steel mat underneath. They were nearing the outer limits when Petrie lifted the wheels.

Sam took a deep breath. "You don't have to cut it so close, you know."

"'This bucket of bolts is not a P51. And that grass held us back. Besides that, there's thirty people on board. I thought it

335

was supposed to be twenty-five. But we made it with a foot to spare."

"There're more kids than we thought there would be; ten instead of five. But that was too close," Sam said.

It was a bumpy ride back to the base, because of the low altitude. Many of the people were airsick. With a curtain separating the cockpit from the cabin and all the windows blacked out, there was plenty of light. Sam stood outside the airplane cockpit and looked at the passengers, old men, women and children, ill clothed and hungry looking. All looked back at him, unsmiling, with sad eyes.

"Does anyone speak English?" He asked.

For a few moments no one moved or spoke. Then a young woman timidly held up her hand. Then another, then some of the children, until a good half of them had their hands up.

Sam moved among them, providing all the comfort he could. He gave candy to the children and airsick pouches to those who needed them. And he gave words of encouragement to all. He asked the young woman to tell the non English-speaking passengers what he was saying.

"Soon we will be in England," he said, "It's a free country. You don't have to be afraid anymore. When we get there, warm food will be available at the base. There will be a place to rest. And tomorrow you will be moved to a place that has been provided for refugees. People who understand what you have been through run it. Is there anything I can do for you?"

One old man spoke in French for a few moments. The young woman translated.

"Mr Gruenwald wants to know who you are and asks if he can shake your hand."

"I'm Colonel Sam Warden, United States Air Force, and tell him I'd be honored to shake hands with him," Sam replied.

The young woman spoke rapidly and Sam walked over to the old man and stuck out his hand. The old man held Sam's hand with both his while looking up at Sam with tears in his eyes. Then all the passengers wanted to shake his hand. It was an emotional moment for him.

Sam went back to the cockpit and told Petrie. "I'll fly this crate for awhile. Why don't you go back and see your fan club?"

Petrie was gone for a while and came back into the cockpit. Sitting down, he buckled his flight harness and said nothing.

"What do you think?" Sam asked.

"You don't want to see a grown man cry, do you?" He replied.

The trip was completed without incident. The passengers were cared for, as Sam had told them they would be.

The next day Sam met with General Lockwood, who had high praise for the successful operation.

"What now?" Sam asked.

"We'll see what the French underground people report. If there's no sign of detection we'll continue as soon as all the factors are in place. In the meantime we'll fly our usual search and destroy missions. You'll lead squadron A."

It was a month before another rescue mission was flown with the C47. It was a repeat of the first. Sam and Petrie had become the accepted crew for that mission. Petrie called the operation, "Warden Airline."

They ran eight flights before the Germans discovered the landing strip. The discovery was made when a member of the underground revealed it to the enemy and then had an attack of conscience when he learned the Germans were planning to slaughter the next group of refugees while the plane was on the ground. He confessed his treachery and was promptly shot. But the damage was done.

The rescue flights had been, roughly, one month apart. It was now early June 1944 and the invasion of France was near. Reconnaissance and fighter sorties were the order of the day.

The Night Hawks continued to play a vital role in the successful defeat of the Germans, as they retreated across France and into the borders of their homeland.

In early 1945 there was no doubt about the ultimate unconditional defeat of the Nazis. Germany lay in ruins. The Russian Red Army was rolling relentlessly toward Berlin.

The Night Hawks had moved their base to France, near Paris. Captain Petrie was the most popular member of the squadron. With his knowledge of Paris and of the language, the Night Hawk personnel had access to the many delights of nightlife in that city. It was a heady time. Champagne flowed and the girls were many, and friendly. The German occupation had left its mark. One of the more pronounced was the number of young women with shaved heads. It was a mark of distinction for collaborating with the enemy.

Sam's P51 Mustang fighter plane had thirty-one swastikas painted along the fuselage, signifying the number of enemy planes he had shot down. He had long since passed the required number of missions to be relieved of combat duty. Each time he was given the opportunity to leave the war zone and return to the states he had turned it

341

down. Many of the Night Hawks had left the squadron, Colonel Mimba and Jim Holland among them. With the war winding down Sam decided it was time for him to leave combat duty. But first, he felt he must pay a debt of gratitude to the French people who had helped when he had been shot down behind enemy lines.

He explained his desire to Captain Petrie and asked for his help. He was not sure of the location of the Duloc farm but with Captain Petrie's knowledge of the country it was located in a short time.

The roads were filled with military vehicles rushing to and fro. No one paid the slightest attention to two Air Force officers in a Jeep driving through the countryside. That is no one paid any attention until they drove into the Duloc farmyard.

The Duloc family was having a celebration. There was a crowd of people in the yard and in the house. They stared at the two officers, as they got out of the Jeep, not completely without apprehension. Many unpleasant experiences with military personnel had left them cautious. These were the first Americans to visit the farm since the Germans had departed.

In his native language Captain Petrie asked to see Pierre Duloc. A young boy ran into the house and in a few minutes Pierre came to the door. Sam removed his cap and was instantly recognized. Pierre called over his shoulder, "Mama, Simone, come quick." He ran to Sam and embraced him.

Nicole and Simone came running. Nicole hugged him and stepped back and touched the scar on his cheek.

"It just makes you look more dashing," she said.

Claude Eldridge

Simone was ten years old shy as she smiled at Sam. He held out his arms and she rushed in. Then everyone was talking at the same time. Pierre waved for silence and said, "I want everyone to meet our soldier. He used to live in our wine cellar." The crowd cheered.

Captain Petrie was introduced and in nothing flat they all knew he was a native serving with the United States Air Force. Sam knew enough French to understand most of what Petrie was saying. In typical Petrie fashion he was not above stretching the truth, especially about how he and Sam had freed the country of the Nazis.

"Can you imagine," he told the crowd, "An American soldier that doesn't drink or smoke? But be sure you lock your women in the cellar, but not with him." Everyone loved it.

The two men were invited to join the party. Sam said, "We would love to stay, but we have to get back. I'm going home as soon as I can make the arrangements. I wanted to thank you folks for taking such good care of me when I was injured."

"We did nothing compared to what you have done," Pierre replied, "You and the other Allies have freed our nation of the German scourge. We shall always be indebted to you." The crowd cheered wildly.

"I have brought some presents from Paris." Sam said, as he started passing out packages. There was a warm jacket for Pierre, also a pair of heavy work gloves. And the most desired and welcome gift, ten cartons of American cigarettes. For Nicole he had brought yards of colorful material for dressmaking. And following Petrie's advice, he had gift wrapped several sets of feminine under garments, which he had

345

purchased at the PX in the camp where he was stationed. Simone's gifts were enough to bring joy to a little girl who had been deprived of things a child loves.

There was a box of chocolate bars. There was a bag of fresh fruit, and a doll that Alicia had sent from America. The Duloc family was overwhelmed with the unexpected gifts. The emotional Pierre grabbed Sam and kissed him on each cheek. Sam blushed to the roots of his hair. Then it was Nicole's turn to blush when she unwrapped the packages containing the under garments. Petrie whooped with laughter at the red faces. The crowd finally joined in the merriment after Petrie informed them of the cause for Sam's embarrassment.

Sam was most touched by the reaction of little Simone. She ran to him and he lifted her and cradled her in his arms. Sobbing she said, "I will never see you again but you will always be our soldier."

The two officers said their goodbyes but before they could depart Pierre insisted they take a dozen bottles of his best wine.

On the way back to camp Sam explained to Captain Petrie that he had another call to make when he could find the location. He wanted to thank Frank and especially the young boy, Charles, for their help when he and Malone had escaped from the German prison.

"Do you know the name of the town?" Petrie asked.

"No, I don't, I was too busy trying to stay alive to worry about the name of a French village."

"We'll find it, "Petrie promised, "I can find anything with nothing to go on."

"Your modesty is the most attractive thing about you Captain Petrie."

"As you Yanks say, some folks got it and some ain't."

A few days passed and Captain Petrie had been busy trying to locate Frank and his family. He met Colonel Sam on the parade ground and fell into step by his side. "I've got some news."

"I'm glad. I was beginning to think I would be here for the duration."

"It's not good news," Petrie said, soberly.

Sam stopped walking and looked at his friend. "What?" he asked.

"They were pretty easy to locate. It took a couple of days to verify what happened. They are all dead, Frank, his wife, Jolene, and the young nephew Charles. The Gestapo found a sub machine gun in Frank's possession, it was a marked gun issued to a collaborator. The sons a bitches executed the entire family because of the gun."

"I gave that gun to Frank. They helped me and now I feel like I caused their deaths."

"Don't feel that way, my friend. You can't be responsible for the actions of the German bastards. You've done your share to get rid of them. Go home to America and have a good life."

"I will be glad to get away from all the senseless destruction. The only regret is leaving friends like you."

"I plan to see you again someday," Petrie said, with his trademark grin breaking through.

Sam made the necessary arrangements to return to the states and asked General Lockwood to make the announcement.

Night Hawk personnel were surprised to learn that Sam was leaving. One said, "Hey, it's time to reap the rewards. We're winning. Don't leave now we've just begun to celebrate. Wait until it's over and the city is yours."

"You take the glory, I'm going back to the U.S.A. Write me a letter," Sam replied.

The Night Hawks held a farewell dinner for Sam. The Duloc gift of wine was used for a toast. General Lockwood made a short speech.

"This is a most unusual group of men, with most unusual talents. It is a miracle that any survived. I salute those who did and did not survive. To Colonel Samuel Warden, I say may God bless you all the days of your life. And to the rest of the Night Hawks I say, a man is leaving your ranks."

The next day Sam boarded a military transport and after a few stops enroute, he was back in the states He had been away over three years. He reported to Andrews Air Force base where he was notified that his assignment was the Air Force training command at Key Field, Meridian, Mississippi.

When he arrived there he promptly applied

for, and was granted a four-week leave.

Chapter 8

Sam caught a bus in the city of Meridian and headed for his home in the same manner in which he had left. The only difference was now he was alone and when he had last traveled this route, his friend, Tump had been with him.

As the bus swayed along the road, he wondered about Tump. For a while they had written to each other, but then the letters stopped. The last he had heard was what Alicia had told him that night in London. Sam had never been punctual about correspondence. He had written to his parents sporadically. Writing to Alicia followed the same pattern.

The bus arrived in Parkersville in the early evening. The streets were almost deserted. Sam used a pay phone to call

Alicia. The housekeeper answered the phone and told him Alicia was away until the weekend. "May I say who called?" the housekeeper asked.

"Just tell her Sam called," he replied.

It was two miles to Lone Pine. Sam decided to walk instead of calling his parents, or hiring a taxi. He swung his duffel bag over his shoulder and set out down the street, past the courthouse and the drug store and the jail. All signs of the gallows had long since been removed. But it was still clear in Sam's mind.

It was a soft April evening, quiet and still, waiting for the blanket of darkness. In the distance a whippoorwill was calling. Blooming dogwood and red bud could be seen in the faint light. A flood of nostalgia swept over the young officer as he strode along. Everything was just the way he remembered it.

He had walked about a mile when an automobile came down the road behind him. It slowed to a stop and a voice said, "Hey, soldier, let me give you a lift."

Sam tossed his bag in the back seat and climbed into the front. He recognized the driver to be Lee Brown

"How are you Lee?" he asked.

Lee looked closely in the dim light, "Damn," he said, "It's Sam, Sam Warden. How are you, boy? What are you doing out here in the dark, walking? Damn, I'm glad to see you. I saw your daddy today. He didn't say anything about you coming home."

"They don't know."

"You're liable to give 'em a heart attack popping in like that."

"Do you think so?" Sam's voice had a worried sound.

"They'll be too happy to see you to let anything matter."

Sam had barely finished telling Lee that he was walking home just to enjoy the evening, when they arrived at Lone Pine.

"I'm gonna drop you off here at the end of the drive and leave. I don't want to intrude on this home coming," Lee said, as he pulled to a stop. "But I would sure like for you to come by to see me sometime while you're here."

"I'll do that Lee," Sam promised, as he got out of the car and retrieved his bag. He stood by the side of the road gazing at the house where he had lived until he went away to college. The lights were on in the living room and he walked toward that beacon in the darkness. He passed Jose and Ava's house and their dog began to bark. "Same old hound," he thought.

He walked up on the porch and he could see his father sitting by a lamp, reading the paper. He knocked on the door and through the small glass at the top he could see Ava come bustling to answer. She opened the door and Sam stepped into the lighted room. Ava let out a shriek that brought Angela and Henry on the run. When they got to the door they saw Ava with her arms around a tall soldier and she was sobbing, "Mistah Sam, Mistah Sam." They rushed in and arms hugging him and his mother's tears of joy wetting his face surrounded Sam.

"You just in time fo' supper, let me set another plate," Ava said, as she hurried away. "I'll go tell Jose you is here. He'll want to know."

Henry and Angela continued to cling to Sam. Angela was sobbing and Henry's eyes were wet. Jose came into the room with his hand extended. "Lawd have mercy, he done answered my prayers. Mistuh Sam you done gone and made a man out of yo' self."

"Come along now Jose and let these people have some time to their selves," Ava said as she led her husband away.

"Why didn't you call and let us know you were coming?" Henry asked

"I'm sorry, I know I should have called, but I thought it would be nice to just come home and walk down the road and remember how beautiful a Mississippi night could be, without any body knowing I was here. But I am sorry. It was cruel. I know it now. Please forgive me."

"Don't you worry one minute. You're here and that's all that matters," Angela said. "Here, let me look at you. My, you don't look like a boy anymore." She touched the scar on his cheek. "It's a wonder you didn't lose an eye."

Sam was wearing his dress uniform. The left breast was covered with ribbons. The colonel's eagles on his epaulets, his hair

close cropped and his lean, broad shouldered
figure caused his parents to be filled with
pride and awe.

While the family was talking Ava had
changed her dinner plans. She remembered
Sam's favorite dishes and she took the time
to prepare them. Golden fried chicken and
light fluffy biscuits and gravy. "I wants
you to eat. You're just plain skinny," she
said as they sat down at the dinner table.

"This is the best food I've ever eaten,"
Sam said, as he took his third helping.

"Chile, you always had a good appetite,"
Ava said with pleasure in her voice.

Sam and his parents sat and talked long
into the night. They had much to tell about
what had happened since he had been away.
Tump's injuries were serious enough to cause
him to be discharged. "By the way," Angela
said, "He doesn't want to be called Tump
anymore. It's Tj now. He said it was tough

enough to be a marine without having a handle like Tump stuck on you."

"Is he home now?" Sam asked.

"He was for awhile. But he's back in the hospital in Jackson, he got bunged up pretty badly," Henry replied. "He almost lost a leg. The military hospital is trying some reconstruction work on it."

"Did you know he got married?" Angela asked.

"Tump? Married? I can't believe it," Sam replied.

"Was married," Henry corrected, "She sent TJ a Dear John letter. It made him pretty bitter. That and Joe getting killed changed him a lot."

"Alicia told us you two are engaged. Do you have any wedding plans?" Angela asked. "I'll be most happy to help anyway I can." She could visualize a big church affair.

"No definite plans. I tried to call her, but the housekeeper said she was away until the weekend. I'm anxious to see her," Sam replied.

"I can't believe you and Alicia Steinberg," Henry said, "you never gave her any attention that I knew about."

"She changed a lot in a couple of years," Sam replied.

"And I expect you changed some too," his mother said.

Henry and Angela told him of the number of his schoolmates and others in the county who had lost their lives in the war.

"There were three brothers and two cousins, from the Bakertown neighborhood, on the same ship that went down off the Solomon Islands. All hands, everybody on board, were lost," Henry stated sadly. "When you were missing in action, we thought you were dead." Tears rolled down his cheeks and he hastily wiped them away with the back of his hand.

"I never did think he was dead," Angela stated emphatically. "I told you he would be alright. Didn't I?"

"Yes, yes you did. And I'm so glad you were right."

It was after midnight when they retired. Angela said, "I'm so excited I know I won't sleep a wink."

Sam lay in his old bed, in the same room he had grown up in and thought about his time before the war. He tried not to think of the bluffs overlooking Squaw Creek, off old sawmill road. He dropped off to sleep and when he opened his eyes, sunlight was streaming through the windows.

He was shaved and dressed and ready for the day when he heard a commotion downstairs. His heart began to beat faster. He recognized Alicia's voice.

Claude Eldridge

He hurried down the stairs and met her hurrying up. She backed down slowly, never taking her eyes from his. "Why didn't you let me know, you bum?" And before he could answer she was in his arms. Sam never bothered to try answering the question.

There followed days of happy reunion. Sam's car had been stored at Lone Pine. Henry had kept it in good working order. He managed to get rationed gasoline from Lee Brown, who told him not to worry, there was plenty more, for him, where that came from. They roamed the countryside and stopped and had picnics and made love on a blanket, and in the back seat of the car at night.

Angela was happy. She took Sam and Alicia to a luncheon given by her ladies church group. It was held in the church fellowship hall. Attendance was usually light and most of those were older women. But the word had gotten around that Colonel Sam "Bat" Warden

362

was going to be present and the place was
jammed.

As more and more people filled the hall
and more chairs were brought in, Sam said to
his mother, "I thought you said there would
be just a few people here."

"Oh, there usually is about twenty, but
I'm so glad there's a good turnout. It shows
how much people care for you." She was
beaming with joy.

Alicia was radiant. She waved and smiled
to friends as they came into the hall. Some
came by their table to hug Sam and tell him
how happy they were to see him.

Angela was the president of the group.
She opened the meeting and had the usual
reports of the activities since the last
meeting. She then said, "I'm happy to see
such a good turnout. Everyone must have
brought a friend. I would like to recognize

any visitors and then I have someone I want to introduce."

There were a large number of visitors. The majority was young women. Two members of the local press were men. When all had been introduced, Angela said, "I have a visitor that I hold most dear. My son, United States Air Force, Colonel Samuel Alexander Warden."

There had been a spattering of applause when each of the other visitors had been introduced, but now the entire audience stood and applauded and it continued, it seemed to Sam, for a long time. Only he and Alicia were still seated. He leaned over to her and whispered, "What've I gotten into?" She whispered back, "Stand and maybe they'll stop."

Slowly he got to his feet. The applause quieted and the audience began to sit. Turning to face the front of the hall he bowed slightly, thinking that should be enough. One of the men from the press yelled, "Speech, speech."

Taking Alicia by the hand, they walked to the podium where Angela was standing. He stood between the two women and began to speak in a quiet, even voice.

"I thought I was going to a quiet luncheon with my mother and my fiancée," Sam paused and there was a ripple of laughter. "I want to thank my mother for that warm introduction and for this quiet luncheon." There was more laughter. "I want to thank all of you for the warm welcome. I see many people in the audience I've known all my life. I had forgotten how important you are to me. I had forgotten how good southern food is. I had forgotten how good it feels to hold my mother in my arms. I had forgotten the touch of my father's hand. I had forgotten how sweet the flowers are in the Mississippi springtime. I had forgotten how warm the Mississippi sun is on my bare skin. I had forgotten the sound of a whip-poor-will in a quiet spring night. I had forgotten how sweet everything smells. I had forgotten because it hurt too bad to remember. This week I remembered. I remembered to thank God that I'm here. And I remembered why we are fighting a war on the other side of the world."

He turned and kissed his mother and then he kissed Alicia. Angela held him and sobbed brokenly. Sam's were the only dry eyes in the hall.

The next edition of the Parkersville Sun printed the speech on the front page. A picture of Sam with the caption: "Colonel Warden Remembers His Heritage."

When his leave was over, Sam returned to his military base. President Roosevelt died and Harry Truman became President. And as was expected the war was over in Europe.

Key Field was close enough to Lone Pine and Parkersville that Sam could spend the weekend at home and with Alicia. In June the Parkersville Sun carried the announcement of the wedding plans of Sam and Alicia.

Tump came home from the hospital in time to be best man. Sam met him on the street one day and the friendship was rekindled immediately. Both men were dressed in their military uniforms. Tump, a Marine sergeant, and Sam an Air Force Colonel. They gravely shook hands, and Tump said, "Hell, I didn't know whether to salute you or hug you."

Tump was on crutches and Sam said, "You hug me and I'll take away your wooden legs. What're you doing, gold bricking as usual? Damn, Tump it's good to see you."

"Don't call me Tump. It's Tj now. Being a Marine is tough enough without having a handle like that. And I read in the papers that you and Alicia are getting married. You kids are too damn young for that stuff."

They kidded around for a while in the same manner as when they were younger. Tj told Sam that he would always have a limp from the wounded leg. It was difficult for Sam not to sympathize but he was afraid to do that because he could see the pain in his old friend's face as they talked about the injury.

Sam and Alicia were married in August. The Japanese surrendered. The war was over. Sam was discharged from the US Air Force. He and Alicia enrolled in the University of Mississippi in September.

Their plans were straightforward. They would live off campus. They would graduate with degrees in Business Administration. They would become business partners. Alicia's father had given her one hundred thousand dollars for a wedding present and

368

Sam had money he had saved from his officer's pay. Finances were not a problem.

Sam's school record was not favorable in the university. He had simply walked away when he enlisted in the army. But now he turned his ability toward making good, and doing it quickly. He doubled up the load he took. School was a year around task. There was no time out for a vacation. His energy, a photographic memory and the ability to get by on very little sleep made it possible for him to graduate with a bachelor's degree in two years. He absorbed books. His grades were perfect. When he graduated his counselor wrote in his yearbook. "Sam Warden, a young man for the future."

Alicia was the perfect mate for Sam. She was a top student, but she couldn't match the pace set by her husband. After two years she still had two years of work toward her degree. It was decided Sam would attend

369

graduate school at the University of Virginia. Alicia would transfer with him.

There were many young couples in the same, or similar circumstances as the Wardens. But none seemed to be as intense. Therefore, they made few friends. An occasional dinner, a night at the movies was the extent of their social life. They shared everything. Alicia would do Sam's typing and he would do research for her. Sam would do the cooking and Alicia would do the dishes, vice versa. They created excitement about completing their education.

They had been at Charlottesville about two months when Sam received a call from Tex Malone. Sam had last talked to Tex in 1945 before he left Paris.

After saying hello and how are you, Malone got right to the point. "Sam, I got a deal that will make a lot of money. Remember, I used to talk to you about the

oil business. Well, I've got my own drilling
rig. I got a real good lease. I know there's
oil in that place. I got to raise some money
to operate on. Do you want a piece of the
action?"

"How big a piece? I don't have any
money," Sam replied.

"I need fifty thousand bucks."

There was a long pause before Sam
answered. "I was thinking," he said, "I
haven't drawn a pay check since I was
discharged from the Air Force. I've been
going to business school where one of the
first things they teach is to watch out for
smooth talking Texas oilmen. If I had the
money, which I don't, what makes you think I
would stick it in a hole in the ground?"

Tex laughed, "I hope they teach you about
risk and reward. The time I spent with you
made me think you were the world's greatest
risk taker. How about friendship and trust?

Sure it might be a dry hole, but I'm gonna drill it. Why don't you come down and see me? Bring your lawyer. You'll see it's strictly on the up and up. And another thing don't they teach you how to raise capital?"

Sam was intrigued by the sincerity in Tex's voice. "I can't see any way to raise that much money. But I'll talk to my wife and get back to you."

"You mean you're a married man now? So am I. I've got the sweetest little Texas gal you ever saw. Bring your wife and we'll barbecue a steak. Seriously, Sam this looks like a big deal. I'd like to see you get in on the ground floor. I know I can raise the money some other way. I just thought this might be a chance to repay a big debt."

"You don't owe me anything."

"Just my sanity and maybe my life. You let me know."

Sam told Alicia about the conversation. "Fifty thousand dollars. He's dreaming, but I would like to see what he's doing."

"Let's go," Alicia said. "We've had our noses to the grind stone too long. We can spare a couple of days toward the end of the week and take the weekend, that'll give us enough time."

"You would like to go, wouldn't you?"

"Sure, let's call it a vacation." Alicia snuffed out her cigarette and said, "I'll call the airport."

Sam called Malone and the next morning they departed for Texas.

Tex and his wife, Dolly, met the Wardens at the airport and the men agreed there would be no business until the next day. Alicia and Dolly became instant friends; they had very little in common except ex-fighter pilot husbands. But sometimes people take an instant liking for each other, and so it was with the two women.

The men had a lot of catching up to do. While Tex grilled steaks and drank beer, the two men talked about the war and the last time they had seen each other. The extent of Sam's drinking was one beer, or one anything else. The two women drank wine and all had a good time.

The next morning Tex went over the geological survey data with Sam and told him how promising they looked. They drove out to the site where Malone planned to drill the first hole. Equipment was being moved in and workmen were clearing the scrub oak trees that covered the land. Bulldozers roared and groaned as they leveled the ground and graded the road that would permit access for the drilling equipment that would follow.

"It looks impressive," Sam said, "But I have no idea what you're doing."

"We're gonna drill for oil. And this is just some of the necessary work that must be done." There was contagious excitement in Malone's voice. "We figure four partners in this little venture. And we have three, my father and Dolly's father and you will make the fourth. We would have done it on our own but the three of us have hocked all we have, and it's not enough. There are other people we can get but I told the other partners if we have to go outside the family I wanted you. They are willing to go along with my judgment."

"When I was discharged from the Air Force," Tex continued, "I went to school for one year. Then I decided that was not for me. My old man has been in the oil field business all his life, and when I got a chance to get this oil lease, he encouraged me to go ahead. After I sealed the lease up tight he suggested we form our own company."

"I worry when I don't know a thing about something that I'm about to get involved in," Sam said, shaking his head in doubt.

"Sure I know how you feel. We've got the papers drawn that shows the entire charter, the terms and conditions, all legal and above board," Malone was serious as he reached over and caught Sam by the arm. "Get your lawyer to come down and check it out. We want you to do that, we insist that you feel comfortable with what we're doing."

"I don't know if I should go any further. I'm sure my college professors would advise against getting involved with a start up under funded oil drilling venture."

"I'm sure they would, and I'm just as sure they could tell you horror stories about people losing their shirts. And I can tell you the same thing. I can also tell you there have been fortunes made in this business and there will be many more made and I plan for mine to be one of them." Tex Malone was silent for a moment. "I have five hundred acres under lease. There's oil here. I know it and my father knows it."

On the way back to Malone's house they talked about other things but when they pulled into the drive, Tex said, "Sam,

I'm not trying to sell you a bill of goods; I think I'm offering you an opportunity. But believe me I know how you feel. Why don't you take the partnership papers, the leases, the incorporation papers and all the other legal mumbo jumbo we have, talk it over with Alicia, get her opinion, and then have your father check it all out and call me in two days. If you're in, fine, if you're not, there's no harm done."

"I don't believe I'd be—" Sam started to say.

"Wait, don't turn it down yet. Take the two days, OK?" Tex insisted.

On the way to the airport in their rental car Sam told Alicia the details. He gave her the folder filled with legal papers and they rode in silence as she read the stack of information.

"It sure looks like a straight forward business deal," she declared. "I'd sure like to hear what Dad Warden would have to say about it."

"He'd say run, do not walk to the nearest exit. Even if he said it's a good deal, we don't have fifty grand to invest in a wild cat oil venture."

"I liked the Malones, Dolly told me how hard Tex worked to put this thing together. I liked Dolly," Alicia repeated.

"I liked them too, but that doesn't mean we should get involved in this deal," Sam was emphatic.

"I've got my wedding present money," Alicia said.

Sam looked at his wife in complete amazement. "You must be kidding. Do you think I would even consider letting you use that money? Your father would have a conniption fit."

"It's my money," Alicia insisted, stubbornly.

"Right, in your father's bank."

"Let's go home by way of Parkersville," Alicia said.

"Do you really want to get involved in this thing?" Sam asked.

"We could at least let Judge Warden take a look," Alicia replied.

In Parkersville Alicia went straight to her father with the proposition she was going to withdraw her money to invest in a business deal. At first he was pleased until he heard what the business deal was. Sam was right. Maybe he didn't have a conniption fit but he was outraged. And even suggested a sanity check for Alicia, and something worse for Sam. Alicia in turn was furious.

"Let it rest, baby," Sam tried to soothe her, blaming himself for causing her to go to her father, "It'll take Dad a few days to check this out. Let's go back to Charlottesville and we'll see what happens."

That's what they agreed to do. Before they left Sam slipped away and paid a visit to his old friend Lee Brown. He told him the story and asked for a loan of fifty thousand dollars, with no collateral and no assurance when it would be paid back.

Lee said, "I don't know if this oil thing is a good deal or not. But I believe you are a good risk. All you have to do is sign a note saying you owe me fifty Gs and when you are ready I'll send you a cashier's check. If this deal doesn't pan out, you can pay me when you get a job. I've always believed you

have what it takes to be a big success. And
I haven't been wrong so far."

Sam and Alicia went back to school and in
two days Judge Warden called and said that
he had called on a Texas law firm for help.
The firm had given the Malone oil venture a
clean bill of health. Judge Warden was so
favorably impressed he offered to lend Sam
the money, which, of course, was declined
because other arrangements had been made.
The transfer of funds was made and the legal
documents were dispatched by the most rapid
method available

It was a few weeks later when Tex called.
"We struck oil," he said, "Not a lot, but
enough to keep us going for awhile."

Sam told Alicia he could hear the
disappointment in Tex's voice.

The next report was even worse. A dry
hole. Sam and Alicia were extremely busy.
Sam, especially, he was trying to cram two

381

years of graduate work into one year and he resented any distraction. Tex always called at night, often when he was near exhaustion from a day of hard labor. It was to his credit that he was brief and did not ramble on with the drilling news. He did tell Sam that the drilling crew was working in an area where the oil was near the surface. Once he said, "The oil is so close to the surface that I can't wear cowboy boots for fear the heels will punch holes in the ground and fill up with oil."

After two more shallow, low producing wells, Sam started getting a check each month. The first was one hundred dollars. After four months, the amount had increased to one thousand dollars each month. He and Alicia put all the money in a savings account for the purpose of paying the Lee Brown debt. "If it keeps coming and we live

8101214161820222426283032343638404244464850525456586062646668707274767880828486889092949698100102104106108110112114116118120122124126128130132134136138140142144146148150

long enough we'll finally get Lee paid off," Sam said.

It was springtime in Virginia and close to graduation for Sam. He was working late at night preparing a final paper. Alicia was asleep, when Tex called. And it was not just another call. He was excited and drunk.

"Throw away them damn books and get down here. We got the biggest well I ever did see. It's been spewing oil all over the county since it blew in early this morning. We just got it under control a little bit ago. I ain't had a bite to eat all day. Been running on hundred proof Old Rub of The Brush and now it's all gone."

Sam finally got Tex to quiet down, some. "You had better get some food and rest and I'll call you in the morning," he cautioned the excited man.

"I know you'll want to grab that pretty wife of yours and be on the way as soon as

you can. Dolly and me will be waiting for
you. We'll have the biggest party you ever
did see."

Tex was beginning to run down. The
excitement, the hard work, the lack of food
and the dying effects of the alcohol were
beginning to take their toll. Dolly took the
phone and told Sam that he was just about
out on his feet.

"I'm going to put him to bed," she said,
"It does look like the crew has hit a big
one. Call him tomorrow."

"I'll call, but I'm in the middle of
winding up my graduate work and there's no
way I can get away at this time."

"I understand, but you call and tell him
that. He'll probably sleep until noon; he's
sound asleep on the floor now. I'll probably
have to leave him there until he wakes. Bye
for now." Dolly said as she hung up the
phone.

The phone and the conversation had awakened Alicia. "What's that all about?" She asked.

Sam told her what had happened. "Anything to interrupt what I'm trying to finish. I'll never get it done," he griped.

"My, aren't we the excited one? I think your friend just told you that you're a rich man, or going to be one and you're bitchin' because he delayed your work a bit. What would it take to excite you?" Alicia was sitting up in bed as she looked across the room at Sam.

He turned and winked at her. "Take off your pajama top if you want to see excitement."

"It's late, my gosh look at the time. I assume we are not going to Texas tomorrow, I mean today?" Alicia asked.

"You assume right. We'll go when we can. I'll call Tex in the afternoon. Dolly thinks he might be able to comprehend a conversation by then.

When Sam called, Tex was suffering from a giant sized hangover, and a celebration was not high on his priority list. It took little persuasion to convince him to wait until Sam could finish his schoolwork.

Sam graduated at the top of his class. His parents were there to congratulate him and beam with pride. Several corporations had representatives present to offer him employment. His reputation for brilliance had circulated through the business community. He thanked each representative with grave politeness and said he was not interested. The next morning he and Alicia loaded their possessions in the old prewar car and headed for Texas.

Chapter 9

The going was not speedy. The car was old
and unairconditioned. The Southern part of
the United States was in a late spring heat
wave. They stopped early in the day at an
air-conditioned motel and decided to travel
at night to avoid the heat.

When they arrived in Texas they found the
drilling crew was busy drilling another
well. Tex was trying to manage what was
turning out to be a very lucrative oil
producing company.

"This thing is driving me crazy as hell.
The phone rings all day. People are lined up
to talk to me. I can't get a damn thing
done. It goes on night and day. What am I
gonna do?" Tex moaned.

"Let Alicia and me help," Sam offered.

"Sure you can help. You're a partner. What can you do?"

"We'll set up an office and take all the paper work, phone calls and visitors off your back. You can get back out in the field and make us more money."

Tex thought for a moment. "Yeah, yes that would do it. Dolly has been trying to handle the bills and it's driving her nuts also. We'll turn them over to you. She'll love you for it."

Sam and Alicia had a private conversation about what needed to be done. It was obvious the Malone team was all experienced in oil production and not in running a business office.

The small Texas town was Malzone, where office space was unavailable. They rented a house trailer and set it up in a vacant lot. After utilities were installed they were in business. It took about two weeks for Sam and Alicia to get to the bottom of the stack of unpaid bills and outdated correspondence. During that time they lived in a couple of rooms in the office trailer house. The weather was scorching hot, but they had room air-conditioners installed and it was livable.

One day they went out to the oil-drilling site, past the first big well that had gushed in with a roar. They were shocked by the damage done by the oil spewing over the landscape. The grass and scrub trees, everything, was lifeless, covered with a thick layer of black goo. The hot sun filled the air with the stench of oil. "Smells just like money to me," Alicia smiled as she looked at her husband. She was used to his unsmiling, no expression face.

"It looks like a disaster area," he replied.

They went to the current site where Tex was overseeing the drilling operation. "We are close to the depth where the other one blew in," he said, wiping sweat from his grimy brow. "Maybe you'll get to see this one come in. Looks like we're in a major strike."

"How about all the damage around the first big one?" Sam asked.

"Damage, what damage?" Tex asked.

Before Sam could reply, one of the drilling crew called with a problem and the question was left unanswered.

On the way back to town Alicia said, "Maybe that's the way an oil well site is supposed to look. Tex didn't even see any damage."

"He didn't see anything wrong, that's for sure." Sam was silent for a few moments. "That's probably a part of the problem," he added as they rolled along.

That night the second big gusher came in, as strong as the first. The crew was better prepared and it was brought under control in a short time. It was now obvious the partners were going to make some serious money. The checks to Sam and Alicia were growing each month. The first thing they did was pay off the Lee Brown loan.

Tex Malone began expanding the business as rapidly as he could. A second drilling rig was added and then a third. The payroll grew and the other activities created a lot of work for the office. One day after an almost non stop from morning to night session of work, Alicia asked Sam," How long are we going to keep up this crap?"

"You are right, it's time for us to bail out of this job," he replied, "I didn't intend for it to go this long. This is not my intended career."

"What do you intend to do about all this activity? After all you have a stake in this operation, and it looks as if it's going to get really big," Alicia was frowning as she spoke.

"We'll hire an office staff. A manager, a steno or two, an accountant and whatever else we think is needed. Then we'll take a vacation," Sam replied.

They informed the other partners what they were going to do. It took a month to hire a staff of competent people. Office space was rented in a new building in Malzone and the other partners agreed to a name for the budding company. It was officially named: Malzone Oil Company, Incorporated. Tex Malone was the president, his father was vice president and Dolly's father was treasurer. Sam and Alicia were named directors.

The officers of Malzone Oil threw a farewell party for the departing Wardens. There was much food and drink and dancing. Dolly and Alicia were among the celebrants who over indulged.

Dolly's father was Bill Browning, a salty old oil field worker who had spent his life working for hard-nosed bosses, and now he was beginning to realize he could quit slaving and be the boss himself. He really disliked Sam Warden, with the poker face and the clean shirt and clean fingernails. After about a half dozen bourbon cocktails, he walked over to Sam and said, "You're a lucky bastard, you get a quarter interest in a gold mine just because you know Tex Malone,"

The scar on Sam's cheek turned a bright red. Alicia dancing with Tex saw her husband's face, and she immediately started for him.

Claude Eldridge

"How did you get your quarter share, Mr Browning?" Sam asked, his eyes boring into the older man's eyes.

Browning was taken aback, before he could answer, Alicia was by Sam's side. "Come," she said, taking him by the arm, "Let's get some food," she had been frightened by the look on Sam's face.

They said their goodbyes and the next day before they left town they traded their old car for a new one. They drove to the Texas coast and rented a condo. They swam and loafed and made love at night. Early in the mornings they would jog, barefoot, on the wet sand. Sam told Alicia to run ahead of him.

"Why do you want me to do that?" She asked.

"I'm trying to figure out why your behind moves like it does, and why your hips swivel like they do."

"You don't like it?" She said, looking over her shoulder.

"I'll show you how much I like it," Sam said, as he ran to her and lifted her into the air and then laid her on the sand. As he slipped his hand inside her shorts leg, she wiggled free and said, "You idiot, not here, this place is full of people."

Sam held her in his arms and started kissing her. "We've been too busy for me to show you how much I love you, but we're not too busy now."

"Let's go back to the condo," Alicia replied.

They spent two weeks loafing and enjoying each other's love before leaving for the trip back to Parkersville.

They discussed what they would do in the future. Alicia would return to college at Ole Miss in the fall. They would get an apartment and Sam could pursue what they had decided would be the future business for them.

They had decided to form a corporation. They talked to Lee Brown about serving as one of the officers. He was designated as the Vice President for: Warberg, Incorporated.

While Alicia was completing her bachelor's degree, Sam began buying timberland in the counties surrounding Parkersville. The income from Malzone Oil, Inc. continued to increase, thereby giving them a lot of latitude about purchase decisions. At first they paid cash for everything, but as opportunities increased they began to leverage all purchases. When Alicia graduated they were the owners of five thousand acres of land covered with the soft near white pine common to that area.

The building boom that began after World War Two was in full swing when they purchased the lumber mill in Parkersville. From there they expanded to construction of houses. They had the best of business conditions. They owned the timber, the processed lumber, the construction and the sales of the end product.

It was the best of times for the young people. They built a new house on property adjoining Lone Pine. They agreed it was time to start a family.

Their first child, a boy, Michael Alexander Warden, was born May the first, 1951. That was the same year Sam's picture appeared on the cover of the magazine, South Wind. The caption stated: Young Man In a Hurry. The article, written without his consent and over his objections, depicted him as a multimillionaire.

Their second child was born three years later, a girl, Patricia Ann, born April twelve, 1954.

Although Sam and Alicia were wealthy, Sam seemed driven to exceed over past accomplishments. Malzone Oil management planned to take the company public and Sam and Alicia took their share of the company in common stock before the initial public offering. The stock soared from the first day it opened on the New York stock exchange. A year later the Wardens traded their stock for timberland along the Mississippi coast and for real estate in California. It was property that Tex Malone had accumulated and he was pleased to add the Warden's stock to his without having to go to the market place.

It was a profitable deal for the Wardens. Oil was discovered on part of the land. Sam had an independent oil drilling company develop the field. He made strict rules about protecting the environment. If there was an oil spill, it was the responsibility of the drilling contractor to clean up the place and leave it as it was before. If oil spewed over the trees and they could not be saved. He required they be taken down and new trees planted. The contractor protested long and loud. But Sam was adamant. It was a part of the contract. He was instrumental in starting a movement that became the standard for the industry. Warberg, Inc. built a reputation for being a good neighbor

Warberg Inc. was one of the first to become involved in off shore oil exploration. At one time all the oil producers thought it was too expensive to drill off shore, but Sam had the foresight to determine what the future would be like.

His old friend Tex Malone bumped into him in the airport in Dallas one day. After shaking hands Tex cocked his head to one side and said, "You know my friend I never did understand you. You made a lot of easy money on Malzone oil and could have made a lot more. That stock you traded me just keeps going up. You cause everybody to keep things clean and ship shape around your drilling sites. That costs a lot of money. You go out into the gulf and start producing oil and you can't be making a lot of money at that venture. It costs too damn much to pump oil out there. Tell me what's your objective"

"I like to try new things," Sam replied, "We're making ends meet. That first big oil well in Malzone left the area looking like the end of the world. I just knew there had to be a better way."

"Well," Tex replied, "You have your ways and I have mine. I wish you a lot of luck." He turned and walked away.

Flying was the recreation best liked by the Wardens. For a while they used Lee Brown's biplane, My Baby. Sam purchased a

World War Two P51 Mustang. He had it completely restored. It was named My Baby II. When he needed to unwind he would take the P51 and climb as high as it would go, then turn its nose down and hurtle toward the ground. At a low level he would pull out with a window-rattling roar. He stayed away from the heavily populated areas. But the residents of Parkersville could hear the bellow of the engine as the plane was pulled from the dive. Jose Williams would shake his head and say, "The Kun'l sho like that ole plane."

Angela was happy with her grandchildren living close to Lone Pine. Both she and Henry delighted in spoiling the kids. The years slipped by and Michael started to school.

Someone once said, the rich get richer, and that was true in the Wardens case. Alicia's father had died and she was the sole heir to a considerable fortune, which included the Parkersville National Bank. Sam and Alicia tried to avoid publicity, but it was difficult to do so. They were generous donors to local charities. Sam had financed the building of a school in Bakertown, a school that was open to all races. Its grades were kindergarten through high school and it had a vocational training unit that taught subjects the farm boys could use immediately.

He had established a trust fund to assure the continuation of what he believed in. And that was a simple belief, an education for everyone who was interested.

At first the school created a storm of protest in the community. Sam was called a "nigger' lover. And some of the more rowdy boys said flatly, "I ain't going to school with no negra." And some of the old timers backed up the young boys. But times were changing. Some of the Bakertown veterans of World War Two and the Korean War had married girls from different areas; girls who were more enlightened and who had a lot of influence on their husbands. During the war some of the local girls had left the area and had married men from other areas. Nearly all of them were strong supporters of the school.

All the controversy caused the Wardens to get more publicity than they desired. The danger to them was brought forcibly to their attention one day when a strange man showed up at Michael's school and informed the teacher that Mr Warden had asked him to pick up the boy and take him to the airport.

The tall well-dressed man had come to the classroom door and stood waiting. The teacher had started to say that Michael had gone down the hall to the bathroom, when she happened to glance out the window and saw a car waiting with two other men standing outside the two front doors. Sudden dread struck her heart and she heard herself say, "Mr Warden picked the boy up about thirty minutes ago."

The man looked wildly about the room. It was obvious he did not know Michael. And about that time Michael walked past the man and took his seat. The man hurried down the hall and out to the waiting automobile. The terrified teacher quickly took the bewildered boy to the principal's office.

The principal called Alicia and when he told her what had happened, she promptly said, "Call the police, I'm on my way, Sam's out of town."

The police, Alicia and the would be abductors got to the school about the same time. One of the abductors had convinced the other two that Sam Warden was out of town and that the teacher had been "Jerking your chain." Their decision to return to the school was a big mistake.

Just one week before the Parkersville police had hired a new policeman. The rookie was one of the two officers to answer the principal's call. His name was Thomas Jefferson Johnson. When he had attended this school he was called Tump and now answered to TJ.

Alicia's car skidded to a halt and she jumped out and ran across the lawn toward the school's front door. The abductors ran their car onto the lawn and stopped just behind the running woman. The passenger's door swung open knocking her to the ground. Two men, with guns in hand, jumped out at the moment the police car turned the corner.

TJ was riding on the passenger side. He had a cool head and deadly aim. The first man died as he reached for Alicia. The second turned his gun and fired one time before Tj's shot struck, knocking him back into the open door of the car. The driver stomped on the gas and tore up the turf as he sped away with a hail of lead to urge him on.

Alicia had the wind knocked out when the door struck her in the back. She was gasping and struggling to her feet when a pair of strong hands lifted her and a familiar voice said, "Alicia? Are you alright?"

"TJ, Michael, is Michael safe?"

"I think he's OK. We'll know in just a minute," TJ said.

He helped Alicia to the school door where she was met by the principal and Michael. She grabbed the boy in her arms. Tj's partner had been busy on the radio and in a few minutes the place was swarming with police, sheriffs officers, an ambulance and even a fire engine. Several surrounding counties were alerted and late in the afternoon the abductor's car was found with a dead man inside. The other one escaped, for a while.

When Alicia regained her composure she went to where TJ was telling his chief what had happened. She walked up to him and said, "How can I ever thank you for what you've done?" She put her arms around him and hugged him close.

TJ grinned, "Just doing my job, but for you I would do the same again even if it were not my job."

"I didn't even know you were in Parkersville. When did you get a job as a police officer here?" Alicia asked.

"This is my first week on the job. And I thought it was going to be dull. Now look at all this fuss," waving his arms at all the activity going on around the school.

"Thank God you were here. I'll tell Sam when he gets home. He'll be so pleased."

"Well, OK, I've gotta go now, the chief is jumping up and down to get my attention. You take care of the boy and your bruises. You'll be sore all over tomorrow," TJ said, as he turned to walk away. Alicia noticed that his limp was barely noticeable.

Sam was on board a commercial flight bound for Parkersville. He had drifted off to sleep and was dreaming he was standing on the bluff overlooking Squaw Creek where Camille had died. The roiling water was rising rapidly and he could not move, it had climbed to the edge of his feet when he jerked awake. Shaking with dread he looked around the cabin, he listened to the engines. They droned their song of confident power. He could detect nothing out of the ordinary. Still he was on the edge of his seat until the plane landed. When he stepped off the plane he understood. The local press and radio personnel were waiting. That's when he learned of the attempted abduction of his son.

Alicia gave him the details when he got home. He held Michael on his lap and listened to his wife without interrupting. Michael said, "Daddy, I walked right by that bad man and he didn't say a word to me."

"I'm glad you didn't say anything to him either, Michael."

"I was scared," Michael said, snuggling down in the safety of his father's arms.

"You're my brave boy," Sam said, squeezing Michael until he began to giggle.

The sheriff posted guards around the house for the night. The kids were in bed fast asleep and for the first time since Sam got home, he and Alicia, were alone.

"This is the reason I've shunned publicity. I should have seen it coming. I feel so stupid," Sam said, as he held his wife's hands in his.

A doctor had examined Alicia; who found only bruises from her encounter with the car door. He had prescribed a sedative, which she had refused to take. The ordeal had left her shaken but undaunted. "What are we going to do?" It was more of a command than a question.

"What do you want to do?"

"I want my kids to be safe."

Sam pulled her close to his chest and stroked her hair. "I want all of us to be safe. Let's get some sleep and tomorrow we'll decide what to do. The sheriff's people are here tonight. If the bad guys show up we'll sic Tump, I mean TJ, on them. Why don't you show me your bruises?"

Alicia slipped off her blouse and turned her bare back to Sam. Dark bruises ran down her back from her shoulders to the top of her buttocks. Sam pulled her panties down and looked at her well-rounded bottom. It was smooth and unmarked. Patting her behind gently he said, "It's a good thing the door hit this first or you might have been really hurt"

Alicia turned and retorted, "Well, thanks a hell of a lot." Then the floodgates opened and she clung to him and sobbed uncontrollably.

The next morning they decided they would hire security guards; to guard the house day and night, go to school with Michael and stay in and around the school all day and escort him home at the end of the day.

Sam went to the Police station and thanked his boyhood friend for what he had done the day before. TJ was getting a little bit unhappy about all the publicity. The newspapers all over the country had carried the story of how in a fierce gun battle he had thwarted the would be kidnappers; the hero of the day, ex-marine, up to the challenge and a lot more.

"Hey Sammy," he growled, "I didn't think you'd buy that hero bull. You of all people know I never do anything I don't have to. Those bastards pulled a gun on me. I always get pissed when people do that."

Sam took a good hard look at the man standing before him.

Tj was a muscular, wide shouldered six-footer, and was beginning to get thick around the middle. There was a thin hard line around his mouth and although he smiled often, his eyes were hard as steel and they looked right through a person. It had been over ten years since they had seen each other, and Sam wasn't sure he knew this stranger at all.

"Where have you been all these years? What have you been doing?" Sam asked.

Tj smiled and waved his hand, "Oh, just around. I was on the police force in New Orleans, too much temptation there. I decided to take a job in a quiet place. I figured nothing ever happened here. I was in New Orleans five years and never shot one man. Been here a week and look what happened."

Sam told him about how concerned he and Alicia were about the safety of the children, and that they had decided to hire a security force.

Tj said, "That's probably a good idea. I reckon it's one of the curses of having a lot of money." There was no rancor in his voice, just a touch of sympathy. "I know some good people. If you want me to I'll contact a couple of guys and send them to talk to you, or have them send you a resume."

"I would appreciate that," Sam replied, "And thanks for the offer, and thanks again for the good work you did yesterday."

Tj smiled and waved to Sam as he walked away.

Sam asked the sheriff to keep his men on the job around Lone Pine until he could hire suitable guards. He told Alicia of his conversation with Tj and what had been suggested.

"Why don't you hire Tj?" Alicia asked." Then he could select people who are qualified."

Sam called Tj and told him what Alicia had suggested.

"I think I'll pass, Sammy. I just got on this job and they are running short handed. I'm obligated to give sixty-day notice before I leave and you need somebody now. I'll get you a couple of candidates right away. People you can trust. I guarantee it.

Tell 'Licia I said thanks for the vote of confidence."

The first man Tj recommended was a local ex-sheriff. Fifty-year-old Willie Williams was a known fearless person of high integrity. The second was a graduate of the Louisiana police academy, and Tj recommended he be assigned to the school as an assistant to the principal. "You don't want Michael to think he's in jail. You pay the guy's salary and he'll be free to do the guard job without looking like a cop. Only the school officials and a few others will know what his real job is."

Sam and Alicia thought Tj had an excellent idea, and they accepted it immediately.

There were two more men hired, and the guards around the clock activity began in earnest. It was a deadly boring job. There was not an abduction attempt ever again, but

the guards became a part of life for the
Wardens, including Henry and Angela, as well
as Jose and Ave Williams.

The business interests of Warberg, Inc.
became worldwide. Sam made contact with
World War Two acquaintances and their
influence helped break into markets that
might have been more difficult under
different circumstances. It was a game to
Sam. He loved the big deals. He made a lot
of money and the amount he owed was
staggering, because of his leveraging
activity.

He was bidding for an oil company in an
African country when he ran across his ex-
partner, Tex Malone. It was customary for
all such bids to be secret. No company was
supposed to know what any other company was
bidding. Vast oil reserves were involved and
a more lucrative one countered each bid Sam
offered. The Warberg, Inc. bid had started

at five hundred million dollars. It had gone up fifty million at a time until Warberg, Inc had almost all assets involved in the last bid; one and one half billion dollars.

In the capitol city of that country Sam was walking across the lobby of the King George hotel when he saw Malone going into the bar. Sam followed and stood behind him at the bar. Malone ordered a double shot of bourbon whiskey and as he took a long swig, Sam spoke. "Still drinking old rub of the brush, I see."

Malone swung around and growled, "Sam Warden, now it all makes sense. I wondered who the hell was pushing this thing beyond reason. We're being suckered, my friend. They got a great thing going and they intend to get what it's worth."

The two men shook hands and Sam said, "I've gone as far as I'm going. I've got a bid on the table and that's it."

"Then you win," Malone said, with relief in his voice. "I had decided the last bid Malzone Oil submitted was as far as we would go."

The settlement date was set and the final transaction was scheduled to be made in New York City.

The night before the closing date, Sam was in a hotel room at the Waldorf Astoria. In his dream he was standing on the bluffs overlooking Squaw Creek, the water was roaring as it rushed by where he was standing. He awoke with a start. Alicia was sleeping quietly by his side. He turned over and after awhile he drifted off to sleep, and immediately he began to dream the same dream, except this time Alicia was standing with him. Somewhere in his mind he knew he was dreaming and struggled to wake. He began to thrash around and Alicia shook him awake.

"Wake up honey, you're having a nightmare," she said. Sam awoke and found he was shivering. "Just a bad dream, I reckon."

Alicia wrapped her arms around him and asked, "What was it all about?"

"Just an old war scare."

He lay staring at the ceiling until he could hear the quiet even breathing of his sleeping wife. Then he slipped out of bed. He went to a telephone in the next room and called the guards at Lone Pine. He instructed the guard to personally check each member of his family and assure him they were safe. The time was four am.

The guard first went to Judge Warden and told him of Sam's request. The judge then went with the guard and they roused the housekeeper, the children were checked and found to be safe. The Judge called his son and told him that he had seen everyone and they were ok.

"What's happening son?" Henry asked.

"A bad dream I guess, sorry to be such a worry wart. Have the guard doubled just to humor me."

Sam walked to the window and looked out over the city. His mind was racing. In the distance he could see a neon lighted sign advertising Shell Oil. His thoughts turned to the oil deal he had scheduled for that day.

He wondered what could be wrong with the biggest deal he had ever put together. He went over the details in his mind. His constant review had engraved each detail in his memory. Warberg, Inc. attorneys had checked each legal aspect of every conceivable thing. All were clean.

It was six o'clock in the morning when he called Jim Sloan, his congressman from Mississippi. The phone was answered on the first ring. "Jim, what do you know about Micron?" he said by way of greeting.

"Good morning to you too. Nothing much, except it floats on oil. What's going on?" Jim answered

Sam quickly told him about the business deal he was scheduled to complete this date.

"What makes you think something is wrong?" Jim asked.

"Just a gut feel. Just a feeling that something is not right."

I'll make a couple of quick phone calls and get right back to you," the congressman said.

In about an hour Jim called back. "I don't know what it is, but something is cooking in that little oil patch. Stall your deal for a couple of days and I'll have the straight scoop on what's what."

Sam told Alicia at breakfast he was going to delay the purchase of the oil company. He then called a meeting with his top legal counsel and informed him of the decision.

The signing ceremonies were being held in a conference room in the same hotel where Sam and Alicia were staying. There was a round table, and all the principals were milling around drinking coffee when the Warberg, Inc. people walked in. Each person took a designated seat. Sam remained standing.

"Ladies and gentlemen," he began, "Something has happened that makes it necessary for Warburg, Inc. to ask for a two day extension on the contract signing date. I'm sorry for any inconvenience this might cause. My attorney will stay and work out any details. There was a stunned silence for a full minute. Sam picked up his brief case and stood by Alicia's chair as she rose. They walked from the room.

Mark Whelan was the Warberg attorney, and now the wrath of the sellers broke around his head. They were livid with rage. He sat quietly as everyone else was talking at the same time. "We want to know what happened. We know your company had the financing. We checked all this out with the banks."

"Mr Warden wants two more days," Whelan smiled as he looked around at the angry group. "Why are you so upset? Delays happen all the time in business deals as large as this."

"We have another buyer just waiting for an opportunity. Warburg, Incorporated does not get another day. You tell Warden that he either settles this day or we'll go to our other buyer," the oil company attorney shouted.

Whelan quit smiling. "Put that in writing and I'll take it to him."

The oil company attorney dictated a note to a secretary they had brought along, she quickly typed it, the attorney and the contracts administrator signed, dated and affixed the exact time of day. The necessary copies were made, the original given to Whelan who bade the group good day and promised he would call in a few minutes.

Whelan took the note to Sam, who read it and asked, "Why bring this to me? I said two days and two days it is."

Whelan was smiling his best lawyer's smile. "I'll tell you why. This note is worth two million to you. That's your deposit, your earnest money. I call them back, they run to another buyer, you get your money back."

"Good thinking, call them and tell them two days," Sam nodded his approval as he spoke.

The other buyer was Malzone Oil. That afternoon Tex Malone called and said, "Sam, tell me what the hell is going on. Are you really about to back out on the best opportunity to come along in our life time?"

"I didn't back out. I asked for a two-day extension. The sellers gave me an ultimatum. I don't take kindly to that kind of tactic."

"Why did you need a two day extension?" Tex wanted to know.

"There was something I wanted to check out and it takes a couple of days," Sam replied.

"Sam, is there something I need to know? These guys are anxious and I told them I was ready to step in, but for some reason I feel uneasy. What do you think?"

"I don't know what to say. I've got it pretty straight that something's going on in that country, and I don't know what it is, but as soon as I know, you will also know."

Jim Sloan called at ten pm that night. "Sam, don't touch that deal with a ten foot pole. The government is going to nationalize the oil business. That means you would lose your shirt and everything else. They simply confiscate foreign business, and especially where it's a natural resource like oil in the ground. They will say it belongs to the state in the first place."

"Thanks Jim, I won't forget this," Sam answered.

"Look Sam, no one is supposed to know about this. I would be in big trouble if it leaked. Don't mention it to Alicia or to your lawyers or to no one. Understand?"

Sam called Tex and said, "I can only tell you that I wouldn't touch that deal at any price."

Tex was silent for a few moments. "You can't tell me why?"

"No, a serious breech of confidence is involved," Sam replied. "I hope you haven't invested much money yet."

"My bank has been notified to transfer the earnest money early tomorrow morning."

"That could still be stopped."

"Yeah, I guess that's what I should do. Thanks Sam. That sure looked like a good deal, on the surface."

Tex informed the sellers he was no longer interested. They quickly held a conference and then called the Warberg attorney to inform him they would accept the two-day delay. Whelan told them Warberg was working another deal and all their assets were tied up.

The next day when Sam and Alicia were walking through the hotel lobby, a member of the Micron delegation attacked Sam. The man was armed with a knife and the first swipe slashed Sam's clothing through to the skin.

427

He swung around to face his attacker and as the man lunged again he raised his brief case and the knife buried to the hilt in the soft leather. Sam let go of the brief case and dropped the man with a hard right to the side of the head.

The commotion had attracted the hotel security forces and they swarmed over the attacker and quickly subdued him. He was babbling about Sam messing up a business deal and screamed that he was going to kill him if it was the last thing he ever did.

Two days later Micron nationalized the oil industry.

Alicia had watched the action in the hotel lobby with complete helpless horror. On the way to the airport she insisted that Sam get a security guard to travel with him.

"I don't want some joker tagging along with me every place I go," he retorted.

"Then quit running around all over the country."

"You don't mean that. This is what I do. This is what we do. This is our business."

"You could retire," Alicia suggested.

"You know you don't mean that," Sam was becoming annoyed.

"I know I want to feel you are safe when you leave home. Get someone you would like to travel with you. Give Tj a job. He would make an excellent bodyguard. I don't believe he is afraid of anything."

Sam knew she had made up her mind. And he thought she might be right. "I'll do something," he promised.

Warberg, Inc had built a ten-story office building in Parkersville. The company corporate headquarters were located there. The divisions of the company were all represented. The managers who were instrumental in making Warburg, Inc. a success were all available for the morning staff meeting. Sam thought one essential element was missing. There was no corporate wide security representative

Sam called his old friend Thomas J. Johnson and made a luncheon appointment. They met in the Warburg building cafeteria.

After the initial greetings Tj looked around the cafeteria and said, "This is a pretty nice place. Any chance of getting a drink here?"

Sam replied, "This is a dry state, in case you have forgotten, and besides that, you are working."

"Nah, I'm not working, this is my day off. And I do know it's a dry state. I've been drinking moonshine for a week. The law has gotten so tough on the bootleggers that the cops don't have any good drinking whiskey."

Sam sighed, "It's good to know it didn't take you long to corrupt the sheriff's office."

"I didn't have to corrupt them. Being a cop is just about the same as being a crook. It's just the opposite side of the same thing. Show me a good cop and I'll show you a person who would make a good crook. He knows all the angles."

Tj stuck a cigarette in his mouth and struck a match with his thumbnail. He exhaled a cloud of smoke and said, "Sammy, I understand you don't waste a lot of time. I usually drink my lunch when I'm off duty. That's the only way I can keep my belly flat. And you can't buy me a drink, so what's left for us to do?"

"How would you like to go to work for me?" Sam asked.

"We discussed that once before, when you hired the guards for Lone Pine. I don't care about being a night watchman."

"I'm not talking about a guard job, I'm talking about a job as security chief for Warberg, Inc. We are an inter-national company. And we think the head of security for the entire operation should be here in corporate headquarters."

Tj rubbed his hand across his chin as he squinted at Sam through half closed eyes. "That sounds like a hell of a big deal to me. You need some pin stripe college man, maybe an ex F.B.I. agent."

Sam shook his head, "No, we don't need someone to hold down an office chair and go to meetings. We want someone who can talk to the working people. When there is a strike brewing, we need someone who can handle that sort of situation. We need someone who has the guts to do what needs to be done."

"And what makes you think I fit that bill of goods?" Tj's voice was almost belligerent.

"We've known you all of our lives, Alicia and me. We've checked your record from birth to now. We know you went to the Police Academy and graduated—barely. We know that your trouble in New Orleans stemmed from your refusal to participate in bribery. And above all else I trust you."

Tj grinned his easy grin; "Damn, you didn't have to throw in that "graduated barely" crap. I never was long on the books." He turned serious and frowned, "I don't know, Sammy. I would hate to let you down and you have to fire me."

The Warberg personnel Vice President had written a job description and had included and offer of employment to Thomas J. Johnson. The title would be: Corporate Vice President of Security, salary, sixty thousand dollars per annum, full expenses when traveling, a company car and the use of a corporate airplane when deemed necessary. After one year the salary would be reviewed and a retirement plan with profit sharing would be negotiated.

Sam pushed the paper across the table to Tj and said, "This is the offer. Don't give me an answer now. Sleep on it and let me know tomorrow," he looked at his watch, "I've got to run, I'm late for a meeting." And he hurried away, leaving Tj staring in disbelief at the sheet of paper.

The next morning Tj called, "Who do I have to kill?" He asked when Sam answered the phone.

"I take it that means yes?" Sam queried.

"Yeah, if you are foolish enough to pay that kind of dough, I'm sure dumb enough to take it."

It was a better job than Tj had ever dreamed he would have. And to his surprise he fit right into the Warberg corporate structure. By way of indoctrination Sam took him on all trips. "Just to give you a feel for what we're doing and to make Angela think you are my body guard."

Chapter 10

Tj began to earn his pay when he was assigned to report on a labor strike at a lumber mill in Alabama. After arriving at the mill and listening to what management had to say, he went to the picket line and talked to the workers who were striking. He found that an accident in the mill had escalated into a wildcat strike when management had refused to correct the unsafe condition. Hardheaded management and equally hardheaded union leaders had caused the original grievance to get lost in the heat of insults being tossed back and forth. A fight had broken out between strikers, and non-strikers who were attempting to cross the picket line. Two injured men were hospitalized. Management had requested police protection. The union had made

outrageous   demands.   Communications   had
broken down.

Tj had been dispatched to the mill to
make sure company property was secure. He
was a natural mixer and had insight into the
thinking of working people. The first night
he was in the city where the mill was
located, he went into a local bar and
ordered a drink. It was a hangout for
working men and their wives. Some of the
strikers were there, gathered around a large
table, drinking beer and trying to have a
little fun. The wives had a worried crease
between their eyes. The strike was one week
old.

Tj ordered a round of drinks for the
table. The men waved their thanks and one of
them walked over and invited him to sit with
them.

Tj joined the group. He was dressed in
jeans and a shirt open at the throat. He

looked like any other southern workingman. And when he introduced himself, there could be no doubt about his origin.

"Where are you from?" one of the ladies asked.

"Mississippi," Tj replied, with his big smile breaking through.

"What do you do there?" she asked.

His smile widened, "I work for Warberg, Inc."

A silence fell over the group. One of the men started to get up from the table. "I ain't drinking with no company man," he growled.

Tj held up his hand, "Wait, I'm here to see if the company property is secure. We want to make sure you have something to go back to when this is over. If somebody burns the place down we all lose. My job is to make sure that doesn't happen. If there's no job to go back to, why go through all this

misery? Just go look for another job now.
I'm really on your side you know."

The man slowly sat down again. His wife
was looking at him and holding on to his
arm.

Tj took a sip of his beer and continued,
"It looks to me as if some rival company is
behind this unrest," he lied, "It might be
their intent to close the place and keep it
closed."

The men at the table had been with the
company for a number of years. The pay was
good and usually the working conditions were
acceptable.

"I never thought about the mill closing,"
one of the men said.

"Well, of course the company has no
intention of closing the place. But things
have gotten out of control. It might be
something that can't be helped," Tj shook
his head as he talked.

439

Tj excused himself and left the bar. By the next morning the rumor was rampant that a Warberg, Inc. rival was trying to close the mill and the company had sent a man to protect the property. It had an extremely sobering effect on the workmen, probably caused by the concern of the wives. The union people asked for a negotiating session and before it started Tj called Sam and told him what was needed to settle the strike. Tj was given the authority to make whatever concessions he thought necessary.

The union had toned down its demands, and more importantly were willing to negotiate without the previous hostility. Management had agreed to improve the safety of the mill by appointing a safety committee made up of the work force. Tj had made that recommendation to the management and had included a recommendation that a grievance committee be established which included a member from the office work force, a member from the lumber yard, one from the mill and one from the delivery truck drivers.

The mill manager said, "Hell, they didn't even ask for that. Why give away the farm?"

Tj smiled, "Call it leadership. They'll be so surprised you'll have labor peace for awhile, and who knows, you might be setting a precedent for the future."

The strike was settled that day. The next morning the mill steam whistle echoed throughout the area, calling the people back to work.

Sam was favorably impressed with the work Tj did at the mill. In the staff meeting at headquarters Tj made his report, and when John Rausch from the New York office asked how he had managed that feat he replied simply. "If you want something done you have to appeal to the people who are affected. Get them involved. If there are wives involved and milk for the baby is an issue use that to your advantage."

"In other words you're just one of the redneck good old boys, is that right?" Rausch asked, with a smirk creasing his handsome face.

Tj replied with his best hillbilly accent, "That's keerect, Mistah Rausch, suh, I'm just a Mississippi redneck."

Sam looked up quickly at the tone of Tj's voice. He was not surprised to see a smiling Tj, nor was he surprised to see the hard glint in his security chief's eyes.

Rausch was a Harvard graduate, a snob who looked down his nose at anyone who was not a graduate of an Ivy League school. He had flaming red hair and a temper to match. He was about to prod Tj verbally again when Sam spoke.

"That was a good job Tj. We could use a lot of that kind of initiative."

Rausch changed his mind and held his peace, but Tj knew there would be another day, he could tell John Rausch was not pleased about Sam's words of praise.

A lumber mill near Pine Bluff, Arkansas had a series of incidents that interrupted production. It was obvious sabotage was intended when the high-speed saws that turned a log into lumber with one pass, struck a steel pin driven into the log. The saws broke under the impact and pieces of steel screamed like shrapnel through the work area. Two men were injured and the mill shut down for repairs. And after the second incident the men were afraid to return to work.

Sam asked Tj to see what he could do to get the operation back into production. "I'm not sure this is in your job description, but somebody needs to see what's wrong at that place."

443

"The job description is whatever you want it to be," Tj replied as he headed for the airport.

When he arrived at the mill he met with Albert Jenkins, the mill manager. "What's it take to get this thing up and running, Al?" he asked as soon as he introduced himself.

Al was a big grizzly tough man about fifty years of age. He squinted at Tj and replied, "We gotta make sure the men know they ain't gonna get killed when they go back to work. We got a hell of a scary thing going on here. Chunks of saw blades flying all over the place."

"What's been done so far to make sure the saws hit no more steel pins?"

"We started building a shield to contain the fragments in case we hit another one. We think that'll work."

"If you hit another pin, you'll be shut down. Right?"

444

"That's true," Al replied, "But it's a random thing. We've examined a lot of logs and can't find a thing. We thought we would run as long as we can and when we hit a pin, we'll fix damage and go again. The shield will at least keep people from being hurt, or worse."

"How about a metal detector?" Tj asked.

"We didn't think about that," Jenkins replied.

"Let's see if we can work out something. I'll call a company in Little Rock that has some experts in that field And have them send a couple of guys down here."

Ozark Electronics in Little Rock sent two representatives armed with the latest in metal detection equipment. Tj had informed the company of what was needed and they were prepared to work the problem. The equipment utilized a loop antenna that was passed over the logs, one at a time. If metal was present an audible beep was sounded. There were no pins found in the first dozen logs, but to prove to the mill workers that the system worked, pins were driven into selected logs without the electronics people knowing which ones. The equipment never failed to detect the metal.

Very little training was needed for a trusted mill worker to be qualified to use the detection equipment and in a short time the mill resumed production. The shield was in place just in case one of the pins should slip by the detector. In the first day of operation three logs were found to have steel pins driven into them.

The logs were pulled aside and the pins extracted. Tj and Al examined the eighteen inch long, one half inch pins. They were sharpened at one end to facilitate driving into the soft pinewood.

"Looks like they were manufactured for the job," Tj said.

"Nah", Al said, "They look like ordinary drift pins construction workers use. They are so common finding who bought them would be like looking for a needle in a haystack."

"Yeah, I guess you are right about that. What's the chance of catching the guy in the act of pounding the pins into the logs? Or do you think he pounds them in before the trees are cut down?"

Al pushed his hat back and rubbed his hand over his face. "I think he drives the pins into the logs after the trees are felled."

"What makes you think that?" Tj asked.

"We had the timber cutters looking for telltale resin seeps. If the tree has been injured the sap starts to ooze and forms resin. So far we haven't found any sign of that sort. And the chance of catching him in the act is slim and none. The logging site covers a wide area. It would take an army to cover that much territory."

Tj looked thoughtful. "Tell me about the work activity in the woods. When is there none of the company employees in the logging area?"

"Well, of course at night there is no one there and we never work in the woods on weekends," Al replied.

"Has anyone ever gone there at night or on the weekend? Just to sit and listen?"

Al glowered at Tj. "Hell no, it'd be a big waste of time."

"This is Friday night. Why don't you and me go out to the logging area and ride quietly around and see what we might be able to see and hear."

"Hell I ain't gonna waste my Friday night in them frigging woods. I'm going home and drink me a little whiskey and scorch a big steak on the grill. You're welcome to come with me. You look like a fellow who might enjoy both those things." Al was emphatic.

"Al, I wasn't *asking* you to go." Tj was smiling and his voice had gone soft.

Al looked at him quickly. "Oh, it's like that, huh?"

"That's the way it is. The booze and the steak sound mighty temptin', maybe some other time."

The sun was slanting down the western sky when they went out into the logging area in Tj's rental car. He drove slowly along the logging roads where the heavy trucks had gouged deep ruts in the soft soil. The dust was heavy and rose behind his car in a thick cloud. The surrounding hills cast deep shadows across the land Thunder rumbled in the distance.

Al broke the silence. "If it rains we'll be here until someone finds us on Monday.

Either that or We'll have to walk out. These roads will become a swamp."

Tj knew Al was an unhappy man. He drove past a road that branched off to the right and showed signs of very little traffic.

"Where does that go?" he asked.

"There's a new staging area up the valley and we've just started hauling out of that area."

Tj turned into the road, turned off the engine and the two men sat silently in the gathering shadows. It was still and quiet. Suddenly there was the ringing sound of steel on steel echoing loudly in the quiet valley.

"Who you got working up here tonight?" Tj whispered.

"Nobody," Al whispered back.

The two men eased out of the car and left the doors open. They walked quickly up the road toward the sound. As they rounded a bend in the road they came up on the staging area piled high with logs. A man with a sledgehammer was in the process of driving a pin into a log. He tapped the pin to get it started and then swung the twelve-pound sledge with powerful strokes. When the pin was flush with the outer surface of the log, he used another pin to sink it even further. He then rubbed a handful of dirt in the wound to make it appear as the rest of the dirt-covered surface.

Al gasped and crumpled to the ground as the whiplash crack of a rifle echoed in the valley. Tj instinctively dived for cover as the rifle cracked again and he felt a searing pain as a bullet creased his head. Tj lay behind a pile of logs and he could feel blood running down his cheek. He slid his hand down to the leg holster where he carried a snub-nosed thirty-eight special. It felt cool and reassuring to his grasp. He thought Al was probably dead. Then he heard footsteps approaching and the two men began to talk.

"Damn, Buck, you kilt them both." The pin driver said.

"That's what I meant to do, Bud. That one's that Jenkins bastard from the mill and I don't know who the other son of a bitch is. It's a damn good thing I was standing guard. I'll just make shore they are both dead."

Buck raised the rifle to shoot Al again, at that moment Tj sat up. The thirty-eight special spoke three times in rapid succession and the rifleman crumpled to the ground. The man called Bud jumped to retrieve his fallen comrade's rifle.

"Hold it," Tj's voice cracked, "Touch that rifle and you're a dead man."

Bud froze in his tracks and turned slowly to face a bloody faced Tj. Blood mixed with the dust of the staging area gave him a grotesque appearance.

"Back off, hands behind your head," Tj commanded, his voice hard and crisp.

Bud quickly obeyed. Tj picked up the rifle.

:"Turn around," he told Bud.

Bud began babbling, "Oh, please don't kill me. I got a wife and kids. I'll do anything if you just won't shoot me."

With the butt of the rifle Tj struck him behind the head, knocking him unconscious. He quickly removed Bud's bootlaces and tied his hands behind his back. Then removing Bud's belt he used it to tie his feet together. He rushed to Al's side and found that he was still alive.

The rifle bullet had struck Al in the back, low on the left side of the rib cage. It had passed all the way through his body. There was very little blood on the entrance and exit wounds, but there was bloody froth on Al's lips as he struggled for breath.

"Oh my God," Tj groaned as he jumped to his feet and raced for the parked car. Lightening was flashing and thunder was rumbling through the hills and valleys. He knew he must hurry, he remembered Al's warning about what would happen if it should rain on the soft, churned up ground. He placed the badly injured Al on the back seat of the car and left Bud and the dead man where they had fallen. He drove the car roaring down the dusty road, leaving a cloud of dust in his wake. When he reached the highway, just as rain began to fall, he drove as fast as the car would move. He was an excellent driver with years of experience on different police forces. He was trying desperately to attract attention. He reached the city limits and did not slow down. With the car horn blaring he dodged traffic and ran stop signs and red lights. Under his breath he cursed, "Where the hell is a cop when you need one?" He was preparing to stop and ask directions to a hospital when a black and white police cruiser turned into the street behind his racing car. The flashing red lights and wailing siren were most welcome. Tj stopped and as the police car pulled alongside the startled officer saw a bloody, mud caked man. Before the officer could speak Tj shouted, "I've got a badly injured man in my car, please lead me to a hospital."

Without a word the officer complied. With red light and siren the two cars raced through the streets. The officer radioed the hospital and the emergency ward personnel were waiting. That action helped save Al's life. The doctors said they arrived just in time.

The police waited until Tj's wound had been cared for before they questioned him. Tj began by identifying himself. He was a duly authorized deputy sheriff of Warden county Mississippi. And he spoke the language of law enforcement people. He quickly explained what had happened and ended by saying, "There's a dead man and another one getting mighty wet out in the woods somewhere and I'm damned if I know how to get back out there in the dark."

The police knew the mill personnel and from Tj's description they were able to find knowledgeable people to lead them to the site. With four-wheel drive vehicles they plowed through the mud to where they found Buck sprawled on the soggy ground where he had fallen. Bud was huddled against a pile of logs in an attempt to get away from the falling rain. The dead man was loaded in the back of one of the four-wheel drive vehicles. A thoroughly miserable Bud, with teeth chattering from the cold rain was placed in a police vehicle and the caravan headed back to the city.

The police investigation found that Bud had been fired by the lumber mill management and was an easy mark when Buck sought someone to help with the sabotage of that facility. There was no record of Buck. He had just drifted into the area. A loner who lived in a boarding house and no one knew anything about him. There were no fingerprints on record, anywhere. He carried no identification. He had always paid Bud in cash. He had a large amount of cash in a money belt strapped around his waist. No one knew what motivated him to try to wreck the Warburg mill. Tj summed it up correctly when he said; "There are a lot of people in this part of the world just like this guy, no official record."

On his way out of town Tj went by the hospital to visit the recovering man. Al was a tough and very seasoned lumberman.

"You sure as hell know how to screw up a man's weekend," he told Tj, with a wry smile.

"That was a hell of a close call man," Tj said with genuine regret in his voice. "I never dreamed we would run into that sort of thing. I thought it was just some joker who was pissed off at you or some other boss man." He told Al what little information the law enforcement officials had found about the man called Buck.

Al looked thoughtful and said, "Warburg has been dealing for the Anderson tract, hundreds of acres of prime timber. Might be some other company trying to take out the competition."

"It beats the hell out of me," Tj said, extending his hand in goodbye.

Al said, "I wish I could have scorched you a good steak and maybe enjoyed a shot of whiskey together. You're a good man Johnson."

"We'll make it another time, when you get well. I promise I'll be back." Tj replied

"Don't come on business." Al cautioned.

Tj smiled and headed for the door. When he arrived back in Parkersville he reported the events of his trip to Sam.

Sam leaned back in his chair and frowned. "Look", he said, "I don't want you doing that sort of thing again. You were just lucky. You'll wind up dead. It's not worth the risk. And besides, we lost the Anderson tract. We were outbid by Arrowsmith, Inc."

"I never in my wildest dreams thought there would be violence out in the woods like that," Tj said.

"Yeah," Sam replied dryly, "You just carry that gun strapped to your leg for ballast."

"You think this steel pin business had any bearing on the bids? Like maybe distract us while they made an end run?"

"I don't see any connection. We were just outbid. It happens. It seems we've been on the losing end of a lot of bids lately. Lost some big government contract by being underbid. Just have to sharpen the pencil, I guess." Sam's voice was troubled.

Contracts was not Tj's concern. After leaving Sam he was hurrying down the hall to his office when he met John Rausch.

"Well," Rausch said, with his usual smirk, "I hear you added another notch to your gun."

"Where did you hear that, Mr Rausch?" Tj asked innocently.

"Oh, you made the newspapers. You're a regular John Wayne."

Tj did a slow burn and without replying walked into his office. Rausch got under his skin. And he was sure Rausch was aware of that also. As he passed his secretary's desk he said, "Have Chuck Mitchell come see me."

When Mitchell came in Tj said, "I want you to find everything there is to know about John Rausch."

"You mean *the* John Rausch? Like Vice President John Rausch from the new York office?"

"That's the guy," Tj replied. Chuck Mitchell was his most trusted subordinate and he knew he could level with him.

"That's one of Mr Warden's heavy weights. I don't want to get fired. What am I looking for?"

"If anybody gets fired it'll be me. I don't know what I'm looking for. I just want to know something that'll shut the bastard's big mouth. It's either that or I shut him up with my fist in his face. And I don't want to do that to Sam. That would make boardroom news," Tj said angrily.

Chuck grinned and said, "I don't see you riled very often. I'll use a private detective agency to get all the good stuff, OK?"

"Do what you have to do, just don't let him get wise."

"You don't have to tell me that. How about the cost?"

"You don't have to ask that do you?"

"Just checking." Chuck grinned, as he headed for the door.

It was three weeks later when Chuck reported to Tj on the Rausch investigation. They were in a closed-door meeting, just the two of them. It was obvious Chuck was enjoying himself.

"Mr Rausch is squeaky clean," he began. "Clean, that is, back in New York, but right here in little ole Parkersville it's a different story. He's been banging Dolores from Contract Administration."

A light came on in Tj's head. "That could explain a few things," he mused. "I had just planned to shut his big mouth, but this puts a different slant on things. You may have just uncovered something important. What kind of evidence do you have?"

Chuck was thorough. "Oh, the usual things, photographs, motel registrations, under a phony name of course. They never arrive together and they leave separately as well. But the photos show all the right stuff. A divorce lawyer would love this much evidence."

"What about a bug in the room? What do you think that would tell us?" Tj spoke quietly.

Chuck had a puzzled look. "What're you looking for? You've got enough to rock the old boy back on his heels."

"What you've found makes me rethink my objective. I'll give you the details later. I want to know what goes on in their room, other that the obvious."

"You got it," Chuck replied.

Tj instructed his secretary to make an appointment with Sam

It was late afternoon when Tj walked into Sam's office. He quickly got to the business he had in mind. "I think through just plain dumb assed luck I've stumbled onto something about contracts. I need you to let me do some snooping around in that department. Who knows what the final bid is, on any contract?"

"Just a few people, the vice president of the department, his assistant, a couple of secretaries, and myself if it's a big one. What's going on?" Sam was curious.

"I don't really know. It's just a gut feel. But, I need your help to either prove or disprove my suspicions," Tj replied.

"What do you want me to do?"

"Do you have a big contract in the works that's just about complete?"

"Sure," Sam replied, "A cruise ship to be built in the Pascagoula ship yard if we are successful."

"Competitive bid?"

"Two other bidders."

"Have your people put out a phony final bid. You know just put it in the hands of the usual people who would handle it, but don't send it to the requesting company."

"I'll have to let Joe Warren in on this, if I don't he'll think I've lost my mind."

When Sam explained to Warren what Tj had requested he was not pleased. With fire in his eyes he snapped at Tj, "You've got a hell of a nerve snooping around in my department. You suspect someone leaking information, don't you?"

"Wait," Sam said, holding up his hand. "There's a simple way to find out. Do what security is asking and if no one is guilty, there's no harm done. Either way we'll know for sure."

The word, security, cooled Warren's temper. "I've wondered if we might have a leak. I've made sure only the necessary people know the final numbers. What is it you want?" he asked Tj.

"Finalize the cruise ship contract this weekend. Have complete numbers by Monday. But don't send the contract. Have your courier take a delayed trip. Give me two days. And by the way, who are the necessary people who need to know the numbers?"

"My assistant, Bill Jones, myself, Mr Warden and the two secretaries, Rita and Dolores."

When Tj heard Dolores' name he felt a tinge of excitement and thought, "bingo".

At the Monday staff meeting John Rausch was his usual suave self. Before the meeting started he looked across the table at Tj and said, "Johnson, You shoot anybody this past week?"

Tj felt the slow burn start in his belly and start to move up. Before he could reply Sam walked into the room and the meeting got underway.

The meeting was routine. Department heads made their reports and Joe Warren announced that the cruise ship contract had been finalized and was being submitted this date. Sam was watching Rausch but there was no outward indication of interest. His eyes were downcast as he took notes.

467

The next morning Chuck Mitchell was waiting when Tj walked into his office. "Boss, you gonna love this," he said, waving a small cassette tape. He put the tape on the player and it began to unwind. You could plainly hear the door rattle as Rausch entered the motel room. There were noises of using the bathroom, the sounds of a drink being poured. Then a knock on the door and the sound of another person entering the room. There were the muffled noises of embraces and kisses and the unmistakable voice of John Rausch.

"You got something for me baby?"

The breathless voice of Dolores answered. "The cruise ship contract numbers." She quoted the exact numbers Sam's people had agreed upon.

"That's a good girl. You've got a reward coming." There was the gasping sound of an excited woman and the rustle of clothing.

468

"That's all I need," Tj said.

"Oh hell boss it gets good from now on. There's lots of really hot stuff going on." Chuck was obviously enjoying his latest assignment.

"I make my own music," Tj said as he headed for Sam's office with the cassette player in his hand.

After Sam and Joe Warren had heard the pertinent parts of the tape and had reviewed the photograph, they were both ready to discharge the two people immediately. But Tj cautioned them to go slow.

"What's the rush? They have no idea we are on to their game. We need a confession from the girl. What kind of person is she?" His years of police work were becoming evident.

"I guess I don't know what kind of person she is. I thought I knew. She comes from a good family. She's an excellent secretary. I think she's planning to marry some local guy. I would not have dreamed she would be involved in this sort of thing," Warren said, puzzled and with genuine sadness in his voice.

"We need for her to admit she was involved in industrial espionage. There's no telling where this will go; surely to a court of law. Joe, Let's you and me confront her and see what happens," Tj proposed.

"I've got a better idea. You and one of the legal staff talk to her," Warren offered, "I'm so mad at the bitch I'd fire her the minute she walked into the room."

Warren's suggestion became the plan. Tj selected a woman from the legal staff to be the witness. Dolores was told to go to Tj's office for a job interview. When she came into the room her head was held proudly crowned with a wealth of coal black hair. She was five feet three inches tall and weighed about one hundred and five pounds. Her legs were long and slim and her figure was well rounded. She was so young and beautiful Tj felt a moment of sadness as he introduced himself. The small hand she offered was firm and warm and she looked him straight in the eyes. He introduced the legal staff person by name only and asked Dolores to have a seat. She sat with her knees together and her feet flat on the floor.

"Your name is Dolores Cummings. Is that right?" TJ asked.

"Yes sir," she replied smiling, her voice was low and slightly husky. Dolores was the picture of a self confident, poised young woman.

"Miss Cummings you've been selling secret company information to a Mr John Rausch. Isn't that right?" Tj's abruptness was like a slap in the face.

471

The color drained from her face and the smile fled.

She stammered, "No, no no, I haven't. Why would you say such a thing? I wouldn't do that."

"Isn't it true Miss Cummings, you and John Rausch are lovers?"

"I don't have to listen to this, I'm leaving." She rose from her chair.

Tj had been speaking in a soft voice, now it changed to a harsh accusing tone. "Sit down. You can talk here or down at the police station." The girl quickly sat down and looked at Tj with eyes brimming with tears.

"We know all about you and Rausch. In fact he admitted everything and said it was your idea in the first place," Tj lied.

That opened the floodgates and the tears and a torrent of words flowed from the girl. She told the whole sordid story. She had

472

found Rausch exciting, he had promised marriage, she had believed him, she had never received money for supplying contract information to Rausch. He had convinced her that the information was being used to enhance his standing with the company by giving him an advantage over his competitors within the company. She couldn't believe he would betray her by saying it was her idea. Tj couldn't help but feel sorry for the miserable girl. He asked the legal representative to take her to the restroom and help her regain her composure.

After they left the room Tj called Sam and told him what had happened. He recommended to Sam that the girl not be fired but transferred to a non-sensitive area.

"I'm flying to New York tonight to take care of Mr Rausch, and I want you to go with me," Sam said

"I wouldn't miss it for the world," Tj replied.

John Rausch had an office on the thirty-fourth floor of an office building near Wall Street. It can best be described as posh. Sam and Tj had spent the night in a nearby hotel and in the early morning they walked, unannounced, into the office. A surprised Rausch was as cordial as a man could be, and that included Tj.

"What can I get you gentlemen to drink?" Rausch asked;

"What kind of booze do you have?" Tj wanted to know.

Before Rausch could answer Sam said, "Cut the crap Rausch, you're fired. Get out of my building today."

A stunned John Rausch looked from one man to the other. "You can't fire me I've got a contract with Warberg, Inc."

"Does it include industrial espionage? I know all about the stolen contracts. I've got a signed confession from the girl. I'm filing charges with the district attorney." Sam's face was grim.

John Rausch wilted. There was no sign of his usual bravado. Sam led the way to the door with Tj following. When they got to the door Tj turned toward Rausch and with his fore finger extended like a gun and his thumb raised he made the sound of a shot like kids do when they play. It sounded like a soft, "Que".

On the flight back to Parkersville the two men discussed the possibility that Rausch was involved in the Pine Bluff, Arkansas mill incident and very likely had something to do with the loss of the Anderson tract. But it would be difficult to prove.

"I guess old Rausch will get off Scott free if you don't try to nail his ass to the barn door," Tj observed.

"I'm not getting tangled in a long drawn out legal action. Let Mr Rausch try getting another good job in this country. He's been with Warberg for fifteen years. He'll have to account for those years in his resume. He'll pay and pay and pay," Sam replied with grim satisfaction.

Thereafter when Warburg Inc. had a problem area, Tj was the trouble shooter given the task to make it right. He often went with Sam in a company owned plane. Sam was always the pilot. Although Tj had never learned to like flying he tolerated it because that was the way Sam always traveled.

When it was just Sam and Tj on a trip the comradeship of their youth was evident. Tj liked to drink and have a good time with the ladies. He always invited Sam to go along. But Sam would say, "I'm a married man. Alicia would be unhappy if she even suspected I was playing around."

Tj would laugh and come back with some comment like, "Sex and marriage have nothing to do with each other. Sex is like food; it's a necessity of life. Marriage I can get along without." None of the delights he described to Sam caused him to waver.

It was in the spring of 1960 when Sam met Maryrose Boden. She was a sixth grade teacher at the Warden school. He had gone there for the dedication of a new gymnasium. The principal had asked Sam to speak to the sixth grade class because that was the age when boys started to drop out of school to work on their father's farm. The principal said, "Some of these old guys still think the earth is flat, and they are sure that going to school is a waste of time."

Claude Eldridge

The principal walked Sam to the sixth grade class. As they walked into the room the teacher had her back to the door. As she turned to face them a shock ran through Sam. She looked so much like Camille Dotson it was startling, the Camille of long ago. The one person Sam could never forget.

Smiling she walked across the room to meet the two men. She extended her hand when the introductions were made. When their hands touched Sam could feel his fingers tingle. Maryrose said, "I've heard so much about you Colonel Warden, it's very nice to meet you."

She introduced Sam to the class. "Students this is Colonel Samuel Warden. He is the World War Two hero this school was named for. He's going to speak to you today."

Sam thanked her for the introduction and then he walked to the front of the teacher's

478

desk and sat on the edge of it, in a relaxed casual manner. "I don't want to make a speech today. I just want to visit with you young people for a while. I would like to know what you would like to do when you grow up," he looked around the room, "Anyone?" he asked.

The young people were a little shy at first. A little urging from the teacher caused them to start talking. One girl said she wanted to be a teacher, like Mrs Boden.

"Then you know what you have to do. You have to complete high school and then go to college. Isn't that right?" The girl acknowledged she knew what she had to do. Other girls joined in the conversation. One boy had the ambition to be a doctor and Sam told him how proud he was to hear the boy set his career goal so early in life. One of the boys said, "I want to be a farmer, and I can't wait until this year is over. I never

479

intend to set foot back in another schoolhouse. It's a waste of time."

Sam looked at the speaker. He was larger than the other kids; obviously a couple of grades behind the others. He was so freckled his skin looked rusty. A shock of red hair hung down over his face.

"I wish I could say something that would make you change your mind about school," Sam began, "Farming is a fine profession. Schooling just makes it better. You have to be able to keep a book of accounts. That means you need the skills you are learning here. If you go on and finish high school you will learn to be a more successful farmer. If you go to college you will be even more successful. The great advances in agriculture in the past few years have come out of the universities of this country."

"All of you young people are right on the threshold of life. The doors to the world

480

are just starting to open for you. To pass through those doors you are required to have a ticket. And that ticket is education. The years of formal education are short. If you don't have the ticket when the doors begin to close it will probably be too late. You can do anything you make up your mind to do, if you have the education. The world is yours, if you have the education. Without it you will be stuck in the lowest paying jobs, doomed to a life of hard labor and not knowing what is waiting for you."

The rusty-faced boy shook his shaggy head of hair. "I know all I need to know. My Pa needs me to help work. He can't read or write and he owns his own farm. He says school is a waste of time."

"Who does his book work? Who writes his checks?" Sam asked.

"My Maw does all that."

481

"What would he do if something happened to your mother?"

The boy was at a loss for an answer.

"Some day you will want to own your own farm," Sam continued, "A high school education, at least, will help you achieve that goal. It is your defense against failure. It takes a strong person to take on a tough task and see it through to the end. The easy way for you is to drop out of school and go work on the farm. Do you have what it takes to stick it out through high school? You're a big strong fellow. You would make a good high-school football player. All the girls love football players. Maybe you would be good enough to get a college scholarship, then maybe good enough to become a pro football player. But you can't do those things if you drop out of school. You only have one chance."

The boy didn't answer, but Sam could see he had struck a responsive chord in the young person.

The school day ended as Sam finished his talk. Most of the young people scampered for the exit as soon as the bell rang. A few came to where Sam and Maryrose were standing, and shyly introduced themselves. They talked for a few minutes about their educational goals. Sam was surprised at the maturity of the few who stayed to talk. He was also surprised to see the rusty-faced boy waiting in the background. After the others had gone the boy introduced himself as Marvin Baker, but was better known as Rusty. When he shook hands Sam could feel the rough calluses from the hard work the boy had been doing.

"I would really like to stay in school," Rusty said, "but I've missed so much school because I had to work on the farm I'm behind all the other kids. And it ain't gonna get any better. Did you mean it about football and stuff?"

"Oh, yes that's the gospel truth," Sam replied, "Just ask Miss Boden."

"Rusty it's true that you can do whatever you set your mind to do," Maryrose said. "We could set up a program for you to do extra studies and that way you could make up lost ground. But the real task is to convince your father to let you stay in school."

"I think my Maw could help with that," Rusty said as he shook hands with Sam again as he departed.

"I would like to see what happens to these ambitious ones in the future, especially how Rusty makes out," Sam told Maryrose, after the boy had left the building.

"Maybe I could see that you get a progress report each year," Maryrose stated.

484

Sam stared at this beautiful young woman so long she began to blush.

"I'm sorry," he apologized, "But you remind me so much of someone I used to know. I'll take your offer of the progress report if it means I'll get to see you again."

Maryrose smiled, and looked away, "A year is a long time and you are a busy man. You will have forgotten by that time."

"I won't forget," Sam replied. He said goodbye and Maryrose held out her hand. Sam took it and she tipped her head back to look up at him The gesture was so like Camille that he once again felt a shock run through his body He held her hand and she made no attempt to withdraw it, neither did she look away as he stared into her eyes.

Sam left the building and as he drove toward Lone Pine his thoughts were in turmoil. Forget it, he ordered himself. At home he was busy with his children and later when Alicia came home and put her arms around him all thoughts of Maryrose left his mind.

During the night he dreamed he was with her. They were walking along a beach, kicking the sand with their bare feet. She turned and tipped her head to look up at him. He looked away and when he turned back to her she was gone. He awoke and lay staring at the ceiling for an hour before he dropped off to sleep.

As the days passed Sam found Maryrose slipping into his consciousness more and more often. It was very disturbing. He had always been faithful to his wife and had no intention of doing otherwise. After about a week he told Tj about meeting a beautiful schoolteacher. "Don't get any ideas, I understand she's married."

"Was married," Tj corrected, "Her husband was killed in an automobile accident about two years ago. I see her sometimes when I go hunting with the guys over in Bakertown. Did you know she is a cousin, or some kin to that girl that Woody Baker killed? It's pretty hard to tell who is kin to whom with those people. Not as much inter-marrying now as there used to be."

Tj's casual voice droned on but Sam did not hear. He understood the resemblance to Camille now. He promised himself he would just forget.

The next day he was hurrying through the lobby of the Warberg building when he met her face to face. "What a surprise to see you again, so soon," he exclaimed.

She smiled a radiant smile and replied, "It's nice to see you. I'm on my way to see the dentist. He has an office in this building."

"I've thought about you a lot," he blurted, and then quickly, "I know I

487

shouldn't talk like that, I'm a married man."

"I've thought about you a lot also, she replied, "And I know you're married," the last was said in a low voice, almost a whisper.

"I guess there's nothing we can do about it," he replied.

"I'm going to Meridian next week for a teacher's meeting. I could get away for awhile if you could be there."

"I'll be there," Sam promised.

Sam knew that a clandestine affair, of any duration, was out of the question. Body guards, or at the least one bodyguard, was his constant companion. He decided to confide in Tj.

"I want to talk to you about something personal," he said to Tj that afternoon, as he prepared to close his office for the day.

"What's on your mind boss," Tj asked, in his usual congenial manner.

Sam felt a little embarrassment. It wasn't going to be as easy as he had first thought.

"Ah, maybe I'll just forget all about it," Sam replied.

There was silence in the room for a good two minutes as Sam busied himself putting papers away.

"Is it about the cutesy little school teacher?" Tj asked.

"How could you possibly guess that?"

"Hell, Sammy, you're an open book. You are as predictable as the sun coming up. Do you know when you talked about that teacher the other day, I remember thinking that's the first female, other than family, you've mentioned to me since we came home from the war. It only takes a genius to figure that out."

"You got it right. She gave me a chance to see her next week, but I never have a minute alone. I thought you might know of some way."

"Hey, look Sammy, this is ole Tj you're talking to. That's the easiest assignment I've ever had. Leave it to me. Since she's willing, I'll get in touch with her and make all the arrangements."

And that's the way it began. Tj would make hotel reservations, in his own name, and when Maryrose arrived she would go to Mr. Johnson's room, which was an adjoining room to Sam's. It was a perfect cover for a straying husband.

The time Sam spent with Maryrose was exciting and satisfying. Every thing about her reminded him of Camille, her beautiful body, her passion and even the slight musty smell of her breath. Sam was reliving his youth.

The relationship ended on the same sort of condition. Their liaison had been in effect about three months, when she, with her face buried in her pillow, announced; "I'm pregnant."

A chill ran through Sam. His mind raced back in time to the bluffs overlooking Squaw Creek. He lay looking at the naked young woman lying beside him. She was on her stomach and the smooth curves of her rounded behind and legs were prominently displayed. There was no joy or excitement in the sight today. After a long wait, while neither moved nor spoke, Sam asked, "How could that happen? You said you were using a diaphragm."

"I did use it. I don't know how it happened. I'm so embarrassed," she answered.

Sam reached over and patted her smooth round bottom. "Don't worry," he said. "We'll

491

get you to a good doctor. He'll take care of it in short order."

Maryrose turned over and looked at him with cool blue eyes. "I hope you don't mean what I think you mean," she said. Her voice had a tone Sam had not heard before.

"You're a smart girl. What do you think I meant?" Sam's voice had also become crisp and hard.

Maryrose slid off the bed and started putting her clothes on. "I'm not going to abort this baby. It's the same as murder. I believe it's a mortal sin. God would never forgive me."

"How do you feel about breaking the seventh commandment?" he asked, with sarcasm in his voice.

"At least I wasn't married," she shot back, very heatedly.

"Wait a minute," Sam insisted, "Fighting won't solve a thing. We can work this out. What would you like for me to do"

"I don't want anything from you. Just get me out of here and on my way home. I never want to see you again," she said, in cool even tones.

A tinge of fear entered Sam's mind. He had visions of a pregnant woman near his home, announcing to the world who the father might be.

"I can imagine how it will be in your home community. I think forgiveness is not a part of their makeup. You won't be able to teach. What will you do?" He asked, his voice becoming more sympathetic.

Maryrose sat down as the truth of his statement sank in. Her big blue eyes filled with tears and her chin began to quiver.

Sam did not go to her, but he did offer some comfort with words. "You have a problem

493

with maintaining your reputation. And I have the same problem. It would benefit each of us if we would work together."

She dabbed at her eyes and in a small voice asked, "What do you have in mind?"

"Give me a few days to work it out and I'll get back to you," he replied.

The next day Tj listened as Sam explained the problem. Tj smiled but there was no mirth in his eyes. "It would sure cast a shadow on your image in the business world," his smile widened as he continued, "Alicia would kill you, after she wrecked this empire you two have built on love and trust."

"I don't need your sarcasm," Sam growled, "I know what the consequences will be if this thing gets out. I'm telling you this because I need some help, or at least some advice."

"Do you want me to take care of it?" Tj asked.

"I'd like to know what you do, before you do anything," Sam replied.

"The way I see it, she has a couple of options. One, she can abort, which you say she won't hear of, two, she can elect to have the baby and keep it. Which is not much of a choice if she plans to live in Bakertown. And the third choice is to put it up for adoption. How do you think she feels about choice number three?"

"I don't have any idea what this woman thinks, or what she might say," Sam replied.

"I'll see what I can do and let you know."

The next day Tj was back in Sam's office with a deal worked out. "The lady has agreed to put the baby up for adoption. She will move out of state. You provide her with a job until she can no longer work, pay all expenses, arrange for a job after the baby is born and she will call it even."

"That sounds like something you dreamed up and offered her," Sam guessed correctly.

"I had to have something to bargain with. There's just one problem. She's afraid to live alone in a strange city," Tj replied.

"The job and expenses I can take care of, I don't know about the living alone, I can't do anything about that. I don't want to involve another person, some one like a companion or nurse. And besides, I want to make sure the pregnancy can never be traced to me," Sam was emphatic.

"Sammy, with your money and my cunning we can fix this so no one could ever trace it back to you. Don't you know an obstetrician out of state?"

"Yeah, I know one. One of my war buddies. Jim Holland in Wichita, Kansas. I saw him

not long ago when I went to the Beech
Aircraft factory to pick a plane."

"You don't have to give him the details,
just get him to handle the adoption and I'll
take care of the rest. Tell him Tj will get
in touch in a couple of months."

"Why a couple of months?" Sam was
curious.

Tj smiled his mirthless smile, "No use
being in a hurry. It'll be a few months
before she starts to look pregnant. Give me
plenty of time to work out the details. And
to guarantee you won't be involved, I think
I should be her companion. You'll have to be
lenient with my time for me to work that
part. That way there will be only three
people who know who's guilty of what."

Sam had complete confidence in his friend
and employee, but he often did not
understand the cynicism that was a part of
Tj's personality.

"What do you get out of it?" Sam wanted to know.

"You pay me big bucks to work for you. Whatever you need is a part of the job. I'd just as soon be sitting on my ass in Kansas waiting for this lady to domino as to be on the way to Paris. It's just a part of the job."

"Seems to me you don't have much of a life. Don't you ever think about getting married?"

The smile left Tj's face and the eyes became even harder. "I was married-once. I got a Dear John letter when I was ass deep in mud and blood on a little island in the Pacific. That cured me. All broads are the same. You turn your back and they jump into the sack with the first bastard that comes along with a hard dick. I used to think you and Alicia had the ideal marriage, but you've probably fucked that up."

498

Sam was taken aback by the bitterness displayed by his friend who, outwardly, appeared happy go lucky. "I'm sorry," he said, "I didn't mean to stir up bad memories."

Tj waved his hand, "No problem. What is to be will be and what's done is done. You can forget about this little chore. I'll see that it never gets back to you."

Maryrose was four months pregnant when she and Tj moved to Wichita. They moved into an apartment in the Hillcrest apartment building. It was fairly luxurious and it had a security system that would allay Maryrose's fear of being alone when Tj was out of town. They posed as man and wife and used the names Thomas and Mary Brown. Tj had fake social security numbers made for each. They were actual numbers of people long dead. He got the names of the people who had owned the numbers from tombstones in a graveyard on North Hillside. He used just the numbers. This was a part of his plan to assure the anonymity of Sam Warden.

Tj contacted Doctor Holland and Maryrose signed the necessary papers using the name Mary Brown. The adoption was assured.

The Browns settled into a quiet life. Tj spent about half the time out of town taking care of his Warberg, Inc security job. He reported his activities at the monthly staff meetings in Parkersville. He and Sam never spoke of Maryrose. He spent the rest of his time in Wichita, much of it with Maryrose. He had his nights out "with the boys ", like any married man, he joked.

Tj discovered that Maryrose was a religious person. She loved to go to church and asked him to accompany her. He was surprised to find he was enjoying the service. He limited his drinking while in the apartment. He found himself looking forward to getting "home" when he was out of town.

Tj's talent for drawing became an asset when he was idle in Wichita. He and Maryrose would take a picnic basket to Riverside Park. They would have lunch and while she relaxed in the warm autumn sun, Tj would sketch the river scenery.

Maryrose told him he was the best artist she had ever seen. And she had seen a lot of them when she was going to college to become a teacher.

Tj asked her to pose for him in the apartment. She sat gazing out the window toward the city skyline. In the best oil painting he had done, he captured, not only her great beauty, but also the sadness of her eyes. He wouldn't let Maryrose see it until he was finished. When he unveiled it tears welled up in her eyes and she said, "I'm overwhelmed."

"It's for you, I want you to have it," Tj said.

She touched his hand and said, "Thank you, thank you for everything. You're a good friend."

"Think nothing of it," he replied. He started to say, its just part of the job, but changed his mind.

One of their neighbors was a young couple named Manning. They had a beautiful little girl named Julie. Outside of the Manning apartment there was a sun deck where little Julie played. The Brown's sun deck was adjacent to the Manning deck.

One day Julie fell asleep in her sandbox. The sun in her blonde hair formed a halo around her pink face. In one hand she held a ragged old doll, in the other hand she held a small spade. Tj quickly sketched the child as she slept; he then took several photographs with his camera in order to capture the light and the coloring. When the film was developed he painted an outstanding portrait of the child and titled it: Julie Sleeping. When it was complete, he asked Maryrose to invite the Manning's over for coffee.

Mr. Manning was out of town but Mrs. Manning accepted. When she and Maryrose were chatting, Tj brought the portrait of Julie and said, "Here is something I want you to have," and he handed it to her. The mother gazed at the beautiful work and burst into tears.

A few days later Mr. Manning stopped by the Brown's apartment. "I want to pay you for the painting of my daughter, it must have taken a tremendous amount of work."

Tj smiled and said, "I was paid more than money when Mrs. Manning burst into tears. That told me how much she cherished it."

"I want to thank you. It is outstanding. We'll never part with it." He shook hands with Tj and thanked him again and again.

It was February when labor pains began for Maryrose. She called out to Tj who was in the adjacent room. He hurried to her side. "We'd better go to the hospital," she said.

Tj found himself fumbling in his haste. He dropped the telephone, then dialed the wrong number. When he reached Dr Holland, he could her a groan on the other end of the line.

When Maryrose and Tj got to the parking garage and opened the door they discovered why the doctor had groaned. Sleet and snow was blowing horizontally across the landscape. It was a Kansas blizzard, driven by a thirty mile per hour wind.

Tj cursed the weather and was glad they were close to Wesley Hospital. He drove with utmost caution through the mounting drifts. They arrived at the hospital without mishap.

"It's a good thing you didn't wait an hour or two," he said to Maryrose. "We might have had to use the kitchen table."

Tj began the vigil that most fathers experience. It went on through the night. Early the next morning Dr Holland came by the waiting room and told Tj it was all over. The doctor had made all the arrangements and had planned that Maryrose would never see the child.

"Can I see the baby?" Tj asked.

"This way," Dr Holland said, "I take it you're not the father."

"That's right. I'm not," Tj replied.

The baby was a boy, dark haired, with chubby fists pushed up against his face. Tj stared for a few minutes and then walked away. Doctor Holland had told him the adoption was going according to plan.

505

When Maryrose awoke from the drugged sleep, Tj was by her side. He was attentive while she was confined to the hospital. He brought flowers and presents. They did not discuss the baby. A part of the plan was to tell the curious that the baby had been stillborn.

On the third day Maryrose was discharged from the hospital and they went back to the apartment. She had a woebegone look that had grown more pronounced since the birth of the baby. Tj knew she was crying in the night. Once he had heard muffled sobs coming from her room. He thought he had become totally callused to the feelings of people in general and women in particular. But in spite of himself he began to have a deep feeling of pity for the sad young woman.

Tj's plan had been beautiful in its simplicity. He would tie up the loose ends in Wichita, make sure his tracks were covered and he and Maryrose would return to Mississippi, where an apartment and a job awaited Maryrose in the city of Meridian. He would become Tj Johnson again and Mary Brown would vanish and become Maryrose Boden.

When they checked out of the apartment and were on the way to the airport he said, "You need a vacation. How would you like to go to California?"

"I've used enough of your time," she replied, "I'm ready to go back to where I belong."

"Forget about my time. I'm on the old expense account, remember?"

"How can I forget? But, I've never been to California."

"Then it's settled," Tj declared, "California here we come."

They flew to San Diego, rented a car and drove up the coast toward Los Angeles. They walked on wet beaches, bare-foot, and ate in small, off the beaten path, cafes.

When they stopped for the night Tj would get adjoining rooms. They would leave the connecting door open between the rooms. He thought it might make her feel less alone with him being nearby.

One night they stopped at a motel and were told that a festival in town had most of the rooms filled. All they could get was a room with two beds. Tj told Maryrose that maybe they should keep looking.

"What difference does it make?" Maryrose asked, "We are close when we have two rooms. We'll just have to take turns with the bathroom."

It worked well enough to satisfy the weary travelers. They bathed and watched television from their beds before turning off the lights.

During the night Tj awoke to hear muffled sobs coming from Maryrose's bed. He lay staring at the ceiling as the unhappy sounds continued. He slipped from his bed and sat on the floor by her. He whispered, "Are you alright?"

Maryrose reached for him in the dark, and buried her head against his shoulder. Her tears wet his nightshirt as her body jerked with harsh sobs. Tj held her close and stroked her hair.

"Go ahead and cry. It will help you to get over the pain you are feeling," he said gently.

"I, I, I didn't even get to see my baby," she stammered, her voice quavered as she spoke. "I don't even know if it was a boy or a girl. It's not fair. It's cruel."

In his heart Tj was agreeing with her. He had planned to never mention seeing the baby, but here in the dark with the heartbroken mother he changed his mind. "I saw the baby," he said.

The sobs stopped. Maryrose turned on the lights. Her eyes were puffy from crying. "You saw my baby? What was it? How did it look?"

"It was a fine boy. Lots of black hair like yours."

"How did you manage to see him?" Maryrose was tense and looking Tj straight in the eye.

"I asked the doctor and he showed me the baby."

"Why didn't you tell me? I thought he had died."

"I didn't know how to tell you," Tj said, miserably. "I'm sorry I ever had anything to do with this whole affair. I didn't know what I was getting into."

"Don't say that. I don't know what I would have done without you. I feel like you are the only true friend I have in the world," she was thoughtful for a moment, then, "Let's go home tomorrow."

Tj looked at his watch," It's tomorrow already, if we get up now we can make it back to San Diego and be on our way tonight."

Just knowing her baby was alive gave Maryrose a lift. Tj could see a change from the sad young woman that had started the trip. Sometimes she would smile as he cracked some corny joke.

In Meridian Mississippi Tj made sure Maryrose was in her apartment and had the necessities for living and going to work. He was anxious to get away.

Back at Warberg, Inc headquarters, he contacted some of his subordinates to find what had been going on during his latest absence. On Monday he showed up at the staff meeting and made his report in his usual off hand manner. Afterwards he talked to Sam, but did not mention anything about Maryrose.

"I think you should make a trip to New York. We're having some shipping problems. You probably need a change of pace," Sam said, "Strickland can give you the details," (Naming one of Tj's subordinates.) "And by the way, there's a nice bonus for a job well done."

Tj smiled his go to hell smile and said, "Thanks boss I'm on my way."

The company pilot flew him to Jackson where he caught an American Airlines 707. He leaned back in his first class seat with a double shot of Jack Daniels in his hand and took a big sip. The whiskey was warm to his belly and the friendly stewardess made him think of a party at the end of the line. "Tj," he thought, "You old bastard, you've got it made." He sipped his whiskey and when it was gone, the friendly stewardess brought him another one.

He rolled the ice around the glass and thought some more. "If you're so damn lucky why are you so miserable?"

Tj wasn't sure what it was. In New York he spent the night with the stewardess. Local people had solved the shipping problem. He allowed as how he could take the credit. After all it was solved about the time he arrived. He went to a bar that night with a couple of friends and drank too much whiskey. The friends had to leave to go home to waiting wives. He drank some more. He bought a bottle and took it to his room. He had decided to get stoned.

With the bottle in his hand he sat staring out the hotel window. He went to the telephone and dialed Maryrose's number. Her soft voice came over the wire. His tongue thick with liquor he mumbled, "I'se jest wondering if you is alright?"

"I'm fine Tj. Are you alright?"

"Never better. I jest been working and wanted to say hello," he was trying to sound normal.

"Tj, do you know what time it is?"

He looked at his watch through a haze of alcohol and said, "I'll be damned, it's two in the morning."

"Tj, are you drunk?" Maryrose asked.

"Damn near it," he replied.

"Why Tj, why are you getting drunk? I thought you had cut way back on your drinking."

"I'm sorry I called so late. I just lost track of time. I been celebrating something but I can't remember what it was."

"It is nice to hear from you, even at this hour. I'll worry about you. You shouldn't drink like that," Mary rose's voice was gentle.

Tj was beginning to wonder why he was calling her in the middle of the night. "I'd better say goodnight," he said.

"Goodnight Tj," she said, and hung up the phone.

After returning to Parkersville Tj spent the next several weeks being a bodyguard for Sam. The company had purchased a new Beechcraft airplane. Sam was the pilot and most of the time there was only the two of them. On one trip to Los Angeles Alicia went along. While Sam was conducting his business, Alicia asked Tj to accompany her on a shopping trip.

They were good friends and were comfortable with each other. They went into an exclusive ladies apparel shop and as they strolled along Alicia said, "I've always wanted to own a ladies dress shop. I believe

I would be good at managing such an establishment."

"You're one of the owners of this big Warberg, Inc. operation. Whatever would they do without you?" Tj's voice was tinged with sarcasm.

"Don't get smart. You know damn well the company is Sam's toy. I'd like to try something on my own."

"Well, ma'am why don't you just go ahead and jump into the business. You could name it Alicia's. I can see that name in neon lights, winking in my mind's eye," Tj was teasing.

"I had been wondering what to name my new business and you just handed me the right name, thanks," Alicia said.

"You're serious, aren't you?"

"I am now," she replied.

That was the beginning of an independent company, and operated by Alicia Warden. On the way home she was flying copilot in the Beechcraft when she broached the subject to Sam. His response was simple. "If that's what you want to do, by all means have at it."

Alicia's interest in a business separate from Warberg, Inc. consumed a lot of her time. And most of that time was spent away from Sam. Since their marriage they had shared a passionate love life that had satisfied Sam's sexual appetite. Now with her business interest causing her to be away from home, he started feeling neglected.

On one of their frequent business trips out of town he confided in his friend and bodyguard, Tj.

Tj smiled his mirthless smile. "I have a philosophy about pussy," he said, "It's like sleep. You might get some more, but you'll never get what you miss. I try to never miss any."

"You don't have my problem," Sam replied, "I have a wife that I would like to keep. She promised years ago that if she caught me fooling around she would cut off my balls. It would break my mother's heart if we divorced and her grand children were taken some place besides Lone Pine. And I have a reputation to maintain. You're like an old rogue bull. You jump the fence and screw everything you can get your hands on. You don't give a damn what the world thinks of you. And everything you do seems to place you in a more favorable light."

"Man, if I had your dough and your position in the frigging community I would have no trouble getting all the nooky I could handle and no one would be the wiser," Tj stated, emphatically.

"I'm not interested in your tactics, but for the sake of this conversation, what would you do in a situation like mine?"

"There's a place in New Orleans where you can get anything in the world that you can pay for and your anonymity is absolutely guaranteed. I know this guy who has a nation wide chain of call girls. Young, often married women, some of them are college girls working their way through school, are his hookers. You can get an Asian virgin if you have the dough. This guy leases a floor of a top hotel in the city where he has an operation. A hundred grand buys a membership, just a number on a card key. A thousand bucks a night will satisfy the most horny, discriminating man, or woman," Tj finished his explanation with a wave of his hand.

"It sounds like a high priced whorehouse to me," Sam said.

"I guess you're probably right, but a person don't have to worry about his wife or the preacher finding out about his infidelity."

"How do you know so much about this fancy cat house?"

"The guy who runs the operation is a marine buddy of mine. I did him a favor one time and he gave me a night in the New Orleans bordello, on the house," Tj's mouth twisted in a cynical smile.

"This guy is really slick. You know how some hotels don't have a thirteenth floor showing on the elevator. Well, this fellow owns the thirteenth floor. You ride the regular elevator to the top floor, get off and then your card key opens a private elevator door that will take you to the thirteenth. In Vegas all he has is blonde California college girls. If you want to live I recommend that."

"It sounds interesting," Sam admitted.

"I can arrange a sample night with my friend for a thousand bucks. You can select your 'date' from a group of pictures."

"Let's go to New Orleans," Sam said.

The thirteenth floor in the New Orleans hotel was everything Tj had described. Sam became a member of the club. A few weeks later, on the way home from California, Sam set the Beechcraft down in Los Vegas.

"Do you want to go to the thirteenth floor with me?" he asked Tj.

"Not me, that's too rich for my blood," Tj replied.

"Go as my guest. I'll pay, charge it to the expense account," Sam insisted.

"I wouldn't pay a hundred bucks for the best piece of tail in the world, much less a thousand. And it's against my principals to pay anything for it, or let anybody else pay for me. In this town the women pay me," Tj was smiling as he walked away.

Tj walked through the casino on his way to the lobby of the hotel where he had a room reserved. A little cocktail waitress smiled at him and he waved to her. In his room he called Maryrose. She had just arrived home from work. She was well. He stretched out on his bed and fell asleep.

Sam became a regular visitor to the thirteenth floor club as he traveled around the country. That was his only vice. He was good to his wife and kids. He went to church. He gave generously of his wealth. The Warden schools were a model for other states. A poor person could attend and learn a trade, at no charge for tuition. The school worked diligently to place the graduates in good paying jobs, and with Sam's help that endeavor was highly successful. Many of them found employment with Warberg Inc.

One day, out of a clear blue sky, Sam asked Tj. "Do you ever see Maryrose?"

It had been six months since Tj had seen her. In his mind weekly calls didn't count.

"No I haven't. Why?" he could feel himself getting tense.

"I would like to see her. Do you know where to reach her?"

"I could probably find her. You have all the women in the country to pick from. Why this one?" Tj's eyes had hardened.

"It's not the same with all these other women. Find her for me," Sam was bent over his desk and did not see the reaction of his security chief.

The smile had left Tj's face and had been replaced by a grim look. He started to speak, changed his mind and walked from the room.

In the parking lot he sat in his car trying to sort out his emotions. He was angry for some reason that was foreign to his nature. After awhile he drove south to Meridian.

He was parked at the curb in front of her house when Maryrose got off the bus at the corner. She came walking toward him in the warm summer sun. A short dress with no sleeves and a belt at the waist showed her trim shapely figure. She was more beautiful than he remembered.

When she was turning to walk to the house Tj spoke and she turned to face him as he got out of the car. Her eyes shone with pleasure as she recognized who had spoken.

"Tj what are you doing here?" she asked as she ran to him and embraced him.

Tj held her close for a moment. The fragrance of her hair brought back the memories of the trip to California and then he knew. "I just wanted to take you out to dinner," he replied. "That is if you're not busy."

"I'm not busy and even if I were I would change my plans for you," she said.

Arm in arm they walked into her apartment. Tj sat and looked around the tidy place, as Maryrose was getting ready to go out. Everything was as neat as could be. The portrait he had painted of her was hanging in a prominent place. It was the first thing to catch a person's eye when walking into the room.

They dined at a quiet place and talked of Wichita and California and the things they had seen together. When they returned to the apartment, Tj caught her by the arm and turned her to face him.

"Maryrose," he asked, "Will you marry me?"

Her beautiful eyes widened with surprise. "Tj, I never dreamed—of course I will."

He gathered her small body into his arms and held her close. "I love you. I don't know when it started. But I'm miserable when I'm away from you."

"I love you too Tj, you're the best person I've ever known. I've loved you ever since that night in the motel in California."

They were married the next day by a justice of the peace.

Tj returned to Parkersville the following day and met Sam in his office.

"I'm quitting my job. Maryrose and I were married yesterday," he announced.

Sam kept his usual poker face. "Why would getting married cause you to quit your job?"

"I'm tired of pimping for you. I'm tired of doing your dirty work. Alicia is my friend and I'm ashamed of what I've been doing to her by covering your betrayal. And the main reason is; I don't like myself," Tj was brutally frank.

The scar on Sam's cheek was a red streak. "If you feel that way then you had better leave," he said in a calm matter of fact voice. "What will you tell Alicia?"

"I'll tell her I'm married and I want to stay at home with my wife."

And that's what he did. He went to see Alicia and told her he was leaving Warberg, Inc. She was surprised and upset but he didn't wait around for her to question his reasons for leaving a very good job.

Tj and Maryrose moved to Gulfport Mississippi where he got a job as a policeman and she taught in the local grade school. They were happy. Tj had time to pursue his painting and after a few years he made a quiet name for himself as an artist.

Their marriage produced two children, a girl and a boy. Tj's heart was at peace. He loved Maryrose and she loved him in return. They never mentioned Sam Warden, or Warberg, Inc. although both were often in the news.

Sam and Alicia were a good match. Both were successful in any business endeavor they put their efforts into. Lone Pine was home base. Angela and Henry were happy because the grandchildren were near. Secretly, Angela felt as if they raised the kids because Alicia and Sam were away from home so much.

Angela's dreams for Sam had all come true. He was a pillar in the community, active in civil rights, a strong supporter and an innovator for worker's rights. Warberg, Inc.'s employees were among industry's best compensated. They had health insurance, savings plans, and a pension for life. Sam had given Jose and Ava Williams a plot of ground and had built them a new house near Lone Pine. He included them in the Warberg, Inc. corporate pension plan.

Jose Williams summed it up for the county when he said, "Kun'l Sam is the best thing that ever happened to this state."

The aging Lee Brown echoed that statement with, "The best investment I ever made was the day I hired that Warden boy."

Sam was a sought after speaker. He was often quoted in newspapers and magazines. The most often quote was, "We are all part of the same thing, all living things. God has granted humans with the power of reason. We should use that intelligence to take care of all creatures and more especially the young children of the human race."

Sam had always resisted the call of the politicians. The Governor's office, the U.S. congress and the U.S. senate had all been dangled before him. In 1984 the Independent party asked him to be their standard bearer at the convention. The party leaders pleaded with him. "With your record, all of your accomplishments and what you stand for, we believe we can break the two party system."

What convinced Sam to accept was the attitude of his family. Angela thought it was the greatest thing that could happen to her. Alicia said, "I'll make a hell of a first lady." And their daughter chimed in with, "Dad, as handsome as you are you'll get all the ladies' vote".

Sam was indeed a handsome man. His body was slim and hard from a life of discipline. His hair was iron gray and the scar on his cheek called attention to the smooth planes of the rest of his face. A small shiver of excitement ran through him when he thought about being President of the United States. He had accomplished more than most men. His two children had turned out to be good business people. They held positions of importance in companies other than Warberg, Inc. It had been their choice. They were both married and had made Sam and Alicia grandparents. What else is there left for me to do? Sam asked himself. It was 1988 and he was sixty-two years old. He could have passed for forty-five. He could not remember having failed at anything he had tried to do.

Chapter 11

In Seattle Washington, twenty seven year old Kevin Wright walked through his computer factory with a sense of satisfaction. The assembly line was humming with activity. The work moved steadily to the packaging area where the finished product was placed in boxes that proclaimed: The Wright Computer For You.

The Wright Computer was the product of Kevin's years of work on computers. He had become interested when he was in high school and had purchased a kit and assembled his own. He assembled computers for his friends and in his hometown of Tukwila, Washington, if one wanted to know any thing about computers they talked to Kevin Wright. He studied electrical engineering at the University of Washington. His father worked as an electrical engineer for Boeing and had encouraged his son to follow in his footsteps. But in his third year at the university he switched to computer science and took his degree in that field.

He first began assembling computers in his father's garage. He believed computers in general were grossly overpriced and he had been in business only a short time when he proved that to be true. He purchased the components from companies that specialized in that discipline and assembled them in a low cost environment. He made a profit from the beginning. He improved his product and expanded to a small factory, employing four people. When he was twenty-four years old, a computer magazine awarded him: "The Best Computer Of The Year," award, for the PC user. He was swamped with orders, which led to a new building and the new, The Wright

Computer For You, line of personal computers.

Kevin was a happy family man as well as a successful businessman. He had married his high-school sweetheart, Carol Swanson, during his second year at the University. They had a three-year-old daughter named, Clara Joann. The Clara was for Carol's maternal grandmother.

Kevin had lived most of his life in Seattle. His Tukwila home had a clear view of Mt Rainier. Puget sound afforded an abundance of fishing. His father set a good example for his son, by spending a lot of time with the boy and his sister Paula.

Kevin was an adopted son. After he had been with the Wrights for three years Paula was born. Early in his life his parents told him he was adopted. They told him how special he was and they gave him all the love and attention that any boy could wish for. He accepted the adoption without question. It was somewhere in his early memory and he had almost forgotten about it.

One weekend he and his family went to a super bowl celebration at his parents house. Bill and Lucille Wright enjoyed having a party. In addition to Kevin's family, Paula and her boy friend, Carol's parents, her brother and his family, were present. This was a group that had often been together for festive occasions. There was only one difference in this party.

Paula had been working on the Wright family tree. She had made a chart that began in England and moved through the American colonies, through the Western expansion, where Bill's branch of the Wright's had settled in Kansas. Old photographs were shown and many laughs resulted from the comments about who looked like what ancestor. Kevin and Paula were, of course, shown as the son and daughter of Bill and Lucille Wright.

That night when Kevin was preparing for bed, he stared in the mirror. His copper colored hair and brown eyes were in contrast to the blue eyes and almost blonde hair of the Wrights. When he slipped into bed by Carol's side, he lay quietly for a moment and then said, "I wonder who I am, really."

Carol put her arms around him and said, "You're my big handsome husband and I love you."

Kevin held her close. He could smell the fragrance of her hair. He kissed her cheek and said, "You smell like flowers and taste like heaven. And in spite of that pleasant distraction I still wonder who I am, and I intend to find out."

Carol sat up in bed and said, "You might find something you wouldn't like. You have a great life. There must be some unhappiness

associated with your biological parents.
Anyone who would give you up must have been
in dire straits."

"You might be right," Kevin replied, "But
then I'll know."

Carol knew it was useless to argue when
he had made up his mind. She was certain he
would be successful in his quest.

The next day he talked to Paula. She
tried to change his mind. "You're my big
brother. Who has helped me through school
and always tried to protect me from
everything. I don't want that to change, let
it go."

"I don't want to let it go. It won't
change anything between you and me. You did
all this family tree stuff, how can I go
about finding who my real parents were."

Paula winced at "real parents" but she
replied, "It's easy. There's an agency in
Seattle that specializes in that sort of

thing. You were born in Wichita, Kansas. In two days they'll probably have the whole story. They guarantee results"

Paula was dead wrong. Tj had done his work to perfection. Two weeks passed after Kevin had employed the agency when the lady in charge called him on the telephone and gave him a progress report.

"We've struck a blank wall," she said, "Someone took great pains to make sure your parents were never found. And they may have succeeded. We'll keep trying, but it won't be easy."

"Why would they go to all that trouble?" Kevin asked.

"Oh, there are all kinds of reasons. It happens. Not very often, but it still happens. We'll talk to you later," and she hung up.

Days slipped into weeks and the agency had nothing more to add. Kevin talked it over with his father who advised him to use a Wichita detective agency. Bill knew of a good one in that city. Kevin called and employed one of the operatives.

The results were the same as those experienced by the Seattle Adoption Tracing Agency. A dead end street. The detective agency compiled a report and sent it with the bill for services rendered. The report named the couple listed as the parents, Tj and Mary Brown. Social Security numbers taken from deceased people. Phony addresses for references they had given. The detective made a thorough report and a final recommendation. "Give it up. There is no way to locate the people you seek."

When Kevin gave the report to Carol she read it and said, "Honey, maybe it's for the best. Things have a way of working out." She was not surprised, when a few days later he said, "Let's you and me go to Wichita."

They stopped by the Wichita detective agency and went over the report with the man who had been assigned to the case. "I have to be honest with you," he said, "You could spend all kinds of money and the result would be the same. This is a dead end street. The one bit of evidence I got was that both people had a southern accent. The doctor, a Dr.Holland, might have had the answer, but he was killed in an airplane crash a few years ago. I'm sorry we couldn't help."

Kevin said, "I think I'll go talk to the neighbors they had at that time. At least I'll get to talk to someone who has seen my parents."

Kevin and Carol went to the Manning residence listed on the report. Mrs. Manning answered the door and when Kevin stated their purpose, She said, "My goodness that couple is sure getting a lot of attention, you're about the third or fourth group that has been asking about them in the last few weeks. It's such a long time ago it's hard to remember all the details."

Kevin said, "I'm sorry to bother you again. I'm afraid that I'm the cause of all the people nosing around. You see, I'm an adoptee and I think those two people might be my parents."

Mrs. Manning's eyes and mouth both widened with surprise and interest. "Well I declare," she said, "Do come in. I didn't really know what was going on. So many people snooping around it just became a nuisance. Let me get you a cup of coffee. Please sit down."

Mrs. Manning bustled around in the neat house getting the coffee ready. Kevin and Carol sat waiting for the busy lady to stop long enough for them to talk a few minutes.

Carol sat with her "I'm ready for anything" expression on her face.

Mrs. Manning brought the coffee and sat down. She looked at Kevin and said, "You look like Mary. She was so beautiful. We never knew what happened. We were out of town and when we returned they had moved away. We were told the baby had died at birth. I just can't believe they would put their baby up for adoption. They were so devoted."

Kevin explained to Mrs. Manning the process he had initiated and the complete failure to locate Tj and Mary Brown. "I thought I would like to talk to someone who had actually known my parents. That way I wouldn't feel like I had no background at all. I hope you can see my point of view?"

"I sure can," Mrs. Manning, said, "I'll try to remember all I can. They were very nice people. The mister had some kind of traveling job. He was away from home a lot of the time. Mary would sometimes baby sit with our daughter Julie. Oh, and that reminds me, the mister was some sort of painter. He did a portrait of our daughter. I had completely forgotten about it until now. I didn't remember to tell the other people about it. I wonder where that thing is! If you have time to wait I'll see if I can find it."

Kevin looked at Carol, who was beginning to show the wear of the day. He said, "Mrs. Manning, we appreciate all you have done. If we could have your phone number we'll call later in the evening and see if you have located it."

Mrs. Manning agreed and Kevin and Carol went back to their hotel where they had dinner and settled down for an evening of rest and television.

"Let's go home tomorrow," Carol said, "I don't like to leave Clara very long at a time, even if she is with your mother."

"OK, babe," Kevin replied, "I guess this is just a wild goose chase anyway. I might as well give it up. I told that lady I'd call. So let's see if she found anything. Either way it looks like we struck out. An orphan is an orphan is an orphan."

"Damn," Carol said, "I've never heard you feel sorry for yourself before. Poor little orphan."

"Not sorry for myself, just frustrated," Kevin replied.

The next morning Kevin called Mrs. Manning. She was excited. She had found the portrait of Julie and couldn't wait to show it to Kevin and Carol. They went back to the Manning home and found that Mrs. Manning had set the portrait on an easel facing the door. When they walked into the house the first thing they saw was the portrait, Julie Sleeping.

"We just packed it away one time when we moved and as time went by it just slipped our minds. I'd forgotten about it until you people started asking about the Browns," Mrs. Manning said.

"It is a remarkable piece of work," Kevin said, "Don't you think so Carol?"

"It is beautiful," she replied.

Kevin took the portrait and examined it closely. There was no indication of the identity of the artist. "Could I take it out of the frame?"

"Well, sure if you think it will help. Let me get you some tools," Mrs. Manning replied.

Kevin removed the backing and gingerly lifted the portrait from the wide flanged frame. As he turned it over he saw in the lower right hand corner, the initials Tj.

The T was upper case and the j was lower case; the cross bar of the T was long and covered the j like an umbrella.

"Just like all artists, he had to leave his mark," Carol said. "Now if we just knew who Tj is we would have this thing solved."

"Did any of the other investigators see the portrait?" Kevin asked.

"No, I didn't think about it," Mrs. Manning replied.

Kevin started to reassemble the portrait when he noticed a paint smudge on the back. "Look at this Carol, what do you think?"

"Looks like the painter got some wet paint on—you don't think it might be a finger print do you?"

"If it is it is pretty faint. Mrs. Manning could we borrow this long enough to take it to the police department and have them check out this smudge?"

"Well, I don't know, sometimes they destroy things trying to locate something. But if you'll make them be extra careful I guess you can," she reluctantly agreed.

"Why don't you go with us just to keep everyone honest, "Kevin suggested.

A spirit of adventure caused Mrs. Manning to readily agree and in a short time they were at the Police Department. Kevin explained to the officer in charge what they were attempting. The paint smudge was indeed a faint fingerprint. A close scrutiny by the powerful police magnification system revealed two more faint prints.

The police officer said, "They are finger prints, but that's all I can tell you. I can't check them out for you. It's against department policy."

When they were outside the police department, Kevin said, "I believe we should get our private detective back into the picture." They were near the detective agency, which was on Market Street. They stopped by and Kevin explained their trip to the police station.

The private investigator who had worked on the case was an ex-policeman named Carl Wilson. He had been unhappy about his inability to locate the Browns and was ready to help in any way he could. "Leave the portrait with me and I'll have you something tomorrow," he promised.

"No, I can't let you keep the portrait. Something might happen to it," Mrs. Manning protested.

"Look lady," Carl said, "We can cover the portrait with heavy cardboard and just leave the back exposed. I guarantee its safety."

Carl's assurance and the anxious look on Kevin's face caused her to reluctantly agree.

The next day Carl called and said, tersely, "Come see me."

On the way to the agency office the Wrights picked up Mrs. Manning.

When they arrived Carl said, "We picked up enough of a finger print to get an identification. He's an ex-marine named Thomas Jefferson Johnson. He was born in Parkersville, Mississippi. He now lives in Gulfport, Mississippi. Where he lives now was the easy part. I just called the telephone company. Don't ask me about the first part and I won't tell you any lies. And ma'am, he said to Mrs. Manning, "There's not a blemish on the portrait. That sure is a pretty thing."

"Thanks for taking care of it," she replied.

Kevin shook hands with Carl and thanked him. "Just send me a bill," he said. Carl grinned and waved his hand.

549

The Wrights took Mrs. Manning home and thanked her for the only solid lead the investigation had revealed. "I don't know how I can ever thank you enough," Kevin told her as they said goodbye. It was also goodbye to Wichita. That afternoon they caught a flight back to Seattle.

After they changed planes in Denver, Carol was passing time by looking through a magazine. She saw an article titled; Rising Artist. There was a picture of a heavy set, balding, man. Some photographs of his work were displayed on the pages of the magazine. In the right hand corner the initials, Tj, were clearly visible. "Look at this," she said to Kevin.

Kevin read the magazine's biographical article about Tj Johnson, who lived in Gulfport Mississippi. He had lost his wife to an automobile accident the year before. He was becoming renown for his work, etc.

There was no doubt about the signature. "It looks like this just reinforces the information we already have," he said.

"I can't imagine you having any artist genes. You can't draw a straight line using a straight edge," Carol teased.

"I have other qualities, "Kevin replied. "Now that we have all this information, I wonder just how to use it."

"I've been thinking about the same thing. What is our next move? You can't just call him up and say I'm your long lost son."

"That would probably give him one hell of a shock," Kevin was gazing at Tj's picture as he spoke. "I have no feeling at all when I see the photograph of the man who is supposed to be my father. I thought I would be excited. And apparently my mother is dead and I'll never get to see her."

Carol patted his hand and said, "Maybe we should just drop the whole thing. Already there's sadness about the death of the lady, and there's no telling what else you'll uncover."

"You are right about that, uncovering things I mean. But I want to know the story, so I guess I'll just plug along. What do you think I should do next?"

Carol had been enjoying the intrigue of finding lost parents. It was an adventure for her and she loved being included in Kevin's plans. "Maybe I could call him and say I am working for and insurance company and trying to locate someone named Bill Johnson, and does he know of anyone by that name."

"What good would that do?" Kevin asked.

"We would find out if he's at home for one thing."

"What if he really knows a Bill Johnson?"

"Oh, after he described his Bill, I would say it was the wrong man. Then I would find out if he is going to be at home for awhile, and we could fly down there and you could talk to him."

"That could work," Kevin smiled, "You surprise me, once in awhile."

After they were home for a few days Carol tried calling Tj's home but there was no answer. She tried every evening for a week but the result was the same. Kevin became impatient and hired a detective agency in Gulfport to locate him. In a few hours the agency reported that Tj was out of the country on a trip to Europe. Kevin asked the agency to make an appointment for the Wrights to visit him when he returned. "Tell him you have a client on the west coast who is trying to locate a missing relative and thinks he might have some information."

Two weeks later Kevin and Carol were driving down the Mississippi coast toward Gulfport. They had flown into New Orleans and rented a car. "Are you excited?" Carol asked her husband, who had been driving along in silence mile after mile.

"I can't say I am," He replied. It's a bit like a task you set for yourself and you want to see it finished."

"I know, you're not the excitable type." Which was true about Kevin

"I get excited about you."

"I'm thankful for that."

With the small bantering talk time slipped by. They came to the city limits of Gulfport and in a short time were on the street where Tj lived.

It was late afternoon and Tj had been expecting his west coast visitors. When they pulled into his driveway he walked out to meet them. Smiling he held out his hand to Kevin and said, "I'm Tj Johnson."

Shaking his hand Kevin said, "I'm Kevin Wright and this is my Wife Carol."

Tj shook hands with Carol and said, "My, they sure have pretty girls in your part of the coastal area." She liked him immediately.

"Come in, let me get you something to drink. I have a fresh pot of coffee. I hope you like coffee, or I could get you a cola."

They assured him coffee would be fine and while Tj was out of the room, Carol whispered, "I think he's nice." Kevin nodded his agreement. They looked around the living room, which was neat and clean but had a look of not being used very much.

Tj returned with the coffee and when everyone was served, he sat on the sofa by Carol and said, "What can I help you with?" looking at Kevin, with a friendly smile crinkling the corners of his eyes.

Kevin cleared his throat, a little nervously, and said, "I was born in Wichita,

Kansas February 10, 1957, I—" he was cut off by Tj.

"I knew it. I knew it the minute you stepped out of the car. I could see it." Tj spoke with enthusiasm.

Kevin was startled by the reaction, "I was searching for my parents, my biological parents—" he began and was interrupted again.

Tj held up his hand, "First, let me say, I'm not your father. I was there when you were born. I am the man you're searching for. Your mother was my wife. We were married some time after your birth. We used the name Brown in Wichita. I took care of her. I was hired to do that. It was some time later that I realized that I was in love with her. She was the best thing that ever happened in my life. My greatest regret is not acting in time to save you from adoption. She grieved about you all the days of her life. Even though we had two children together. We couldn't find who had adopted you. That door was closed as tightly as the one I tried to close. Tell me, how in the world did you locate me?"

Kevin told him of the efforts they had put forth and the failures. And the success brought about by an old fingerprint in paint on the back of the portrait; Julie Sleeping.

Tj shook his head in disbelief, "That's unbelievable. That's just pure luck young man, or maybe it's fate. Who knows? The older I get the less sure I am about a lot of things."

"I'm sorry to hear about the death of your wife, that is, I should say my mother."

"I was crushed. It almost wrecked me. It was a car accident, if you can call it an accident; she was struck by a drunken driver just a few blocks from the house. The driver got a slap on the wrists and now he's back on the streets." The usual smiling man was misty eyed.

"I thought I had found my father, but you won't claim me so I'm still looking. Can you help me?"

"Let me adopt you," Tj was smiling again, "And we'll forget about you looking further." Then he turned sober. "I can't help you. The man is married and the reasons for secrecy still exist. I gave my word. And I must not go back on my promise."

Kevin looked at Carol, "I guess we can go back home tomorrow hon, this is a dead end street." He started to thank Tj for his help.

"No wait, you have been searching for your roots, let me show you one side of it. You have all kinds of relatives, all in one place not far from here. Stay with me tonight and we'll go up to Bakertown tomorrow. We'll stop at the cemetery where

Maryrose is buried. She'll be pleased that we got together."

Kevin was touched by what Tj said. He looked at Carol and she nodded assent.

In the evening they dined at a seafood restaurant where Tj boasted they had the best seafood in the world and Kevin said that if they did have it must have come from Puget Sound. They talked far into the night. Tj showed family photographs and home movies. It was scene after scene of a happy family and Kevin saw his mother as a living beautiful person. He was touched with sorrow that he would never see her alive. The Johnson children, Thomas and Rose, were shown from babyhood through young adulthood. It was like growing up with them in one evening.

"It would be nice to meet Thomas and Rose," Kevin said as the movie ended

Tj was silent as he rewound the film. Then turning to face Kevin he said, "I don't know how to say this, so I won't even try to be careful. Tom and Rosie are your half brother and sister. It would be nice for you to get to know them, I think. My problem is, I don't know how to tell them about you. They think their mother was a saint. How can I tell them something that would change the way they feel?"

Kevin was quick to grasp the implications. "I can see what you mean. I wouldn't know how to tell you to do that. And I wouldn't want to change the way they feel. If I get a chance to meet them maybe you could just say I am the son of an old friend."

Tj smiled his most disarming smile. "My kids never thought I was a saint. I could claim you as a long lost son. They would believe that."

Kevin and Carol could see the irony of the situation. Kevin replied, "You would make a nice father, but I have one of the best. We're not faced with that problem at the moment, and maybe we won't have to be. Where do they live?"

"Rosie is a nurse in California and Tom is in the army stationed in Germany. I just got back from paying them a visit. My first grandchild is six months old."

"We'll think of something before we have to cross that bridge," Kevin said.

The next morning they drove north through the pine covered forests of Mississippi. Along the way Tj amused the young couple with tales of the south, and especially about Kevin's ancestors. "Your mother was a Baker and the Bakers came to Mississippi before the civil war. They were too poor to own slaves, but were fiercely proud. The big landowners called them poor white trash.

561

They stuck close together. There was a lot of intermarriage and that didn't help their reputation any. During the civil war a lot of the men went to war and didn't come back. The old timers who were left made sure they found the remains of their fallen kin and brought them back from as far away as Gettysburg and buried them in the cemetery at Bakertown. Most of them didn't know what the fighting was all about, but they were fearless soldiers. They are still proud, and independent, and mean as a red dog if they are your enemies."

Carol said, "That explains that mean streak you have, Kevin."

Kevin smiled as he looked through the rear view mirror at his pretty wife in the back seat. "You're really enjoying this aren't you?"

"I always knew you were something besides a Wright. And that temper. It's the worst

I've ever seen." Carol was enjoying the ride and the conversation.

Tj continued, "He probably got that temper from his grandpa Baker. That man had a bad temper. He got in a fight in the store at Baker's corner and cleaned the place out. He knocked three men out cold and yelled at the fourth as he ran away, 'I can lick a cow pen full of the likes of ya'll and mind the gate at the same time.' he was the talk of the county."

When they came to the city of Parkersville Tj told Kevin and Carol that this was his hometown. "This is the place of my birth. I went to the marines from here. I'll never forget the day I left. There was a juke box on the corner, right there," pointing to a street corner, "And it was blaring a hit song of the day; Blues in The Night. For some reason I still remember that trivial incident."

Claude Eldridge

Kevin drove slowly through the streets as Tj talked. It was a prosperous looking city with wide boulevards and tall office buildings. One of the buildings had a large sign that read: Warberg, Inc.

Tj gave directions and they drove through the city toward the southeast. As they approached the sprawling estate of Lone Pine Tj said, "I spent a lot of time here before it covered so much territory. Sam Warden and I went to school together and were best friends."

"I met Mr. Warden once," Kevin said.

"You did? How did that happen?" Tj's voice was full of surprise.

"It was at a trade show in Chicago. He was the principal speaker. I had a computer exhibit there and he came by and introduced himself. You remember me telling you about it, don't you Carol?"

"Oh yes I remember. You were so impressed with this big successful businessman. I didn't know he came from this part of the country," Carol leaned across the back of the front seat to get a better view of Lone Pine.

"Yeah, this is where Sam Warden came from, and is still here," Tj said, dryly. "It's hard to understand people. Why one person is one way and another person from the same environment is different. Sam is and was one of a kind. I guess he's a genius. He has a photographic memory, reads a book by just turning the pages. Never had to work hard in school. Had his own car at sixteen and a private pilot's license before that. Passed a college entrance examination before he finished high school. Ran off and joined the army before he was old enough to enlist. He had some fake identification. He became an air ace and had earned medals from

565

three countries, Came out of the service a full colonel, and a hero. The ugly duckling girl in school turned out to be a beautiful swan. He married her and they were the ideal couple. Everything they touch turns to gold. They are into everything from oil tankers to department stores. Alicia, almost on a whim, started a chain of ladies stores called, what else, Alicia's. A few years back she sold them for millions."

"My goodness, I'm impressed. And they were your boyhood friends?" Carol asked.

"Sam and I were especially close when we were boys. We left Parkersville together and joined the military service during the big war. After it was over we sort of went different ways."

"He sure sounds like an interesting man. And his wife must be some woman also," Carol said. "What about all that money what do they do? Make more money?"

Tj smiled his easy smile, "You know the old saying, them that's got get. But they do a lot of good. Give millions to charity. Sam is a nut about education. That's the reason there are many schools named Warden. He started a free vocational training school in Bakertown that is a fine institution. Graduates from there are actually in demand. The instructors will not turn them loose until they are proficient. And Sam is truly colorblind. He has been a leader in the civil rights movement. That's one reason he's being pushed to run for president of the United States. I guess that's the last challenge for him. Up until now he's dodged publicity like the plague. I brought the paper from home. Got a good picture of him. The advisors say he should learn to smile. Here, take a look." Tj handed the paper to Carol.

"My he is a handsome man. That's my kind of candidate. Smile or no smile," Carol said with admiration.

"He is a charmer. Especially with the ladies," Tj laughed at Carol's enthusiasm.

"He's a great speaker, Kevin said, "His voice is deep, with just a trace of soft southern accent."

They were near Baker's corner when they passed the Samuel A. Warden Vocational School. It had an impressive, well kept campus. The buildings were modern brick and glass; a fitting tribute to the founder. The school was in sharp contrast to the old store at the forks of the road. It had changed very little in the last fifty years. The one addition was a lean-to that served as a restaurant.

"Let's stop here. I want Kevin to sample some of the food his ancestors thrived on," Tj was enjoying himself.

The dinning area was small. There were three tables and two booths and the counter had eight stools. There was a black cook in the kitchen and one elderly lady that did the rest of the work. She had worked there many years and was well acquainted with Tj and his family.

"Hey Tj, where you been keeping yo'self?" she greeted them as they took a seat at the counter.

"Oh I've been here and there, just trying to stay out of trouble," Tj replied, "What's good to eat."

"Same as it was the last time you asked, the answer's the same. We have the best gumbo this side of Noo Orleans."

Tj was sitting between Kevin and Carol at the counter. He introduced them to Emma, the waitress, and said, "Could we have some menus?"

Emma smiled, "Where you fo'ks from?"

569

"Seattle—Washington," Kevin replied.

Still smiling Emma passed out the menus, "I can guess why Tj wants a menu. He's got some visitors, but he'll still order the gumbo and advise you to do the same."

Carol looked at the menu and asked, "What's chitlins?"

"They are soul food. The intestines of a hog," Tj answered with a straight face.

"You mean people eat those things?" she asked in surprise.

"They eat everything but the squeal," Tj replied, enjoying her wonder.

"Yeah, I notice," Kevin said. "How about some mountain oysters Carol?"

"What's that?"

"They are bull testicles," he whispered sotto voice.

Don't let them tease you honey," Emma said.

"Oh I knew what mountain oysters are. I was just surprised for a moment. I'll get you for this Kevin Wright," she said in mock anger.

"What's pot likker?" Kevin asked.

"That's the soup from turnip greens," Tj answered, "Served hot with cornbread it's not bad, if you have a taste for turnips."

"I think I'll have the gumbo," Carol said.

The two men ordered the same. It was served in a large bowl and an ample supply of cornbread was provided. The visitors from Seattle found it delicious. While they were eating Emma kept a running news report of the happenings in and around the neighborhood.

"Yo're in luck Tj. There's a church social tonight. I remember how you and Maryrose and the kids enjoyed the fun and food."

"Well thanks, Emma. I'll try to persuade my visitors to stay."

Emma looked at Carol and smiled, "I'll guarantee they'll have chitlins and mountain oysters."

"I can't wait," Carol said, as her companions laughed.

When they went to the car Tj said, "I would encourage you to stay for that social. You'll see a lot of people you are related to. And the food is good. Lots of things besides chitlins. We can go into town and get some hotel rooms and come back here in time to visit the cemetery where Maryrose is buried, before the festivities start. We'll return to Gulfport tomorrow."

The Wrights agreed and in about two hours they were at the church where the evening's event was scheduled to be held.

They went into the cemetery grounds and Tj led them to Maryrose's grave. There was a double headstone with her name and the dates of birth and death on one side; and the other had Tj's statistics, except date of death, filled in.

It was a somber moment. Tj said quietly, "When I die I'll be with her forever."

Kevin stood with his head bowed. Carol reached for his hand and held it tightly. She knew he was praying. Silently she prayed, "Oh my Lord, please bless the man I love so dearly and give him Peace." When Kevin turned away there were tears in his eyes.

As they strolled through the cemetery Tj pointed out headstones of interest; Civil war veterans, early settlers and the grave of Camille Dotson. He told them the story about her killer hanging himself and then he showed them Woodrow Baker's grave. The inscription on the stone caught Carol's attention: INNOCENT BUT NOBODY CARES.

"How very sad. Let's go, this place gives me the whim whams," she said.

The church social was an unforgettable experience for Kevin, and for Carol also, but more especially Kevin. Tj told him that almost all of the people he met would be related to him. Everyone knew Tj and came to where they were sitting to greet him and were introduced to the Wrights.

"I feel like a politician," Carol said, "I've been shaking hands all evening."

The food was abundant and well prepared. Tj and Kevin did justice to the good cooks who kept insisting they try something more. One time Kevin had some food Carol didn't recognize. "What is that you're eating?" she asked.

"Chitlins."

"Kevin Wright, you're not going to tell me you're eating guts are you?"

"OK I won't tell you. Actually they're pretty good. Have sort of a funky taste."

"I bet they do," Carol retorted. "You'll eat anything."

"You like liver. What's the difference? What's the difference between this and a T bone steak for that matter?"

Tj interrupted with, "Hey don't you two go to fighting over this ethnic food," he was laughing.

Carol wrinkled up her nose and said, "I don't want to discuss it any more."

On the way back to the hotel Kevin and Carol talked about what a good time they had at the church social.

"So many good looking men," Carol said.

"You have one of the good looking ones from the same breed," Tj answered.

"That's a sad story about the Dotson girl," Kevin said.

"Yes it is. She was the only child of Charlie and Cassie Dotson. It just about killed them. Charlie is dead now, but Aunt Cass is still alive. Say, before we leave tomorrow why don't we go by and see her?" Tj said.

"I think I've seen about enough relatives. It's time we head for home. What do you think Carol?" Kevin asked.

"We could stop by for a few minutes. We haven't been in a home here. I would like to see how people live," Carol replied. She was fond of Tj and thought he had been most generous with his time and had been good to them.

"Ok, we'll stop on the way out of town tomorrow," Kevin replied.

The next day they checked out of their hotel rooms and on the way back to Bakertown Tj directed Kevin to turn off on a dirt side road, which led to a one-lane road that showed little use. Weeds had grown in the center between the ruts and as Kevin drove along a cloud of red dust billowed up behind the car. They passed one empty run down house and the next one was the Dotson place at the end of the road.

The house was very old. The roof was corrugated metal, rusty with age. It had an open hall between the two sections. The yard was fenced and weeds had tried to take over and had succeeded to the walk leading to the house.

The yard gate squealed on its rusty hinges as the trio passed through. A slight figure of a woman walked out onto the porch as they approached. She was bone thin and stooped. Her blue eyes were watery and red rimmed and a blue line encircled her lips. Before anyone could speak she said, "Hello Tj."

"Hello Auntie Cass. How are you?" Tj replied.

"I'm tol'able," she replied, "Ya'll come in an' set a spell. I'll get some tea" She shuffled back into the house.

They sat on the porch in straight backed chairs that had been rebottomed with white oak splints. No one spoke, Tj appeared unconcerned as he looked around at the unkept appearance of everything in sight.

Mrs. Dotson reappeared with a pot of tea and the service. Tj introduced her to the Wrights. She peered at them closely and said, "My goodness, Carol is a pretty girl. She 'minds me of my Cammy. Don' you think she looks like Cammy Tj?"

"Auntie Cass, I don't know. It's been a long time ago. And I never knew her very well."

"That's right. I forgot. But she does look like my Cammy. I'll show you." She pushed herself out of the chair and went into the house. In a few minutes she returned with a timeworn diary. "Cammy always kept a derry, every day she kept it. I read it every day since she's gone and I keep her picture in it." From the pages she took a picture of a beautiful young girl and handed it to Kevin. "Don' yo' wife look like my Cammy?" she said

As Kevin studied the photograph, Mrs. Dotson absent-mindedly handed the diary to Tj. He looked at the worn cover and riffled the pages to the last one. The date was August 10, 1941, and then as he read the small handwriting he stiffened to attention. "—tonight I must tell Sam. He said he loved me. I know he will want us to go away together. He must."

Tj flipped back through the pages. Early dates were filled with a young girl's words of hope for the future and her experiences in school and working on her father's farm. He turned to early June and all doubts were dispelled. "Today I met Sam Warden. He is so good looking and he is rich. He has his own car" And then he flipped back to the last page and the damning words jumped into the light of day after all the bygone years. He had been so absorbed he had not noticed the other three staring at him.

Quickly he spoke, "Auntie, did the law see this diary when they were investigating Camille's death?"

"No, she said her derry was secret, she wouldn't even read it to me. I didn't show it to nobody," her voice breaking.

"But Aunt Cass, this is important evidence. It might have cleared Woody. Why didn't you at least tell the law whom she was seeing besides Woody? You could have told them that without showing them the diary" Tj spoke sharply.

Tears welled up in the old woman's eyes and ran down the weathered cheeks. "I couldn't tell them," she whispered, "I didn't know. I can't read."

"But Auntie, everybody thinks you can read," Tj said.

"I know, I allus p'tended I could. I was so 'shamed that I couldn't. When Cammy was alive she would read to me and I would remember what she said, and then I would p'tend to read to Charlie. He would pass on news and tell people I read it to him out of the paper. He was allus so proud," Mrs. Dotson was sobbing.

Carol quickly went to her side and put her arms around the frail shoulders. "Now don't you cry Aunt Cass, it's all right. No one will ever know the difference," She looked at Tj in a reproving manner.

"Aunt Cassie, can I borrow the diary for just a little while? I want to make some copies of the last few pages."

Mrs. Dotson shoved the diary into her apron pocket. "No, that's Cammy's derry and she said it was a secret. No one is supposed to see it."

"But Auntie," Tj pleaded, "Don't you want to see Woody's name cleared and the guilty person brought to justice?"

"I never believed Woody hurt my Cammy no how, so he don't need no clearing with me. And 'sides that I don't care about the guilty person. Hit won't bring my baby back."

"Auntie, it might be obstructing justice and that's against the law," Tj was finding it difficult to speak softly. Mrs. Dotson started to weep again and another look from Carol caused Tj to cease his persuasion.

Under Carol's soothing influence Mrs. Dotson became calm again and Tj gently urged his companions to say their goodbyes.

As he was leaving Tj said, "Auntie, I'll come back to see you soon."

Mrs. Dotson replied, "Hit won't do you no good Tj, you can't have my Cammy's derry."

Kevin turned the car around and as they were leaving, Carol turned and waved at Mrs. Dotson, who was holding herself upright by clutching a porch column with one hand, the other one was deep in her apron pocket. The old woman nodded her head. "That is downright pitiful," she said to no one in particular.

"That is downright stubbornness. Some more of Kevin's relatives," Tj said. "That 'derry' would cause a lot of fuss about an old murder case."

Carol was curious, "What are you going to do? Who was the person named in the diary?"

583

"I don't know what I'm going to do," Tj answered." And I can't tell you who the person was in the diary. At least not for a while."

As they came into the city of Parkersville, Tj said, "Drop me off at the post office. I guess you folks will want to go on, so I'll say my goodbyes now. I can catch the bus when I finish what I have to do."

Kevin and Carol had grown fond of Tj and the feeling was mutual. Carol said, "I'm sorry we have to part so abruptly. We are not in a big hurry. We could wait for you."

"I hate for it to end so quickly also. What I need to do might take some time. You sure you want to wait? It might be a day or two."

Carol looked at Kevin and he nodded his head. "We'll wait," she replied. "Shall we get the hotel rooms again?"

"Yeah, do that, you can get some rest and wait for me there."

Chapter 12

Sam looked out his tenth floor window at the city stretching before him. His eyes were unseeing as he remembered last night. He had been in a deep sleep and for the first time in many years the haunting dream had recurred. He was standing on the bluffs above Squaw Creek. The black water swirled beneath his feet. Suddenly the soil gave way and he fell into the murky stream. He couldn't move or cry out and he couldn't breath. Somewhere deep in his consciousness he knew he was dreaming and he knew if he could even move he would awaken. He was under water and couldn't breathe, his lungs were bursting and the pain in his chest was becoming unbearable. With supreme effort he gave a strangled cry and jerked upright in bed. His heart was hammering, he was gasping for breath and his clothing was soaking with sweat.

Alicia had been awakened by that cry of terror. Snapping on a bed light she was shocked by what she saw. Sam was as white as the bed sheets, gasping and shivering with chill. "My Lord, what is wrong Sam? Are you having a heart attack?" She touched his wet clammy skin and said, "I'm calling an ambulance," as she reached for the bedside phone.

"No, no wait, wait just a minute," he pleaded, "It's just a nightmare. I'll be all right. Indeed he was showing rapid improvement.

"Are you sure? I'll get security to drive you to the hospital."

"We'll do that if I'm not alright in a few minutes," he agreed. Alicia was somewhat appeased because he was speaking in his normal, self-assured manner. He got of bed and changed his pajamas. Together they changed the sheets on the bed. By that time he was almost back to normal. They slipped back into bed and Alicia wrapped her arms around him and held him close.

"That must have been some night horse. You scared the hell out of me. I thought you were dying. What was the dream about?"

"I was dying. I was drowning," he replied, "I'm sorry I woke you; go back to sleep."

"Promise me you'll go see Doctor Scott tomorrow," Alicia insisted.

"I just had my flight physical last week and he said I was in excellent health. Go to sleep, we'll discuss it in the light of day." In a short while her deep rhythmic breathing told him she was sleeping. But for him there was no more sleep. He took comfort in her warm body and the sweet fragrance of her hair. There was dread in his heart and a cold premonition. After awhile he eased out of bed to prevent disturbing her sleep.

Sam took refuge in his time proven stress reliever. He donned his exercise shorts and went down to the basement gym. For a two-hour period he exercised—hard. One phase, the last, was a one-hour run on the treadmill. He showered and stood before the full-length mirror. His flat-bellied body was lean and trim. His eyes were clear and untroubled. He was once again in top form. But he couldn't dismiss the dream. He slipped into their bedroom and kissed Alicia softly on the cheek. She murmured something unintelligible. She had no way of knowing she would never see him again.

Sam had busied himself at the office for a few hours, reading his mail and signing memos. And then he sat staring out the window, remembering the terror of the dark water in Squaw Creek.

The buzzer sounded on his desk telephone and his secretary said, "There's a Mister Johnson to see you."

"Which Mister Johnson?"

"A Mister TJ Johnson."

After a pause and wondering what Tj could possible want after all these years, and remembering their last meeting, he said, "I'll see him."

Tj walked into Sam's office with a confident stride. Sam rose from his desk and walked out to greet his old friend and ex-employee. He extended his hand and Tj took it with his easy smile softening the lines in his face.

Sam was the first to speak. "Tj it's nice to see you. It's been awhile."

"Yeah, it has Sam, You look great. Time treats you real good. Just like good whiskey you improve with age. How's Alicia?"

"Oh, she's fine. I heard about your wife's accident. I was sorry to hear that."

Tj had meant to talk only about Camille Dotson, but the mention of Maryrose caused an old anger to start smoldering in his mind. He suddenly changed his mind as he thought, why you arrogant so and so, see how you like this. Without warning he said, "You remember Wichita, Kansas and the boy born there? Well, I thought you might like to know he's in town."

There was not a glimmer of surprise on Sam's face. "I trust you didn't tell him about me. After all we had a deal and I trusted you, and I still do. Of course I knew about the boy. Kevin Wright. Owns a computer company in Seattle. I've set up a trust for him, not that he needs it, but it will be payable at my death. I've also set up one for each of your kids, payable the same way." He looked at his watch as he turned his back and reached into a desk drawer for some papers. "If that's all you have I have work to do and I hope you'll excuse me."

Tj would always remember thinking; shake this off you bastard. "What I really came to talk about is your 1941 love affair with Camille Dotson."

Sam's body jerked like he had been struck a hard blow. He paused and slowly turned; Tj was startled at the change. His eyes were opened wide and his face was chalk white. The scar on his cheek was a crimson line and his hands holding the sheet of paper were shaking. He stared at Tj as if he were seeing a ghost. He dropped the paper and buried his face in his hands.

Tj had never seen this side of Sam. He could never remember seeing him perturbed about anything. The sight was not pleasant. He thought, it's true he killed her.

Sam regained some composure and when he looked up Tj had another surprise. Sam was smiling.

"That got my attention. How in the world did you find out about Camille and me?"

"Simple, she left a diary. Every detail. The baby. August 10, 1941. The works. You killed her, didn't you?" Tj had a grim satisfaction in seeing Sam wince.

Sam shook his head as if to clear his thinking. "No, I didn't kill her. It was an accident. My crime was in not doing anything or saying anything. That decision didn't hurt Camille, but it did cause the death of Woody Baker."

"What happened?" Tj asked.

Sam started at the beginning and told the entire story. He reminded Tj of that summer when he was working nights at the drugstore and he, Sam, was working for Lee Brown. He left nothing out. The meeting with Camille, the stolen nights, the accident, how he tried to rescue her from Squaw Creek, the Woody Baker trial and the suicide. "That's the reason I joined the army, I thought I would not come back. I was hoping I would be killed, that way my parents would never know of my disgraceful behavior."

It had taken a long time for Sam to tell the story. It had a profound effect on Tj, whose anger had turned to sympathy, to pity for his boyhood friend. "I'm sorry I opened old wounds. I had no idea you were carrying such a load."

Sam smiled, the unfamiliar action made it look more like a grimace. "Don't feel that way. For the first time I feel like a great load has been lifted from my shoulders. I should have told you about it that summer. I could always talk to you and you could always speak your mind. I've missed that these years we've been apart. I always

594

regretted my involvement with Maryrose. It drove a wedge between us. I feel like I've paid a big price for my sin. I lost you as the only true friend I ever had. And I died a thousand deaths because of my actions, or more accurately, my inaction, after Camille's death. Somebody once said, a brave man dies but once, but a coward dies a thousand times, or something like that."

The two men were silent for a few moments as Sam's words hung in the air. Tj said, "I can imagine a lot of things about you, but I could never imagine you being a coward."

"Cowardice has many forms, my friend. When you let it destroy your soul, that is the ultimate cowardice," Sam replied in a low and thoughtful tone.

"Maryrose gave me years of happiness. She was the best thing that ever happened to me. And I've thought about our life together many times, especially since her death. I've come to realize if it had not been for you I never would have married her. It was the time in Wichita that got to me. I have you to thank for that, but I've not always felt that way."

"I regret we spent so much time apart. I didn't know how to make it right with you. Alicia gave me hell for letting you get away."

"I know now it was my fault, but I didn't know how to handle it either," Tj replied.

Smiling, Sam stood and said, "Let's make it a point to get together once in awhile."

"We'll do that," Tj promised.

The two men shook hands warmly and Tj left the office area. He caught a cab to the hotel and as he rode along a deep feeling of remorse set in. He had enjoyed wounding Sam only to have victory turn to a brassy taste in his mouth. He felt ashamed of his actions.

At the hotel he called Kevin and suggested they go for a ride in the country. It was early spring and the air was soft and warm. The first flowers were in bloom and Kevin drove as Tj directed, which was for the most part aimlessly. They went past Baker corner again and Kevin said, "Shall we stop and have some mountain oysters," looking at Carol in the rear view mirror.

"When we get home I'm going to get some and cook them for you," she replied.

"We've got to be on our way tomorrow without fail," Kevin replied. He and Carol had hoped Tj would tell them what he had done about the diary, but they could see he was preoccupied and so they drove along in silence.

Their route took them to the southern end of Old Saw Mill Road. They turned back toward town and as they crossed Squaw Creek Tj realized where they were. Later he would swear he had no intention of going that direction. At the top of the hill near the bluffs he told Kevin to stop the car.

The dim road, little more than a trail, leading to the bluffs was weed grown. It had been raining the night before and the ground was wet. Pointing down the trail toward the bluffs, Tj said, "That's the place where Camille died. The ground is too wet for us to drive there or I would show you the place." Without identifying Sam he described the accident. How Camille had fallen and struck her head and rolled into the flooding stream. How the man involved had followed her into the murky water. As he talked they could hear an airplane engine in the distance.

After Tj left, Sam moved around the office in a hurry. He signed some papers, read some mail, looked at his watch and took the elevator down the back way.

Sam owned, or rather Warberg, Inc. owned a fleet of airplanes. In one hanger there was a Learjet, a Cessna Citation, a Gulf Stream Executive and the two old planes; which belonged exclusively to Sam, My Baby, given to him by Lee Brown, and his most prized possession, a World War Two P51 Mustang. The Mustang was in mint condition. A mechanic who knew the plane inside out maintained it. The Mustang was named My Baby II.

Joe Williams, the chief mechanic, a grandson of Jose and Ava Williams, and a graduate of the Warden Vocational School, saw Sam drive up and park by the hanger. He wiped his hands and waited for what had become a routine. "Good evening, Mr. Warden," he called out. "Going for a ride today."

"Good afternoon Joe. Yes, I believe I'll take My Baby II out for some exercise. She's been getting to much rest lately," Sam replied.

"She's in top shape and ready to go," Williams said, as he began to move the craft out of the hanger.

Sam had always been a careful pilot. He had adopted a slogan and it was on a plaque hanging on the hanger wall. It read: There are old pilots and there are bold pilots. But there are no old bold pilots. He did his walk around check and made sure every item was as it should be, Williams walked with him, just in case there was something the 'Colonel' might not like. Joe was a graduate of the Warden A&E School and prided himself on being thorough.

When the check was over Sam climbed into the cockpit and went through that check. Satisfied that the plane met his rigid specifications, he started the engine. The

Allison coughed a couple of times and then came to life.

Sam gave a thumbs up at Williams and taxied to the end of the runway. Joe would remember later that Sam smiled as he waved to him. He thought what a great airplane that Mustang is as he waited for the takeoff roll.

Sam did all the usual things at the end of the runway. He did the engine run up and checked the controls. He turned the plane left then right and finally completely around in one complete circle. He turned My Baby II into the slight breeze and stood on the brakes as the engine roared toward full power, then he released the brakes and pushed the throttle to the firewall. The P51, a veteran of many breath taking air shows, streaked down the runway and was airborne before it passed the hanger where Williams was standing.

Joe had returned to work on an airplane instrument when he heard the sound of the P51 coming across the field. He looked up in time to see the plane scream by at low level. He thought, that's not like Mr. Warden, he never buzzes the field.

The plane roared over Lone Pine so low it rattled the windows and the dishes in the cupboards. Angela saw it pass and said to Henry. "I wonder what he thinks he's doing? Won't that old plane ever wear out?"

The plane made a wide swing to the south and came over Baker Corner at the same tree top level. It then pointed its nose at the sky and climbed out of sight. When it turned into a dive and came hurtling toward the earth, its engine bellowing at full throttle, is when Tj and his two companions first heard the sound. As they stood by the side of the road and looked toward the sky they saw the sleek craft pull out of the dive, shattering the quiet of the late afternoon, as it turned and flew nearby they could see the pilot. The plane climbed at a steep angle again, out of sight and the sound faded.

"That's Sam Warden," Tj said.

"What a beautiful airplane," Kevin said. "And a great pilot."

"Only the best," Tj replied.

They looked skyward as they heard the sound of the airplane engine. The P51 came straight down, at full throttle. The late sun glinted against its polished skin for the last time. The full power bellow turned into a shriek of protest, and then into a death scream.

"Pull up Sammy, pull up Sammy, pull up you son of a bitch," Tj shouted.

The plane struck Squaw Creek with a crash like a clap of thunder. The noise echoed up the hollows and rolled back and back again.

A flock of birds flew screeching from the wooded area. A fireball billowed into the sky as the fuel ignited. Then all was quiet.

"Oh my God, how awful" Carol gasped.

The three ran down the grass-covered trail to the bluffs. The plane had struck where Camille had fallen when she died. A crater had been gouged into the bottom of the creek and it had filled with murky water, which completely hid the wreckage. The vertical stabilizer had broken off and was lying on the far bank, propped against a tree. The name, My Baby II, was spattered with mud, but was clearly visible.

"Sammy, what have I done," Tj said with anguish in his voice.

The funeral was three days later. There had never been anything like it before in Parkersville. Sam was known and highly respected throughout the world. He had military medals from three countries. People from all walks of life came to pay their last respects. You could not have found anyone who would have hinted at anything but good in his life. The minister of the church where Sam had become a regular attendee conducted the memorial service. The many accomplishments were extolled. Toward the end he said, "—all the factories and ships and buildings are just things of this earth. It has been decreed by the most high God that: man was born once to live and once to die. And Jesus said, that whosoever believes in me shall not perish but have everlasting life. And that's where Sam Warden is today. But he is not gone from us. I see him in the level gaze of his children and I feel his touch when they touch my hand. He was a brave man. He was a good man. There was no meanness in him."

Sam's remains were interred under the large pine tree at Lone Pine. As the casket was lowered into the grave a missing man formation of Air Force planes flew over the site. The lead plane was missing. An honor guard from the Air Force fired their farewell salute. The shots echoed up the valley of Parker Creek and all was quiet. At the very top of the tree a mocking bird began the song of a whip poor will.

The Wright's had stayed for the funeral because of Tj. They feared he might collapse. He had been filled with remorse since the plane crash and had refused to talk about it. Kevin and Carol thought it was because he and Sam had been friends for such a long time.

On the way back to Gulfport Tj told them Sam was the man named in Camille's diary. "I went to see him the day he died. I told him about the diary. He didn't kill her. She was not murdered as everyone thought. It was an accident. Sam's mistake was not telling anyone about what happened. His silence was the cause of Woodrow Baker's suicide. He dragged that around with him all his life." Tj paused for a long minute. "I feel like I caused his death. Barging in on him like I did. I actually enjoyed shocking him out of that cool exterior he always portrayed. I believe he deliberately flew that plane into the ground. He just couldn't live with the thought of being exposed. And I didn't threaten that action."

"How awful," Carol said. "And how sad for you to feel guilty about him."

"I owed him a lot more than I ever admitted, even to myself. He brought Maryrose and me together. She gave me the only peace and happiness I ever knew."

Kevin was pulling into the Johnson driveway as Tj finished speaking. He turned to look at the older man sitting beside him. "You mean he—," he began.

"He was your father."

Mt Rainier slipped past the left wing of the 727 as the pilot began the descent to SeaTac airport. Kevin leaned over Carol who was sitting by the window, to get a better view. "It is nice to get back home where we belong. I feel like I've been sleep walking."

His wife patted his hand and said, "The experiences we had are completely unreal. But at least now you know. Are you sorry you continued to search until you found all the answers?"

"I am sorry. I believe I caused Sam Warden's death. Tj feels guilty, but he just did what I caused," he shook his head sorrowfully. "And another thing; I have two half brothers and two half sisters and I don't dare let any of them know about me. The Warden young people think their father was a saint and the Johnson kids are sure their mother was. You can imagine their reaction if I showed up and claimed to be their brother. Their bastard brother at that."

"I never dreamed you would feel that way. I've never heard you talk like that before. Do I detect a little self pity in your voice?"

"Oh no, not self pity. I know who I am. I'm Kevin Wright. I have a mother and a father, and I'll see them in just a few minutes."

"I'm so glad to hear you say that. The sooner we put this behind us the better off we'll be."

"I'll never forget these past few days," Kevin sighed.

Carol said, "I've been wondering about Woodrow Baker. I guess nobody really cares. On the record he's still guilty of a crime that was never committed."

"I didn't think of that. You're right. In the eyes of the law and the residents of the county he's still guilty."

The plane landed and the Wrights hurried through the concourse into the waiting arms of their families. Everyone went to Kevin's parents' home for dinner. They were curious to know about what had been discovered. Kevin said, "I'll tell you all about it sometime after we've had a chance to rest."

In their own home and Clara tucked into bed, they sat and looked at each other. Carol said, paraphrasing a part of the eulogy, "I see him in the level gaze of his children—," tears came into her eyes Kevin reached for her and his tears wet her cheek. "It's over," she whispered.

As the days passed they talked freely of what had happened in Mississippi. "I feel sorry for Tj, there alone. Let's invite him to visit us. It'll do him a lot of good to get away for a while," Carol said one evening as they were watching television.

"I'll call him right now," Kevin said, reaching for the phone. With Carol on the extension, the three talked for over an hour. Tj promised to visit Seattle the next time he went west. They had said all the things that friends talk about and were about ready to hang up when Kevin said. "Carol was wondering about that tombstone on Woodrow Baker's grave. She thinks nobody really cares that an innocent man is still falsely accused."

"Doesn't that bother you Tj? You know he's innocent, and we know he's innocent and poor Mrs. Dotson knows he's innocent," Carol asked.

There was a long pause before Tj answered. "You know, it's kinda strange you mention that. I've been wondering the same thing. I'll be damned if I know what to do about it. I think I've done enough damage. What do you think should be done?"

"The law should be shown the diary and his name cleared. Maybe it could be done quietly without the attention of the media," Carol was quick to reply.

"There's no case without the diary. Do you think you could get it?" Kevin asked.

"You saw what happened when I asked Aunt Cass for it. No, I don't believe I could get it. And if someone goes to the law and a search warrant is issued and the diary is not found, I shudder to think what the attitude of the law would be, especially if I'm the one involved. And I don't intend to be involved."

On that note they said goodbye.

Tj could not escape that easily. He found himself thinking more and more about what Kevin and Carol had said. It was as if he were guilty of something he could not fathom. He had always been a sound sleeper and he liked to say "I sleep so sound because I have a clear conscience when I first lie down," he now found his sleep disturbed by dreams: crazy dreams that had no meaning. One night he dreamed he was walking down a dusty road, hitchhiking, and Woody Baker came by driving his old stripped down Ford. The old Ford stopped and Woody waved to him. He couldn't move no matter how hard he tried.

The next day he was in his pickup truck, headed north to Bakertown. He had no idea what to do.

When he came to a the one lane road that led to the Dotson house he turned into it and drove slowly as the pickup bounced over the rough spots. He could still see the track of Kevin's car where there had been puddles of water when they came this way the time before. Spring was in full bloom and everywhere he looked flowers were nodding in the wind. Birds whistled their songs of joy. The scenery was so peaceful that he stopped and looked and listened. One beautiful dogwood caught his attention and he photographed it, thinking that he might paint that scene in the future. He thought about his mission and came to a decision of sorts. He looked at the sky and said aloud, "Thank you Lord."

At the end of the lane Aunt Cassie was sitting in her rocking chair. She was motionless and for a terrible moment Tj feared she was dead. When he slammed the door of his truck she raised her head. "Hello Auntie," he said, feeling a great sense of relief.

"Hidy, Tj, you ain't getting my derry," she said, her voice querulous.

The gate squealed in protest as he walked into the yard. "Auntie, I knew you wouldn't give it to me. That's not the reason I came out here. I'm concerned about you living alone. Have you ever thought about moving into some place where you can be cared for?"

"I ain't goin' nowhere. When I go anywhere it will be to join my Charlie and Cammy," she said, most emphatically in her dry squeaky voice.

"How about social services? They have nurses and other people who will look in on you every day to make sure you have food and that you are not sick."

"I ain't' no welfare case and I ain't gonna stand for some stranger nosing around. I'll thank you to keep your nose outa my business."

"I was just trying to help, Auntie, honest."

"I know what you want. You want my derry. You or nobody else will ever see it again. I put it in a safe place where it will never

615

be found." The old woman got shakily to her feet and went into the house.

Well I'll be damned, Tj thought as he returned to his truck. His next stop took him down another one lane road, far back into the hill country. The road had deep ruts and places where water had gouged holes as it ran unchecked down the red clay hills. There was no sign that any other vehicle had been over the road since the last rain. He eased along and around a bend at the bottom of the hill there was a fairly prosperous looking farm. A television antenna stretched its sliver colored arms above the treetops. A telephone line came over the hill opposite the road. It was the home of Jacob Baker, the elder brother of Woodrow.

When Tj stopped the pickup in the yard a couple of hound dogs came loping toward him, baying in deep menacing voices. Softly he spoke to them as he got out of the truck,

"Here boy, you ugly son of a bitch, you bite me and it'll be your last act." The dogs began to wag their tails and came to Tj and allowed him to scratch their ears. He had long ago found it was wise not to show fear where dogs were concerned. He and the dogs walked across the yard toward the house. They would run in front of him and turn and bay loudly.

The noise in the yard brought Jacob to the door. Seeing Tj, he walked out onto the porch and waited. He was a big man, over six feet tall and weighed about two hundred fifty pounds. He wore an old felt hat and bib overalls. A week's growth of beard was tobacco stained around his lips. Tj said, "Howdy Jake,"

Jake peered at Tj through bushy brows, Then said, "Howdy," a bit tentatively, then, "Oh, howdy Tj, I didn't recognize you for a minute. Don't see as well as I used to. Must be gittin' old."

"Well now, it happens to all of us," Tj replied.

"Hell Tj you're just a kid. I'm pushing eighty."

"I'll never make it that far Jake."

"You will if you drink good whiskey," He reached inside the door and brought out a stone jug. "This is good stuff. Made it myself. Ten years old in a charred wood keg. Have a drink."

Tj had sworn off drinking, but he remembered this man from the days he and Joe had hunted with him. Drinking was a ritual, refusing would be an affront. He took the jug and held it to his mouth and felt the warmth of the aged whiskey as he swallowed. When he was finished, Jake took the jug and took a long drink. He wiped his mouth and said, "I hate like hell to drink alone. Hate

it but I do it. Where you been Tj? I ain't
seen you in a long time. What brings you to
this neck of the woods? It ain't huntin'
season."

"I got something I want to discuss with
you," Tj replied, thinking rapidly about how
to go about his mission.

"Here have another drink Tj. I got
something I want to discuss with you. I been
watching T.V. and theys showing that shuttle
launch. What do you think of that shit?"

Tj was careful about his answer. He
believed the shuttle missions were a great
accomplishment, but he detected a tone in
the older man's voice. "Ah hell, Jake, I
never did like to fly."

"Have another drink," Jake passed the jug
to Tj and as he drank Jake said, "I think
that whole thing is a crock of shit. It's
government bull. Everybody knows the world
is flat and them bastards just flying around

619

in circles trying to confuse the tax payers." He took the jug and drank deeply.

Tj could feel the whiskey spreading from his belly up to his brain. He wanted to have a clear head for the answers to his questions. "Jake, let me ask you a question."

Jake was beginning to mellow." Shoot," he replied.

"What if I told you Woody didn't kill Camille Dotson?"

"Hell Tj, I allus knowed he didn't kill her."

"How did you know that, Jake?"

"He told me he didn't do it."

"And you believed him?"

"Hell yes, I believed him. He wouldn't lie to me. I'm his brother."

"What if I told you it was an accident and that Woody killed himself for nothing?"

Jake rolled his cud of tobacco around in his cheek and spat a stream of juice at a crawling bug. The bug rolled over and scampered away. He squinted at Tj and his jaw hardened. "What if I told you Woody didn't kill hisself?"

A surprised Tj asked, "Who did kill him?"

"Nobody, he ain't dead."

Tj thought the whiskey was affecting his hearing. "What did you say?"

"You gettin' hard a hearing boy, I said he ain't dead. He come to see me a couple months ago."

A shock ran through Tj. "But Jake, the body, the grave, the tombstone. I don't understand."

Jake passed the jug and said, "Have another drink Tj. I'll tell you something that only a few people know. The only reason I tell you is cause you married one of our girls and yore kids are kin f'oks."

621

Tj now felt like he needed a drink. His head was spinning and he wasn't sure it was Jake's statements or the whiskey. He took a drink from the jug and passed it back to Jake. He knew he was no drinking match for big Jake and he wanted to hear the story with, at least, some memory left.

Jake took a long drink. His Adam's apple bobbing up and down as he swallowed. The jug was beginning to show signs of being empty. He reached inside the open door and brought out a full one. "Plenty more where that come from," he notified Tj.

"Tell me, who is in the grave Jake? People saw the body of Woody. Judge Warden and a lot of other people."

"They saw a body, but not Woody. All of us knowed Woody wouldn't kill that girl. We knew he didn't knock her up. We knew because he told us he had never screwed her. We knew it was somebody else. And his ass would have been mud if we had knowed who it was at that time. Old Charlie Dotson would've made sure of that. All of us Bakers and all our kin were gonna make sure Woody didn't hang. We had a plot to break him out of jail. The sheriff, Ben Hill, was in on it. Hell, he was Woody's lodge brother."

Jake pulled out his pocket knife and started whittling on a piece of wood. He was deep in thought and Tj was about to say something when Jake passed the Jug. Tj had not been drinking any alcoholic beverages for more than a year and the mild tasting whiskey was beginning to cloud his vision. Nonetheless he took another light swig, and passed the jug back to Jake.

"My Pappy and one of his brothers married sisters. They had a house full of kids. Both of them had a house full of kids," Jake paused and spat a stream of tobacco juice at a hapless bug.

Tj thought, oh no, if he gets started on all his kin, I'll be drunk before he tells me what happened.

Jake whittled a little more and got stiffly to his feet. "Tj, I'm stiff as a by George. Gittin' old is shore hell. Let's go down to the barn, I wanna show you my new boar hog. He's a registered Duroc Jersey."

Tj got to his feet and was surprised to find he was steady and could walk straight. Jake hobbled along with the aid of a cane. When they got to the barn Jake opened the door and led the way to a pen in the back. The boar was a fine specimen. His red coat shone with good health and his pen was clean and dry. From the barn Tj could see across the pasture where fat cattle grazed. There was a creek running down the middle. It was a quiet and beautiful scene.

Jake leaned against the pigpen fence and followed Tj's gaze. "I lived here all my life. If I could live here forever, it would suit me jist fine. But I know that can't be." There was sadness in his voice.

"I never knew it was so beautiful back here," Tj said.

"The kids are scattered all over the country. They don't care about things like this. My Paw's brother what married my Maw's sister had a boy named Pete. Same age as Woody. About the same size. Them boys looked so much alike that you'd have to look twice to tell them apart. Same color hair, eyes, everything. Pete was married and had two kids. That year when they wuz gonna hang Woody, Pete was working on his barn roof. He fell and broke his neck. I went into town and told Ben Hill. He wuz the one who thought up the idea of switching Pete for Woody. It was so easy it was scary. We taken Pete into town and Ben and the jailer put Woody's clothes on him and hung him with

Woody's belt. We had a closed casket funeral for Pete who was now Woody. And Woody did write that note."

To Tj's whiskey fogged brain it seemed completely logical.

"How about Pete's family, what did they think? How about his wife?" Tj asked.

"The whole family wuz in on it. Woody had to take Pete's wife and kids. She was Ben Hill's sister. It worked good for everybody but Pete. But he was dead and nobody could help him and we saved Woody. They moved over to the delta, Woody and Pete's wife, had more kids and they turned out good."

"I'll be damned. What about records? Birth certificates and things like that for Woody and Pete?"

"What records? A midwife delivered both boys. Never had been no records. Census maybe had a record, but there wuz nothing else."

Tj's head was spinning more than ever. He still wasn't sure if it was the whiskey or the bizarre story Jake had told him. "Do you want to know who the man was that Camille Dotson was seeing when she died?" he asked.

The old man peered at Tj, tipping his head back to see past the brim of his old felt hat, "I don't care who it was. I know it warn't Woody." He began to shuffle back toward his house. When they reached the porch he reached inside the door and pulled out the jug and offered it to Tj.

Tj shook his head and said, "Jake, I'd sure like another drink, but I have to drive my truck back to town and I don't want to be drunk while I'm doing it. What do you think ought to be done about this situation?"

"What situation?"

"Woody and Pete, Camille Dotson, the whole thing."

"Nothin." Jake's jaw was firm.

"You don't want to clear Woody's name?"

Once again the old man tipped his head and peered past the brim of his hat. "How you ganna do that Tj? Pete ain't gonna admit he's Woody. The law would probably still want to hang him. He ain't dumb. Me and none of the other Bakers is gonna say anything. That leaves you. What kinda proof you got? Is the man who was screwing Camillie still alive?"

"No,he's dead, Jake."

"Tj, you're a good man. You know somebody was done wrong. And you would like to see it fixed. But what would you have to do to make it right? The Dotsons lost a daughter. You can't fix that. Woody was wrongly accused, and his family took care of that. We not gonna let anybody mess it up. We don't care about Woody's name. We gat a saying around these parts. Don't wake a sleeping dog."

Tj stared at the old man for a few moments. "Now that we know what really happened don't you think we ought to set the record straight?"

"What good would that do Tj? Think how many people would be hurt."

Tj could see the wisdom of Jake's comments. He thought of the publicity when it was revealed that Sam Warden was involved in the death of Camille Dotson and the effect on Alicia and the other members of the Warden family. The Baker children would have a severe shock when they learned their father, Pete, was really Woody Baker.

"Jake, I see what you mean." Tj said quietly.

Jake began to whittle again, peeling off long ribbons of wood that fluttered to the ground. He said, "What's done is done and it can't be undone. You can't un-ring a bell. Ain't no use stirring up a hell of a mess.

After you leave I ain't gonna ever think about it agin." He took a long drink from the jug and wiped his mouth with the back of his hand. "Tj I'd shore like for you to come back sometime when you have time to do some serious drinking."

"I'll sure do that Jake," he said as he started walking toward his truck. He stopped and turned, "Why don't you change that marker on what's supposed to be Woody's grave?"

"Why?" Jake responded.

"Well, it seems like the right thing to do."

"That's part of the Bakertown legend. You wouldn't want to screw that up, would you?"

Tj got into his truck and leaned out the window. "Jake why don't you have somebody look in on Cassie Dotson? She's getting mighty feeble."

"She's a stubborn old gal, but our people keep an eye on and they'll know when to hep. That'll be when she's ready to accept it."

Tj was surprised, "Oh, I didn't know someone was watching over her."

"We have our own system, Tj. Some body's always watching over everbody else. You've been watched ever since you've been here."

Tj looked around quickly but didn't see anything out of the ordinary.

"You won't see anything Tj. But if we wanted to we could say you had never been here at all and no one would be able to prove different. You and the truck would just disappear. Tj would you like to have another drink?"

Tj started the truck engine and as he drove away he saw the old man with a big smile on his usually grim face. Careful driving and no traffic saw him arrive safely at Baker's corner. Several cups of Emma's black coffee and a big steak made him feel sober enough to drive into Parkersville. He checked into the hotel where he had stayed with the Wrights. He went into the bathroom and washed his face. Looking in the bathroom mirror, the tired bleary-eyed man stared back. "It's finally over Sammy," he whispered. He went to the bedside telephone and dialed Kevin Wright's number in Seattle. When Carol answered he said, "I won't try to explain what has happened over the phone, but if that invitation still stands, I'll be out in a few days and fill in all the details for you and Kevin."

,"It's a standing invitation," Carol said. "What happened?"

"You won't believe it," he replied.

The End

About the Author

The author is a retired Boeing executive. He studied creative writing at Wichita State University. He and his wife have traveled extensively. He has written many journals recording the events of the traveling experience. He has written two other unpublished books and is the editor of a church newsletter. He is a native of Mississippi, which is the location of this work. He and his wife are avid golfers and gardeners. They have two children and three grandchildren. Their home is in Wichita, Kansas.

Printed in the United States
1490200001B/1